MY PERFECT SILENCE

'I was four when I killed my baby brother'

Rose can't even remember how it happened, but in the aftermath only her older brother Max remained the same, stepping in between her and the world when, at fourteen, she stopped speaking. Twenty years on and the media has fallen in love with Max – and Max has fallen in love with Caroline. When Caroline is killed, suspicion inevitably falls on Rose and she once again looks to Max for protection from the harsh world. Their relationship is cloaked with secrets and lies, hiding the truth behind an obsessive bond that ties brother and sister together.

MY PERFECT SILENCE

MY PERFECT SILENCE

by

Penelope Evans

Magna Large Print Books
Long Preston, North Yorkshire,
BD23 4ND, England.

British Library Cataloguing in Publication Data.

Evans, Penelope
    My perfect silence.

    A catalogue record of this book is
    available from the British Library

    ISBN   0-7505-2575-4
    ISBN   978-0-7505-2575-6

First published in Great Britain in 2006 by Allison & Busby Ltd.

Published in Large Print 2006 by arrangement with
Allison & Busby Ltd.

Magna Large Print is an imprint of Library Magna Books Ltd.

Printed and bound in Great Britain by
T.J. (International) Ltd., Cornwall, PL28 8RW

DEDICATION

For the Amersham Adult Orchestra

Part One

Chapter One

I was four when I killed my baby brother.

I don't remember it but I feel as if I was there. The baby; small, balled fists just visible above the sides of the cot. The banana I happened to be eating at the time. A sweet sponginess to fill his cheeks. Why not? I liked sharing. I liked having a baby brother, not being the youngest any more.

I gave him my banana. Kindly, patiently, pushed it down into his throat like a mother bird with a big stiff worm. All of it. The fists fell back into the cot with contentment. Or something.

I'm told by the time Max ran in it was too late. He shouted for my mother, then stood mutely pointing. The banana peel was spread out over the baby's cheeks like a big star shaped flower. Under the skin the baby was blue, not there any more, not really.

I *seem* to remember looking at her – and wondering what all the fuss was about. She still had us, Max and me. I could be the baby again.

Or do I imagine that too?

Sometimes I imagine it completely different. No generous impulse on my part, just a baby bawling; and me, an infant crosspatch, still wanting to be the baby myself. Cramming the fruit into the noisy pink gap, stopping the din like a cork in a bottle. A child with an answer for everything. That's what they used to say about me, even when I was four. Old enough to know what I was doing.

Except I didn't know. And all I have left is imagination. Because I don't remember anything – except for how everything changed.

Only Max stayed the same. Beautiful Max, my big brother. He never changed. And this I do remember, better than anything in my life. I remember how my brother wrapped his hand around mine, and held it tight. He's been holding it ever since, in a manner of speaking.

Everything else has vanished – even the taste of bananas. All that's left is a vague impression of sweetness. Twenty-five years ago now.

Max was going to be married next week, in his own church with his own congregation all around him. And cameras. Caroline – his bride, his chosen one – had chosen her dress, all sleek lines, long and lean and sophisticated as Caroline herself. I was there when she tried it on. She would have made a beautiful bride. She was beautiful anyway, and clever. And famous. That's why he loved her. Not because she was famous of course – Max is already famous – and not for the reason Caroline was, for talking to famous people on the TV, for finding out their secrets. I mean he loved her because she was beautiful and clever. And I suppose she loved him for the same reasons. Because Max too is beautiful and clever. And famous.

Now he's more famous than ever. A few days ago, Caroline had her head caved in, right on her own doorstep. They found her bleeding, blood dripping down the black painted railings with their shiny brass knobs that everyone has around there, and above them the steps that raised you up to the front door. Five of them.

I was there when it happened. So now they think I did it. The police, I mean. When they found me, Max was washing my hands, sluicing and rinsing. Then he showed them to the police and they were clean. But they had already seen it, the swirl of pink disappearing with the water.

And what can I say? Kill once, kill twice. I don't remember anything about the first time. So what can I say about the second time? Forget once. Forget twice.

'Poor Rosie.'

That's what my father said when the baby died. Struggling to see past the tragedy, to what else had been lost. A big man, big as a bear. A bear who reached out to my mother and said, 'Let's love what we have left.'

Poor Rosie? At the mention of my name, I saw her shudder. At the mention of *love* she turned away. All babies belong to the mothers. She couldn't see past anything. Only the cot, empty now. *Poor Rosie ...* nothing. She shook off his hand and stumbled away into another room, with that new heaviness in her step.

We watched it happen, Max and me, peeping through the gap in the banister. At *poor Rosie,* Max's hand went to touch mine. And as she turned away, the touch became a squeeze. Only six himself, but so much older than me even then. We watched my father sigh, square his shoulders and prepare to follow my mother wherever it was she went. As if it was his duty.

Let's love what we have left. That's what he said.

I must have stirred, ready to run downstairs after him, make him tell me it was all right, and it was enough just to have said I was sorry, like the times I shouted for more ice cream, or kicked my grandmother as she tried to brush my hair. It always had ended up the same way before, with hugs and kisses and chuckles of *Rosie Posie.*

But Max knew. He pulled me away from the stairs, halting the downward tilt.

Rosie, not now. Come with me. Come with me

14

and I'll ... I'll build you a den.

I would have caught my breath at that. Max built such incredible dens. He would pile the furniture and boxes together, cover them with curtains, with spaces for windows and a proper place for a door. He'd spend a whole morning building one, then finally crawl inside – alone. These dens had always been for him, somewhere for him to sit, away from the world. I never even used to be allowed inside. I would hover by the door, breathe down the chimneys like a baby wolf, peering in, looking for the glimmer of his head in the dark.

Go away, Rosie. That's all he would ever say. Until now. And now he was offering to build a den for me. All for me.

So I jumped up to go with Max. But at the bottom of the stairs I saw my father, not gone yet. He had paused, was looking up to where I was. He must have heard a sound.

Rosie?

Was it my imagination or did I, still invisible behind the banister, see my name form itself on his lips? I hesitated, feeling a tug towards him, drawn to him as if he was doing the pulling. And I almost went, following the draw, down to my father big-as-a-bear.

But Max pulled my arm, gently, insistently. *Not now Rosie. Come with me. Stay with me.*

So I went with Max and he built me a den, better than any one I'd ever seen, with a throne made out of piled up magazines. And Max read to me from one of his own books. In the confines of the den, he seemed so big, bigger even than my father. And I forgot that I had wanted to go downstairs. If you forget so much else, you come back to what you do remember. And I keep coming back to Max and me, sitting between the walls he had built just for me.

But sometimes I wonder. What if I had carried on downstairs after all? Would it have changed the way *she* looked at me, if I had caught her then? If I had said something different, if I had said anything at all? Could I have changed anything?

It was – how long? – a week after I had killed the baby. Somewhere in that time they must have had a funeral. A short sharp private affair, it would have been, jagged with grief, to which we were not invited. A week? Maybe it was the same day. Or maybe it was a year, two years later. You remember things in different ways when you are little – if you remember at all.

Whenever it happened, I remember this: the way my mother pulled away at the mention of my name. And I remember Max, holding my hand before he let go to build me a wall.

No one in the family ever mentioned the baby again. But he was always there, growing up beside us. Always in the shadows where I had cast him, those shadows where they all go, the people who vanish for all the different reasons. They might not be visible any more, but they're there forever now, in the empty spaces between ourselves.

Like Caroline. Who would have been a bride next week. Who is also dead.

The police will be back to ask me more questions soon. This time they will want to make sure Max is somewhere else. He keeps too close to me, interrupts when they try to ask me questions. They want to know what I was doing at the house when she died, and he's stopped them finding out even that.

Max. He tries so hard to protect me. He can't stop trying, even now. Still building his walls, keeping me safe.

Right from the start, my mother must have turned, to discover that she was hardly a mother any more. No baby and two children who might just as well have been one child, that's how close they were now.

Things change when a child dies. Obviously. A world splits down the middle and becomes two worlds – Before and After.

Things I remember from Before: my mother growing plumper as the pregnancy progressed. Slower as the baby grew inside her. Noisier, when finally she found it easier to shout than to run after us. My mother laughing because she couldn't see her toes; or eating strawberries in the sun. Kneeling as she tucked me in at night, whispering how she'd love to stay and fall asleep beside me there. Just she and me and the baby inside her. The three of us. Not even Max allowed in.

Other things I remember from Before: my father throwing me up in the air, allowing the world to turn a full three circles before he caught me. Tickling my tummy until I could hardly breathe for laughing. My father eating pastry I had shaped into ducks whose necks had drooped in the oven turning them into fat dying swans. Delicious, *schmecklich*, *delicieux*. He travelled abroad, and could thank waiters in any number of languages.

Things I *don't* remember from Before: Max. Strange – how I barely remember Max. It's only his dens I seem to recall, with his head gleaming inside, just visible in the gloom. Max not wanting to have anything to do with me. Max, trailing instead after my mother, trying to have her to himself, all himself. Small chance with me around – and no chance at all once the baby came along. I think he must have built his dens to get away from me.

So. Memories of what came After: my mother, not plump any more, trying to force the softness back into her lips as she kissed me goodnight. The cake stiff with roses and ballerinas she made for my fifth birthday, icing hard and shining as marble. My mother folding away baby clothes into a bag.

And my father. Still throwing me in the air. Still tickling me in front of the fire. But in his eyes a certain dreaminess as I try to catch his glance. He has tossed me so high above his head. What if he forgets to catch me? What if he tickles me so hard I die for lack of breath? *What if that's the plan?*

And Max. *Now* I remember Max, days filled with him. Six, seven, nine year old Max. Shining at twelve where other boys begin to fade. At fourteen, hair falling into his eyes as he watches out for me. Never so far ahead, never so busy that he can't turn to check I'm there. I remember Max better than I can remember myself – the scraps of me I saw in the mirror. Small and skinny with coarse yellow hair. Like Max but scrawnier, not quite properly put together.

Meanwhile my parents recede – still there, but coming alive only from a distance. People I'd have liked to know better. And already beginning to forget the taste of bananas. Only the memory of sweetness, fading to the memory of a memory.

At nine I went away to school – far away, so that boarding meant a stretch from one holiday's end to the next, and it made no sense to come home even for the occasional weekend. Max's school was closer, and for a long time no one told me he was coming back at weekends, every weekend.

Does that sound sad? It's absolutely and completely not meant to. I *liked* school. Loved it. Even though Max wasn't there. I liked the way the nuns treated every one of us the same – cool, almost sad in the way they called us quietly to attention. As if each little girl reminded them faintly of sins left behind.

Something strange happened the first day I arrived. I looked around at the other children – small, miserable creatures who'd left their mummies and daddies in Africa or Singapore or wherever – and I must have realised there was nothing here I needed to compare myself with. We were in the same boat, every one of us – *all* of our parents were absent. That night, little girls sobbed into their pillows and whispered it was because their mummies weren't there to kiss them goodnight. But they might have been making it all up for all I knew. They might not even have had parents at all. If someone isn't there, you can't question if they exist or not. You can say anything, imagine anything. And they didn't know about me, what I had done. It was nobody's business except mine.

I pulled the covers up to my chin, listened to the muffled sobs around me – and imagined my parents. Within minutes I was sobbing, loudly as the rest. Warmth flooded the surface of my pillow. A lovely, nostalgic warmth. At home, in the World-that-came-After, my mother could rarely bring herself to kiss me. But here I could imagine it happened every night. And, finally, when little by little the sobbing around me stopped, I snuggled down happily, like a child used to kisses.

Next day a letter arrived from her. Long and loving, warmth pouring off the page, love like I remembered. The same thing happened the next week, and the week after and all the months and years that came after. Easier for her now I wasn't there. Somehow school had given me back my mother.

So I loved school. Loved it. Right up until the day I discovered that I was wrong; they knew all about me, even here.

I'd always thought my parents had kept it secret. No one's business but our own. I didn't understand the truth: when you're a child who kills another child, it's everybody's business.

There was another truth as well, and this was a larger one, making every other truth insignificant. It had been there all the time, staring at me out of my mother's eyes, and still somehow they had kept it from me, my mother and father. Struggled and toiled every day to keep it from me.

21

Fourteen years old and I was alone in the gym, on my hands and knees, searching. In a hurry because the next class were already changing into gym knickers and were about to troop in. Too late, though, for here were two girls already picking their way over the rubber mats in their gym shoes. In a small school, these two – Mary and Margi – already had a reputation. They picked on other girls – on any girl – so long as she was alone.

'What are you doing?' This was Mary. She was younger than me, although her breasts were already plumping out her aertex blouse. Her face was dotted with matt patches, not quite skin colour, where she had daubed herself with spot concealer.

'Looking for something.' I kept my head down, sensing the boredom in them, the desire to make something happen.

'What?'

'Nothing.'

They nudged each other, and watched me as I went on searching beneath the ropes. I was wishing the rest of their class would arrive, but they must have been held up. Perhaps Sister Imelda was having a foot inspection.

There was a giggle behind me.

'Look what I've got.' Mary was holding up an object that dangled silkily from her hand. A bracelet.

'That's mine. That's what I was looking for.' I spoke before I could stop myself. Too eager.

'Can't be. You weren't looking for anything, remember.'

'I was looking for that.' I tried to keep my voice cool, the way Max's voice would have been cool. Max was always cool in a crisis.

Margi was triumphant. 'Then you're a liar. We asked you and you said *nothing.*'

Mary began to slip the bracelet over her wrist, admiring it while Margi leered at me.

That bracelet. My mother had given in to me for my last birthday. Passed it across the breakfast table with a quick, tight smile. Always a different mother from the letters, and yet still the same mother. Something understood.

My mother. My bracelet. I made a grab for it, and when Mary dodged, I sprang after her. As she laughed at me, Margi grabbed me from behind, held on to me, sharp nails digging into the skin on my arms. Never mind that she was younger than me, she was much taller – almost everybody was – and strong. It would have taken an adult to haul her off.

Safe now, Mary stepped nearer. Smirking, she shook her wrist inches from my face. The bracelet slid down her arm as if trying to find its way back to me. And before I could think what I was doing, I snapped my head forward, catching the arm and the bracelet with my teeth. Mary squealed.

There was a taste of silver, of metal threaded across my tongue – then something else altogether. Warm flesh, slightly salty, like you'd imagine the skin on a young live pig. Margi's hands pinning my arms injected their nails deeper into me, and goaded, I let my teeth sink, through the salty pink-pig skin.

Mary squealed even louder. Squealed and squealed as if I was killing her.

'Rosie Bryant!'

Sister Imelda's voice bounced off the gym walls. And even then I couldn't seem to let go. My jaws had locked around Mary's arm and I was hypnotised by the taste of flesh and silver.

A hand cuffed me across the head, finally breaking the grip of my teeth.

'Rose Bryant, you will come with me.'

I had a last glimpse of Mary staring in what looked like disbelief at her arm before Sister Imelda thrust me into a side room, so hard I knocked over a chair. I picked it up and faced her.

'She's got my bracelet.' Once again my voice was cool. Here was Max coming out in me yet again. Calm, concentrating on the facts. A child with an answer for everything. They still called me that.

Sister Imelda, her face a sallow wedge

beneath her wimple, ignored this. 'Have you been inoculated against tetanus?'

'What?' I must have sounded insolent in my surprise.

'I said – have you been inoculated against tetanus? It's another name for lockjaw. We'll have to inject the poor child against that, on top of what you've done to her.'

Lockjaw. So that's what had happened. My jaws had locked around Mary's arm. That's why I couldn't stop. I was amazed there was a term for it.

And as I gaped, she leaned forward and wiped something off my chin with a paper handkerchief she had taken from up her sleeve. 'Mother of God,' she muttered with a look of disgust. It was blood.

Mutely she showed me the hanky, and something went cold inside me, making me forget about lockjaw. I had another person's blood smeared on my face. Worse than snot, worse than spit, worse than anything.

I said, 'She deserved it.'

Sister Imelda's face hardened. Everyone knew she liked Mary, named for the mother of God, a girl who could produce real tears every time she took the sacrament. Never mind that she had tasted of pig. Sister Imelda began to talk, in a low voice, as if to herself. 'To think I never believed it. Not a five-year-old – that's what I said to the Reverend Mother when she told me. A five-year-old wouldn't hurt a fly. Or surely not a baby. Not something so small.'

I felt for the chair I had just righted. I needed support, like one of the old nuns we'd see shuffling on Zimmer frames in the walled garden behind the tennis courts, the ones who were in retreat. 'Gaga', some people said.

'I was four, not five.' My voice sounded faint. Almost a whisper.

Again Sister Imelda ignored me. 'What sort of girl are you? Killing one child. Savaging another, biting like an animal.'

I opened my mouth to explain about the baby, the banana and everything. But it was something I had never had to do before: explain. And I couldn't start now.

'Well?' Said Sister Imelda. 'Well?'

'They shouldn't have told you,' I said at last. My voice was cold, matter of fact. 'Not about the baby.'

I saw Sister Imelda give a start. 'And what can you mean by that?'

'It was none of your business. It was nobody's business. I don't know why they told you. *It's not fair.*' The last words said it all, the consequence of the anger building inside me. Not fair that my parents had told them. Not fair that others knew. Not fair I had to be different here, the one place I thought everyone was the same.

Yet what had I said? There was a look on

26

Sister Imelda's face I had never seen before – almost comical, making her look like the child she might once have been, before God and Jesus smoothed over her features. A sharp faced child who had turned over a stone to discover all kinds of evil things beneath.

Finding her voice she said: 'Get out. I'll deal with this later.'

Next day I went and stood before the Reverend Mother. Sister Imelda spoke in front of me and her account was faultless, dry and factual as if she was in court. She didn't try to make anything sound worse than it was, and yet each word seemed to settle on the word that went before, until something entirely new was created, different from the truth; layered and hardening to a picture set in stone. Mother Martha listened to my explanation about the bracelet, and asked me if I was happy at the school, whether I liked the people who were around me.

'Yes,' I said fervently. 'I like everything. I love school.'

I saw her weigh another question, then decide against it. Instead she picked something she had on the desk in front of her. 'Rosie, I want you to take this. Keep it with you.'

I glanced down at what she was giving me. It was a picture of the Virgin Mary staring into the crib that held the baby Jesus, the sort of picture you'd see on a Christmas card. We had the same kind of pictures to keep the pages of our books.

The Reverend Mother sat back and folded her hands, studied the wedding ring on her finger. There was silence now. Apparently the interview was over, which confused me. I had been expecting a punishment. Detention, worse even. I darted a glance at Imelda and found she was watching the Reverend Mother, her mouth twitching as if she too was expecting something else. Moments passed, until she couldn't stand it any more. Loudly, she cleared her throat.

Mother Martha sighed. She looked at me, her face expressionless. 'Rose, I want you to carry the picture with you always. And look at it. Meditate on it when you are alone. See the way the blessed mother observes her child. We call her the mother of God. Yet sometimes we would do well to remember that she is also the mother of a son.'

And that was all. They wanted me to look at a picture. Not even a very good one. Mawkish, is how Max would have described it. Mary was pictured as if she were on the edge of fainting with adoration, in thrall to her child – who for his part was barely visible except for the small, balled fists waving above the sides of the stall.

I nodded. And for days and weeks did what they told me; I kept the picture with

28

me all the time. It was there when I emptied my pockets. It fell on to the floor whenever I reached for a handkerchief. It got covered with crumbs and smeared with butter. I must have looked at it ten times a day without even realising it.

It became crumpled. So much so that, two weeks before term ended I dared to take it out of my pocket to leave it by the side of my bed. Apart from the wrinkles and the grease it looked the same as ever. A tableau of swooning mother love.

About to turn away, I caught sight yet again of the small, balled fists, barely visible above the sides of the cot. And this time, without warning, something began to shake inside me. I had to hold on to my bedside table, ignorant of what was happening to me. I felt like a wall caught in an earthquake as the ground moved, deep and invisible, beneath me. I gripped the table hard. And there was the picture.

Then I understood. It was the picture, its mawkishness a lesson, a weapon. Small, balled fists, and Mary's face, full of hopeless love, knowing what she was going to lose.

And like a wall, I collapsed. It didn't matter that I didn't remember, that I had never meant to harm anything. I collapsed because at long last I understood what I was. I was the child who had a killed a child. I had taken a life, as precious as my own life.

Complete knowledge – this is what my parents had tried to keep from me, to keep me from understanding. And a child was what I had taken from my mother.

If Sister Imelda asked me now what I had to say for myself, I would have to be silent. There was nothing I could say. No defence. No explanation. And no question of fairness. Nothing.

That was the day, the hour and the moment I stopped speaking, the child who had had an answer for everything. Not another word. What else could I do?

Did they see it as a job well done, the nuns who had made it their business to make me understand?

They called a doctor, but he couldn't make me speak. *I* couldn't make me speak. He asked me questions and listened to the silence, and made of it what he could. He was worse off than those doctors from the olden days, who had no stethoscopes to help them, no X-rays or scanners to show what's going on inside.

He needed me to speak to give him a clue. And I had nothing to say. Not now I understood, finally knew what I was.

Chapter Two

I never did get the bracelet back. Mary, named for the mother of God, kept it and probably has it to this day.

At home no one tried to make me speak, not at first. My mother was quieter than ever and my father wrapped around me with bear hugs. But it had been too long since he had hugged me, and both of us were awkward.

In the nights, though, from the other side of the wall, I'd catch his voice rising and falling with anger. Not with me. *'Something happened,'* he kept saying. 'Those bloody bitches of nuns. They know something, and they're not telling us.'

I never heard what my mother had to say in reply. Her voice was too low. The bedroom wall too thick Maybe there was nothing she wanted to say. With me they talked about doctors and treatments, and met with a wall of purest silence – my own. It was the first wall I had ever built for myself. The silence was unavoidable, rooted. Part of me now.

Max understood.

The school had told my parents about

biting Mary – and Max was fascinated by the story. He lay on the lawn and went over it again and again, eyes closed so as to see it all better in his mind. He was sixteen now and his hair was long, springing from his scalp before falling under its own weight. Slightly greasy because he couldn't be bothered to wash it. It was gold, where mine was simply yellow, the colour of straw.

'She deserved it, Rosie. You should have gnawed her fucking arm right off. Eye for an eye and all that.' He opened his own eyes and looked at me. Straight faced he added, 'You've got the teeth for it.' He poked me in my side, where it tickled. 'Little pointed teeth. Like a cat. You should have chewed right through to the bone. And when they came to lock you up, you could just have told them you were mad.'

Mad?

For some reason the word took me aback, filled me with dismay. He saw the change in my expression and he grinned. 'Only joking, stupid.'

And I smiled too, oddly relieved. But a moment later, when he thought I wasn't looking I stole another glance at him, and he was staring at the sky again, not smiling but frowning.

I nudged him.

But he didn't feel me. He was somewhere else now, like when he was very young and would build himself those dens and crawl inside, leaving me outside, forced to be content with catching the gleam of his head in the dark.

Instead of nudging him again, I watched him, the way the sun caught the greasy gold of his head and the finer gold peppering his arms. Max *gleamed* that summer, no other word for it. He reminded me of a young male lion. At sixteen he was tall and skinny – yet shapely, with swathes of muscle smoothed along the bones. Impossible to look at him with the eyes of a stranger, to judge him, yet even I knew he didn't look like most other boys, the ones who came and hung around at our house. Boys who carried their adolescence like a penance, spotty and round shouldered. They hovered on the corners of my mother's rugs, dreading the attention of adults, and unnerved by my new silence. Close up they smelled, very faintly, rank.

Not Max. His face was smooth, except for the down that brushed his cheeks, and he was strong and springy under his skin. If he hadn't had the tendency to slouch required of someone in his teens, he would have been the image of an Enid Blyton boy, the sort that stands up to dogs and hard men with guns. Adults couldn't frighten him.

All at once I was conscious of a sense of ownership, glad he was mine. Grateful I didn't have to share him with anybody else, not even another brother or sister...

At which I felt myself colour. Silence welled up once again inside me – a kind of noise in itself.

'What?'

He had come back from wherever he'd been and caught me staring – and colouring. Now he was looking at me in turn.

I shook my head. I bent forward to pick blades of grass from between my toes. Like him I was barefoot.

He threw back his head again and squinted at the sky. He was beautiful. Girls asked for him on the phone. I'd spoken to them in holidays past, listening to breathy voices that sounded no older than mine.

And I felt a twinge of something. What? Not jealousy, exactly. Maybe a warning fear of the future, of a time when there would be no Max, because he belonged to someone else. Not my Max any more. And no wall against the world.

But now Max was looking at me. He must have caught the sudden misery in my face because his eyes were serious. After a moment he leaned forward and pushed the hair off my forehead and made me look at him – really look at him. I could feel the heat in the tips of his fingers as he guided my stare, the warmth of half a summer's sun stored in his skin.

Max had no need for words. He stared at me and his eyes told me what he wanted me to know. He was making me a promise I didn't need to hear out loud. Max was telling me, making sure I understood: whatever happened, whoever came along, I would never lose him. My wall against the world.

So Max made a promise. He told me he would never leave me. He made me believe it. And then he broke it.

Not because of any breathy girl. As it turned out, there were other ways to lose Max, to be left by him. The truth is, boys are the easiest things in the world to lose. They put themselves in the middle of places and events where they get lost all the time. A teenage boy gets on the back of a motor-bike, rides too fast and, bang – he's lost. He drives a car, ploughs into a wall and, smash – there's another boy lost. He walks into a bar, picks a fight and gets skewered on a kitchen knife. Squelch – another one gone. All of them lost forever. The shadows must be teeming with them.

Boys get lost. We nearly lost Max the summer that I stopped speaking.

Max and I had continued to lie in the long grass at the bottom of the garden – away from the adults, united in silence. Max kept words for when they were needed, like when my parents were present. Then he talked non-stop to cover up the silence, to cover up for me.

It occurs to me now; my parents couldn't have come close to me even if they had tried. They would have had to get past Max.

We read mostly, choosing our subject matter with care. My tastes had changed and I'd finished with children's books. This was the summer I read horror and crime and ghost stories – books with covers of zombies or naked women lying dead. Books full of evil people who knew exactly what they were about, who only killed when they meant to. Who were not accidentally wicked like me, a hapless maker of grief, and forgetful with it.

Max, though, he seemed to have regressed. One day, bored, I breathed down his neck and saw he was reading my old copy of *The Lion the Witch and the Wardrobe*, he was back in the Woods with Edmund and the wicked Snow Queen. At his age! I must have made a noise, a small splutter. Yet even this was speech of sorts and made him look at me, suddenly alert.

'What Rosie?'

In my eagerness to answer I tried to say the words in my head. But of course, they were jammed, the way they had been since the day I had understood the truth of what I had done. So in frustration I reached for the pen and paper I'd taken to carrying for an emergency.

Why are you reading that?

He thought a moment, then he said slowly. 'I suppose it's Edmund. I keep coming back to him. He's interesting.

Why? I hate him, I wrote.

'Who?'

I wrote again. *Edmund. He lies about his little sister, lets everyone think she's made it all up about walking through the wardrobe. He gets her into no end of trouble, and then pretends she's just being a kid or mad. I hate that.*

And it was true. I had always hated the part where Lucy – who never told a lie – was branded a liar, or worse. I never forgave Edmund, ever, not in all the books that came after, when he had long ago redeemed himself. I would have been happy if he had died. Never missed him.

Max rolled over onto his back and looked at me. To my surprise he seemed to be taking me seriously. 'I feel sorry for him.' He offered. 'Don't you?' Then watched my answer from over my shoulder as I wrote:

Why? He's vile. He lies about Lucy, then betrays her – and the rest of his family. You shouldn't be sorry for him.

He shrugged. 'Maybe he thinks once he's started with one lie, he can't stop. He's got to carry on. Besides...'

I raised my eyebrows.

'...he's just a kid himself. A child still. Maybe he doesn't know what he's doing.'

37

I grabbed the pen again. *I'd know. I tell you, he's horrible. He ruins things for everybody. People die because of him. He's a coward and a liar, and he just wants everyone to think the best of him.*

I stared down at my words, surprised by my own vehemence. Then looked up to find Max watching me, his face unreadable. Abruptly he got to his feet. I thought I had irritated him, ranting on about a children's story. I put my hand on his leg to stop him, but he pulled away, began to stride across the lawn. In an instant I was running after him. I had the book in my hand and jogged along beside him, trying to give it back to him, to be helpful.

He ignored me. So still I tried to make him take it, and when even now he wouldn't, I prodded him with it, laughing. With Max I could nearly forget what I was. I could laugh.

Finally, halfway across the lawn, he stopped, and snatched the book off me. Stared at it a moment, with its bent spine and covers all wrinkled and worn. Then suddenly, savagely, he began ripping it to pieces, pulling it apart, sending the pages fluttering across the lawn.

'Hey,' I mouthed in outrage, but he didn't stop. With a last gesture he flung the remnants up in the air so that they blew and settled around me. 'Stupid book,' he said.

And walked off.

I stared after him, bewildered. And furious. The book had been old. I'd been about to put it away forever. But it was my book and suddenly, contrarily, I loved it. And Max had done this. My Max. I looked up to see him disappearing into the house, ignoring our mother as she called out to him. I went around the lawn, picking up the pages, trying to piece them together. But they were past repair. In the end, I got a carrier bag and piled them all in, dumped them in the bin.

And that was the night that I – we – nearly lost Max.

Before that though, he had come in search of me.

'Look...' he began. But I held the book I was reading higher in front of my face and ignored him. It was another Narnia book – *Prince Caspian.* I was challenging him to take and tear this one into pieces as well.

'Rose... Rosie, I'm really sorry. I don't ... I don't know why I did that. I'll get you a new book, Rosie.'

I turned my back on him, on Max who had never turned his back on me.

In the evening his friends came over, the rank spotty friends who stood in the kitchen cowering before my silence, and my father's attempts to make conversation. Max came downstairs and without looking at me, said, 'Let's go.'

And off they went. Like lambs, following Max. People always seemed to follow Max, even in those days. My father raised his eyebrows at me and smiled wryly, acknowledging the fact without needing to put it into words. Sometimes – at moments like this – we verged on being close, my father and I, especially now the words themselves had failed.

But not so close that I felt I could be alone with him. I left and went up to my room. Afterwards the three of us ate in silence. That was what happened when Max wasn't there. Everything became quiet, waiting for him to come back. Then I went to bed. As always, my mother asked if I needed anything and – as always – I shook my head. Sometimes I wished I could say 'yes'. She would have liked there to be something she could do, something I could ask her for. But there never was anything. Distance was our medium – and Max filled the space between. It's why we looked forward to school, my mother and I, to when the letters could start again, love pouring off the page, something understood.

Tonight though, her eyes stayed resting on my face, as if still questioning, reluctant to take *no* for an answer. As if she sensed that a breach had opened between Max and me, a crack that could begin to let anything creep in. Even need.

As for Max, it was ten o'clock, but no one

wondered where he was. He was sixteen. And a boy, not a baby. He could look after himself.

I was sleeping when I heard the crash, a noise that entered my dreams and made me scream out loud. I'd been standing in front of a stone lion, admiring it, when suddenly it shattered and fell with the same crash I had just heard. In the silence that followed, my father's footsteps paused outside my room, snagged by the scream, the first actual sound he had heard from me in months. Then the din started up again, a pounding on our front door, harder than ever, and he moved away.

From the landing I watched him open the door, cautiously at first – then with an exclamation, throwing it wide. Falling into the space came Max's friends – and Max himself, draped over their shoulders. They tripped as they came in and Max slid, too heavy for them to stop, and landed at my father's feet. And didn't move.

Everything had become quiet. Then, panting, the plumpest of the boys – Roger – said: 'We don't think he's breathing, Mr Bryant.'

Behind me, I heard my mother gasp. Slowly my father looked up and spotted us on the landing. Bewilderment and fear stopped him looking like himself, turning him into somebody else's father. It occurred to me I

41

had seen his face like this before, once. Long ago, and as he bent over another child.

My father said, 'Call an ambulance.'

Then, almost wearily, he began to pump my brother's chest. Counting under his breath, *one* two three four five, *one* two three four five. Fear had made my father's movements heavy. A heaviness that had never really gone away, not in all the years since the first time.

The ambulance came. Max was breathing again.

In the wait, the boys told us what had happened. They had spent the evening in the pub. But while they had all been drinking shandy, making their money stretch, Max had been drinking pints.

'He never does that,' Roger said plaintively. He was the son of the woman who ran the post office. The only son, her pride and joy, whom she fed too much. Now his fat cheeks, wobbling with fear, made him look like an eleven-year-old. 'Not ever. He doesn't even like the beer they sell there.'

My mother, cradling Max's head in her lap, said nothing – not about him being only sixteen, too young to be in a pub, too young to be served any brand of beer. Nothing. She was staring into his face, with its skin gone the colour of tallow and his eyes shut fast against her. A tear rolled down her cheek onto his sweatshirt. There was a smell of sick in the hall.

The boys continued with their story. At last orders Max was already roaring drunk. But he spent the rest of his money on a bottle of vodka. No one else had the stomach for it, so they had gone to a bus shelter and watched him drink it – all of it.

'We told him not to, Mrs Bryant.' This was Roger again, his voice plaintive, eager not to be blamed for anything. 'He just kept knocking it back. It was making him sick, but he wouldn't stop.'

And now here he was, his head in my mother's lap, and only the gleam of his hair to remind us it was him. I sat on the stairs and watched him, watched them all. *If he died, what then?* I couldn't think. There was no *then*. I couldn't imagine a future, not after this. Not after Max.

He didn't die, although at the hospital where they pumped him out, they said he should have. Young bodies don't normally survive that kind of assault. *Assault* was the very word they used. As if this was what Max had done – assaulted himself, taken himself to the very edge of the place where boys get lost. He hadn't died, but then again, he wasn't waking up.

'Mr and Mrs Bryant, *Who is Rosie?*'

This was what the doctors wanted to

know. As they had worked to bring him back, as he had risen through the levels of his coma, *Rosie* had been the name on his lips. Over and over again: *Rosie I'm sorry.* Was she his girlfriend, they asked – perhaps the reason he had done this? They put the question as we stood beside his bed. They said they had to ask because it could make all the difference. Max had survived this far, and yet somehow they couldn't wake him. If this Rosie could only come, talk to him, it might get through. The brain responded in so many ways...

I felt my mother go rigid; heard the silence before my father pointed to me.

I was Rosie.

The doctor looked surprised, then touched my arm. 'Will you speak to him then Rosie...? Let him hear your voice. As I said, it could make all the difference.'

Helpless, I stared at him, feeling my mother's eyes on me. Pleading with me. And yet I couldn't move. On the wall, a large white clock ticked off the seconds. The doctor must have wondered why it was I didn't answer and the silence only deepened around us.

At last, keeping my eyes away from my mother, I walked over to the bed. Max's head was sunk into the pillow, his own eyes closed fast against us. He looked as if he were a thousand miles away. Far from us. I took a deep breath.

Max.

Max.

But no sound was made. The air stayed trapped in my lungs and my brother's name no more than a shape on my tongue. I sensed rather than heard another sound, from deep in my mother's throat. I put my head closer to Max's ear.

Max.

But still there was no sound, no voice for him to hear. Nothing to bring Max back.

The doctor turned to my father who murmured something, an explanation perhaps. I stood away from the bed. My father tried to smile at me, but neither of us could look at my mother.

And Max stayed asleep. Lost to us. Lost to me.

In the car home my mother stared out of the window. It was beginning to be dawn, streaks of new sky smearing the edges of the glass. My father drove slowly, talking about what tomorrow would bring. Max would wake up, he said. He was over the worst. He would come back to us.

Nobody spoke. Nobody agreed with him. They had needed me, my *mother* had needed me. She had needed my voice to bring him back and my voice had stayed locked up, not mine to use.

At home my parents went to their room. And I to mine. And now I *could* hear my mother through the wall. She was crying – terrible smothered sobs. If anyone had mentioned my name to her now, she would have turned away forever. The sound drove me out of the house, and into the road. A bus came along taking night shift workers back to their homes. And took me back to the hospital.

In the ward it was still dark, curtains still drawn. Max lay as we had left him – asleep, unwilling to wake. He looked further away than ever. And now the flesh had begun to shrink into the hollows of his face. Hard to think that anything could rouse him now.

I laid my hands on his, and they were cold. He had squandered every ounce of sun stored up in his skin. I put my mouth to his ear, pressed my lips together on the first letter of his name. But still no sound, nothing he could hear.

I gave up, and gave in. My mother was right to cry, right to turn away. I moved my mouth from his ear to his cheeks, pressed my lips against cold downy skin. And kissed him. A long kiss. I must have thought I was saying goodbye.

And it was my mouth that felt him stir, ripples moving under his skin. Beneath my lips, small electric shocks. His eyes fluttered then opened.

He smiled at me. 'Hello Rosie,' he said. 'You're early.'

Later, being Max, he made everything right. Or tried to.

Sitting upright in the hospital bed where he had almost died, grinning and apologetic, he told us it was all because of a bet someone had made in the pub. Not one of the boys, but an older man, having fun at his expense, daring him to drink. No one else had seen it happen. 'Stupid thing to do,' Max said, running his fingers through his hair, which was greasier, more gleaming than ever. 'Really sorry about all this.' He smiled at us, tired and charming. Max could be irresistible when he chose.

And so what could my parents do but smile back? They could smell the unmetabolised alcohol that had nearly killed him, escaping from every pore. But he was unscathed, he had returned to us.

Returned to me.

So we didn't lose Max that time. He came home and for the rest of the holiday allowed himself to be bound to the house, forbidden to go out. It was a kind of fiction we all kept up, pretending that Max was still of the age to be forbidden anything. And kindly, being the boy he was, he went along with the pretence.

My father wanted a different school for me, but I made it clear where I wanted to go. Another school would mean another place and other people who would have to know. Even then he wouldn't listen, not to me. It was my mother who persuaded him, taking my part, making sure I returned to a place where the worst had already happened. Where nothing more could happen. She understood, and it shocked me how much she understood, when never a word was passed between us.

It was the right thing to do. This term the nuns were gentler than I remembered, their faces smoother than ever when set against mine. They were not without imagination. How could they be when they all wore the same rings as the Reverend Mother on their left hands? It takes imagination to be married to an invisible bridegroom. And more than anyone else, more than my father, they understood why the words had failed me. They understood guilt, and their part in it.

Only Sister Imelda kept her distance, never hid her distaste. She must have been broken-hearted when Mary-named-for-the-mother-of-God was discovered smoking cannabis behind the presbytery and expelled.

The doctor continued to visit, and week after week we sat in silence. It became a kind of conspiracy between us, that silence

– an agreement not to probe. We ended up playing Scrabble together, and that was our secret too. Only once did we come close to the edge of a discussion. He made a word on the board: B A B Y, and I came back with another word, one I'd been about to use anyway: D I E. For a moment we both stared at the game, then I shook my head very slightly. He poured the letters back into the box. I got quite fond of him.

Max went back to his school. Two years later he passed all his exams and was able to take his pick of universities. He chose London without ever seeming to have given it much thought.

Except that he *had* thought about it. 'London, Rosie. Hardly any distance. Then you can come live with me.'

I must have looked startled at that. Why should I need to live with him? Eighteen-year-old Max – taller, broader, an adult now – observed me. 'It won't be the same Rosie, at home after I'm gone. You know that don't you?' He paused, then said again: *'Don't you?'*

We were in the garden as usual. He nodded towards the house. *'Look* at her, Rosie.'

He was talking about our mother. Even from out here, we could see her, through all the different windows – vacuuming, dusting, shifting things. From room to room, her slim figure moved with a purpose of its own.

What that purpose was I couldn't have said, wouldn't have wanted to say. But I didn't need to think about it. It seemed to me that Max was simply pointing out the obvious – that our mother was perpetually in motion, never still, her face turned inwards as she moved. I no longer remembered a time when she had ever been different.

Max said, 'Do you think that's all she does when we're not here – hoovers, dusts? Endlessly, like it's important?'

I shrugged. I knew the house slumped into awkward silence the moment he walked out of the door. I knew that all the noise, and the atmosphere – and sometimes, it seemed, the very air we breathed – went with him when he left, like a troupe of actors following him offstage. But I also knew our parents and the way they worked, still trying to mend what had been broken more than ten years ago. And if their house was silent, if my mother was unable to be still, whose fault was that?

Besides, he was leaving out the letters, the warmth that poured off the page. I didn't need anything to be different.

Chapter Three

Two days since Caroline died.

Two days since they found me, blundering through her house, the only other person to have been there. Mute and confused, with only a blank where my memory should be.

Two days and still Max has managed not to leave me alone with the police who want to talk to me. He's determined to stay with me no matter what. He is stricken with loss, sick with grief. You can see it in his face, in the way he stands, in the gleam that's gone from his body. Yet still he is toiling, piling brick upon brick on that wall, trying to keep me safe.

Today the police brought a pile of newspapers with them and put them down in front of me. They must have realised we didn't have any in the house, that Max was trying to keep everything at a distance, protecting me. Trying to make it seem as if nothing had really happened.

And of course, he can't help but fail. I hear him crying for her in his room at night, smothering the sound, trying to keep that from me too. Then there are the police, determined to bring it all home. They make

51

a point of telling me about the way they found her, her tall body foetal and bleeding against those smart railings at the bottom of her smart stone steps. Red against black. They are quite visual in their descriptions. I think they do it to make it real, make me understand that it actually happened. They want to paint a picture of the truth, just like the nuns did.

So they describe Caroline, the blood and the bits of skull. The damage to her face – and they watch me. But *I* watch Max and so long as he looks at me as he always has, his face empty of blame, accusing me of nothing, I can't feel what they want me to feel. So long as Max believes in me, then *I* can believe in me.

But if there was no Max, then what would I believe? Exactly what would I have forgotten...?

Max knows what frightens me. It's the reason he stays, refuses to let down his guard. He knows they are waiting, biding their time, and no wall is going to keep them out.

Chapter Four

I was eighteen when I came home from school for good and discovered Max was right. I didn't know anything about life in our house. I stepped off the train – and Max wasn't there.

No one was there – not even my father. He always had been before, waiting on the platform till the train stopped, ready to greet me with a hug that used to last for one long, long moment. He always hugged me like that, before picking up my bags and carrying them to the car. We wouldn't touch again until we said goodbye, my father and I. But it was always a good hug, that first hug beside the train.

Always my father, then, waiting for me, and more often than not, Max as well. Never my mother though. She said she needed to stay home to get things ready for a home-coming. And she would be as good as her word. I'd walk into the house, where every surface gleamed and whose air was fragrant with the scents of roast chicken and lemon pie, my favourite supper. In my bedroom, even my dolls' faces smelled of polish and my books would be on my shelves, lined up like soldiers. All waiting for me.

A house made ready. Welcoming and warm. My mother's cheek, in contrast, would be cold, as if it had been icy there, in whichever room she'd been, listening for the crunch of gravel in the drive.

This time though, everything was different. I stepped off the train and nobody was waiting for me. I stood as the platform cleared of people, and still there was no one I recognised. Then, at the far end a smallish, stoutish figure appeared in a hurry. And still I didn't know who it was. Didn't recognise it even when the figure waved to me.

I walked up close – and saw the stranger who had arrived to meet me. In three months my mother had changed. Where my father had been large, bear-like in his bulk, she had always been slim and sharp-edged, even in middle age. Not any more; suddenly she was plump, padded out with flesh, and somehow shorter as a result.

I stared at her and she blushed, aware of me marking the changes in her – the coat that had grown too tight, and the hair that needed styling. There were grey roots showing close to the scalp. Eventually she pointed to my luggage, and pretended to laugh. 'Good grief Rose. What on earth are you doing bringing all this home with you?'

I glanced at my trolley with its columns of cases and bags, and objects that couldn't be fitted into any kind of container – cassette player, posters, cushions, a kettle, a toaster. Everything that had furnished a separate life for nine years.

I shrugged apologetically.

My mother frowned. 'Well why ever? I thought all this went into storage until you go back. They have always let you before.'

I blinked at her. I wasn't going back. I'd finished school, even after staying that extra year alongside the girls studying for Oxbridge. Those days were over and I'd come home. Surely she hadn't forgotten?

But she had forgotten. She saw me blink and realisation swept over her. She blushed deeper still, and made a small awkward movement that strained the seams of her coat. I heard something pop.

She turned on her heel and as she did so, staggered. Instinctively I steadied her and just for a moment our hands touched. Quickly, as if she couldn't help herself, she drew away her hand, and we walked on in silence until I couldn't bear it any more. I wanted that hug, brief and tight and heartfelt. I felt for a piece of paper on which to scribble.

Where's Dad?

We had arrived at the car. My mother read the question, but didn't say anything. She seemed to be having difficulty fitting her key in the lock. I knocked on the roof of the car, softly, pleading for an answer.

'Your father?' She blinked once, twice. 'He's not here.'

Well that was obvious. I climbed in, waited as she started up the engine, stalled it and tried again. My father often went away, summonsed by a mysterious thing called 'overseas accounts'. A man who could thank a waiter in any number of languages. But he rarely went away when I was home. Somehow he had always managed to be there, standing in for Max if the silence became too great.

A car blared its horn behind us. My mother had shot backwards out of the parking space without looking behind. Jamming her foot on the brake, she stopped the car and started to shake. With a shock I understood: this woman I could barely recognise was drunk. Not roaring and mad drunk, like drunks on the stage or on the street, but quietly, discreetly drunk.

Finally she spoke. 'I'm sorry, Rose. It's all going to come as a shock for you, what's happened. We wanted you to know, but it just didn't seem ... kind ... to tell you while you were still at school. You had exams, and besides, you know what the nuns are like. Divorce is a dirty word to them...'

Divorce. I stared at her. She looked away.

'It all happened quite quickly, just after you went back. Out of the blue someone made him an offer for the business, and your father took it. It meant early retirement. Freedom for him.'

She laughed suddenly, as if there something funny in what she had just said. *Freedom.* A word to make her wince and smile at the same time.

I listened and waited. She hadn't explained the other word. Divorce.

She glanced quickly at me, then looked away again. 'We should have told you. After the offer he told me he wanted to live in Italy. *Italy!* Can you imagine? When had he ever mentioned Italy? Has he ever mentioned Italy to you, Rose? No, of course not. He asked me if I wanted to go with him. And I told him...' She paused, steadied herself and her eyes met mine. 'And I told him ... *no.* For the first time in my life. *No.*'

With this last word, her voice had softened, making it sound like an appeal.

Then her shoulders sagged. 'Oh Rose, don't look at me like that. It's all right. He wants you to go straight out and join him. He's on the side of some hill somewhere, overlooking a lake. He says it's beautiful. He promises you'll make friends. More importantly, there's a hospital nearby with an excellent occupational therapy unit. He wants you to get your voice back. In fact, he's determined you get your voice back – even if you have to end up speaking Italian!'

She smiled faintly, willing me to see the joke, however slight.

I stared at her. Then mouthed the words. Easy words that anyone could read.

Max. Where's Max?

The smile vanished. Her eyes dropped as she looked at her hands instead. She had taken off her wedding ring.

'I don't know, Rosie. I've no idea where Max is. He said he was coming home two weeks ago, but he hasn't turned up.'

We stared at one another. The man whose car she had nearly driven into had appeared in the window on her side, was shouting through the glass, but neither of us took any notice of him. We scarcely knew he was there.

Both of us thinking the same thing. It was just us now. My mother and me. Distance had been our medium, and now it was gone. And no protective wall between us. Where was Max?

If my mother was different, so was the house.

Inside it was too hot for summer. I touched a radiator and it burned my hand. It was as if someone had gone out one cold spring day with the heating left on, and no one had remembered to switch it off. But, more shockingly, it was untidy, the way my mother had suddenly become untidy, showing signs of neglect.

She had made a kind of effort though.

Scents of roast chicken crept to meet us as we came through the front door, as if to apologise for the dust and the empty wine bottles and the unopened mail stacked up beside the mat.

And she must have been at work in my bedroom too. It was spic and span, smelling as it had always done of polish and talc and toffees. Of me. Years later Max told me the truth about my room. It turned out that my father had slept there every night, all the years I had been away at school. He had gone to bed, woken and got dressed, amongst the talc and toffees, and never left a trace of himself. He had made sure it stayed my room, so that I never guessed.

So much I didn't know.

We ate in front of the television. Then we pretended to watch a film, not taking any of it in. We were missing a third person – and a fourth, other mouths to fill a silence the TV couldn't hope to hide.

Once or twice she would force her gaze towards me and smile. 'This is nice, isn't it, Rosie? Just the two of us?' She had offered me wine, politely, as if I were a guest, from the bottle that was rapidly emptying beside her chair. I turned it down.

The evening wore on and the bottle drained only to be replaced by another. I tried not to watch but I couldn't help it. I had never seen my mother drink before, not like this, gulp after distracted gulp, her eyes distant as if she was somewhere else completely. Eventually she began to nod in her chair. The cushion by her head already had the shape of her face pressed into it. She started to snore gently.

I stood up and touched her arm. Sleepily she opened her eyes – only to shock me with a smile, warm and sunny as a child's. I pointed upstairs and she nodded, struggled to her feet.

I listened to her negotiating the stairs. If you hadn't known, you might have thought there was a little girl in the house, a very large, heavy little girl, making her obedient way to bed.

Next morning I came down early, and everything was different again.

She was in the kitchen, standing ramrod straight in her dressing gown.

'You've been tidying up, Rose.' Her voice crackled as if she was an old woman. 'Whatever possessed you? You must have been at it all night.'

Her eyes were so hostile, I couldn't bring myself to meet them. I turned away to look for cereal, bread – anything would have done – and there was nothing. Nothing in the cupboard, nothing in the fridge. It wasn't food that had been fleshing out my mother.

Her voice crackled again from behind me.

She forced herself to sound calm. 'So ... did anyone call last night, after I went to bed? Max, did he...?'

I shook my head. It was listening for the phone that had kept me up and busy gnawing away at the chaos of the house – washing, scraping, dusting, folding. It had done me good, bringing it back some way to how it used to be.

But the hours had slid past midnight – and Max hadn't phoned.

My mother said: 'I rang his hall of residence last week. And all I got was the janitor. Rude man. He said the students had all left for the summer, made it sound as if I was stupid for asking.'

With the irritation in her voice, she pushed past me to open the fridge door, hand reaching for a bottle. Then, feeling my eyes on her, she flushed faintly. She took her hand away. It was a quarter to eight in the morning. For a moment she continued to stand, breathing hard. She couldn't have hid it even if she had tried; my mother didn't want me home – hated the fact I was home – watching her every move.

I fled so she could be free, get what she wanted out of the fridge. In another part of the house I sat by the phone and waited for Max to ring.

And he didn't ring. It wore me out waiting

61

for him to ring. Meanwhile my mother stayed in the kitchen, banging objects to make it sound as if she was busy, taking her resentment out on the pans, as if now they were the ones who were watching her, passing judgment.

At midday, though, the banging stopped and my mother emerged from the kitchen. And this time she was smiling. She had a cup and saucer brimming with a clear liquid from which she sipped daintily. She curled up in the chair next to mine, plump and catlike. Relaxed now. And still. She leaned towards me, like a conspirator.

'I kept meaning to clean the house, you know. But then...' she giggled. 'The more I didn't clean, the more I didn't clean. And do you know what, Rosie? Nobody died! The roof didn't fall in. The world didn't stop turning. Makes you wonder what it was all for doesn't it, doing all that housework for all those years, like a dog chasing its tail.'

She smiled, her face lighting up so it was impossible not to smile back. She said, 'Your father always told me I did too much. He said I should relax, a little dust didn't matter. I should have listened to him.' She hiccupped, and took another sip from the tea cup, then laid her head back against the sofa and closed her eyes. I had the feeling she had already forgotten what she had been talking about.

I picked up a book and pretended to read, but over the tops of the pages I watched her. She continued to sip from her cup and hummed, apparently happy. But then, as I watched, a frown began to appear in the newly plump features. Minutes passed and the frown deepened, until finally she leaned across and pulled the book away from my face. She didn't look angry or hostile – only anxious. Terribly, terribly anxious.

'Rosie,' she said, spilling the liquor in her cup. 'I know it's stupid, but I keep thinking there's something I should remember. Something I've forgotten. It doesn't matter what I'm doing, sooner or later it hits me – I've forgotten something I shouldn't. It frightens me, Rosie. I'm so sure it's important and I rack my brains and I try and I try to remember, but I never can.'

She thrust her round, frightened face into mine. 'Whatever could it be, Rose? What is it I've forgotten?'

As she spoke her eye seemed to catch sight of something behind me, moving in the shadow of the TV. Something I couldn't see. She gave a small gasp, and I thought fright was set to give way to terror. But she checked it. She dipped her head into her cup, and when she looked up again she was smiling. A minute later she began to talk about the roses taking over the garden.

That was the first time. But it happened

every day after that, at different times and different places. My mother was being haunted by something that had slipped her mind. It never went away. Every day she asked me, anxiously scanning my face as if I, more than anyone, was the one who would know.

What is it Rosie? What have I forgotten?

That second evening was the same as the one before. We sat by the light of the television until she began to nod, and then snore. I touched her arm, and again she woke to give me that smile, sunny and child-like and caught me by surprise. She clutched my hand as I helped her to her feet. And this time she didn't flinch when I touched her. Quite the opposite.

Leaning forward she kissed me lightly on the nose. 'Goodnight Rosie Posie.'

The phone rang. I jumped and ran.

'Rose?'

It was my father's voice. A faint wash of static on the line hinted at distance, of mountains and seas between us. I clutched the phone to my ear.

'Poor Rosie. Not much of a homecoming, eh? We should have told you before. God knows why we thought it was better this way. It was your mother really. She wanted it all finished before you had to know about

64

it. It was in case you thought that something could still be done. She didn't want to get your hopes up.'

He paused, and the only sound was the static on the line. Then his words came in a rush.

'It had to happen, Rosie. Sooner or later. All these years – I couldn't do anything for her, not after the ... well ... you know. She wouldn't be comforted. And she wouldn't forgive herself for feeling the way she did. For grieving too much. The truth is, she found her own way – her own means to stop being unhappy, just for small moments. I guess you know what I'm talking about now. Lots of people get caught that way, through the drink. They can't help it, any more than she could. I gave up trying to help her, Rosie. I needed to make her happy and I couldn't. I failed her.'

He stopped and the wash of static grew louder. He listened to my silence then said: 'Rosie, I want you to come out here, to me. It's all I want, actually. There's sunshine and good food, a different life. There's a ticket in the post. Just get yourself on a plane, soon as you can. Come and see what life can be like when the people around you are happy... It's what your mother wants you to do. Believe it or not, it's all she does want – for you to be happy. So come to me, Rosie. Live with me.'

I heard him and just for a moment I could see it, stepping off the plane, and my father waiting, just like at the station to give me that first good hug. Squeezing me tight.

But the image disappeared, quickly as it arrived. Instead it was my mother I saw, ramrod straight and glaring. My mother catching movements in the shadows, on the edge of terror. Kissing me on the nose. *Good night Rosie Posie.* What had she forgotten?

I held the phone a little further from my ear, and somehow he read the quality of silence. My father sighed. 'Write to me, Rosie. Tell me you'll come.'

Already knowing I wouldn't. That I would never come. In silence we said goodbye, knowing exactly what we were doing. It would always be goodbye now.

Midnight and the phone rang again. This time it could only be one person. It could only be Max. I snatched it up.

And he didn't say anything. Nobody did. Out of the phone came ... nothing. Such a long pause of nothing, you might never have guessed there were two people on the line, that they were connected. I waited as the seconds ticked, until the phone clicked and went dead. I put it back on the hook, telling myself it couldn't have been him. Max would have spoken. He would never have stayed silent.

Silence was my thing.

The next morning I was better prepared for the day ahead. I avoided the kitchen and went shopping instead, in the village post office where they had known me for years. Knew all *about* me. The days when I had believed that killing a child was no one's business but our own were long gone.

In any case, Mrs Platt, mother of fat boy Roger, had made her mind up about me long ago. Her mouth twitched as I came through the door, the way Sister Imelda's used to. She watched me, tight lipped as I filled a basket.

At the counter she raked her eye over what I had picked off the shelves. 'Your brother's finally home then?' When I indicated that he wasn't, she sniffed. 'Well it looks like he is judging by this lot. That everything then?'

I nodded and she smirked. 'Well that's where you're wrong.' She reached under the counter to produce four bottles of wine and two litres of gin. 'You'll be wanting these as well. Better not go home without them.' We observed each other as she dared me to do just that. Defeated I opened my purse – but even this seemed another small victory to her.

'And don't think I'll be taking money off you. Your mother pays me at the end of the month nice and regular. She's got it all sorted, poor lady.'

67

As I left the shop, I heard her say to another woman who had just entered, employing a whisper so loud she could have filled a stage: 'That's the Bryant girl. *Says* she can't speak.'

Mrs Platt was right; it was all Max's stuff I had chosen. Sausages and hummus and oranges. I loaded them into the fridge, ready for him – and there they stayed. A week went by, then two weeks. The fridge began to smell after I forgot to throw away the sausages. I replaced them, but still he wasn't here to eat them. It was still just my mother and me, alone together.

Yet it wasn't so bad. I could have had a mother who stayed all day the way she was in the mornings, angry and itching, when an extra large crash in the kitchen would send me running in, afraid she had come to grief. Or the phone would ring, bringing us together when it was better to have been apart.

Mornings were when she couldn't be trusted by herself. Once she scalded herself with a kettle. Another time she slipped and cut her head on the corner of the table. The doctor sewed up the jagged edges of the wound and never seemed to notice that she was shaking for a different reason altogether.

It was only the mornings though. Come midday and she was relaxed, not the same

68

woman, ready to do her shopping. Wafting down to Mrs Platt's shop, charming every one she met on the way. In the afternoons she was a young woman again, younger than the woman who used to cuddle me close when Max didn't want me near. Before the baby.

She laughed at things in the afternoons.

She laughed at me, she laughed at Mrs Platt. She laughed when she fell over, and when I picked her up again. Most of all she laughed at herself, like when she put ice in her tea and sugar in her gin. Or tried to squeeze into clothes she was too plump for. She never seemed to wonder why nothing seemed to fit any more. And she scarcely mentioned Max or my father.

It was other things that bothered her. Every now and then she'd look at me and frown in bewilderment. *Why are you here, Rose? Are you ill? Why aren't you back at school?*

And once, out of the blue, she asked me: 'Where's the bracelet, Rosie? The one I got you for your birthday. Didn't you like it darling? Did I choose the wrong thing?'

Yet I loved the afternoons. She followed me around the house as I cleaned or read or simply waited, as I was always waiting in those first weeks, for the phone to ring. These were her happy hours, what she had traded everything else in for. And like my father, I didn't have anything more precious to offer.

But then would come the evening and everything changed again. First the smile would disappear, then she would begin to frown and fret, as she wracked her brain trying to remember.

And sooner or later, it came, always the same question, bursting out of her in a wail:

'What is it, Rose? I've forgotten something, and I can't remember what it is, not for the life of me. What is it Rose? What have I forgotten?'

Nothing for it but to watch her drink and wait for sleep to rescue her.

'Good night Rosie Posie.'

Rosie Posie. It made me want to laugh and cry – or reach for other people. One evening I found my father's number in her address book and picked up the phone. A young woman answered in Italian. I put the phone down in a rush. A couple of days later I tried again, and again it was her voice that answered. She sounded friendly – and breathy like the girls who used to ask for Max. When she heard the silence she seemed to know exactly who it was. *'Carissimo, è ki tua Rosa sul telephono.'* She sang the words into the room behind her, untroubled, even by me, the troubling daughter. Is this what my father meant when he invited me to come and try life among people who knew how to be happy?

Carissimo. Whatever else, I knew what that word meant. I put the phone down and when it began to ring again, I let it go.

Anyway, it wasn't my father I wanted. It was Max, who had promised always to be there, and wasn't. I'd been home a month and he was still breaking his promise.

Chapter Five

But that was long ago. Here, it's been three days since Caroline died.

And the police are trying to make him break his promise again, leave me alone again. They don't want him to be there when they talk to me. They already have other sources of 'information' about me, snippets of gossip and make-believe and who knows what else. Now they need to hear what I have to say, confirm what they think they already know. Yet how do they force a speechless woman to speak? They could take me into a room alone and ask me anything they like, but that would be labelled oppression. I know that's true because it's what I heard Max say to them when they all thought I couldn't hear.

I listened to Max through the door, his voice low and reasonable, explaining to them what 'oppression' was. He said it was a legal term, which in this context would mean taking a mute girl with a history of breakdown and mental fragility, depriving her of the one person she could trust, to question her about matters that could only damage her further. Whatever she told them under those circumstances would be seen as unreliable. Inadmissible was the word he used.

If he's right, and oppression is a legal term, then I should have thought the police would know everything about it already. So why tell them? If nothing else it will only put their backs up.

But that's not what bothers me. What makes me fret is that the girl that Max describes to them doesn't sound remotely like me.

He's lying to them, making me seem hopeless and helpless when I am not. I've not been helpless or hopeless in years. Ask down at The Centre. Ask the clients who come to us for help, wrung out by addiction and parched by life. Ask them in the soup kitchen and the dispensary where it's me that runs things – at least I did until the day Caroline died, and Max told me not to go out because the press are there, waiting for me to appear. Ask the people who come to me for help. They'll tell you if I'm helpless or hopeless. I'm neither of those. I just happen to be mute.

It's shocking really, what he's doing on my

behalf. Max is supposed to be a man of God, but he's lying, building me an entire wall out of lies.

Chapter Six

So where *was* Max when I needed him, that summer when I finished school and discovered what life at home was really all about? I found out – eventually.

It had happened in the small hours, when my mother was asleep. I'd tried waking her but she was dead to the world. In the morning, though, she was sober and hard-edged as she always was, fierce and shaking in the kitchen. I looked at her and wondered how I would tell her. Her dressing gown was dirty, and the grey roots had grown a good four inches from her scalp now, like a tree ring measuring the time since she had decided time simply had to stop.

I had the news written down. A lone policeman had arrived in the night, ringing the door bell to bring me out of sleep. He had wanted to talk to my mother but of course that was impossible. At least he had known to expect silence. He was our local PC, and knew all about the sister in the house, the one who couldn't speak.

Now I gave my mother the sheet of writing I had prepared for her, wrapping my fingers around hers to ensure she kept a hold of it. So she could see it was important. She read it standing up, unwilling to sit.

Max has turned up. He is in hospital, but he's safe. It was a drugs overdose. Heroin. They say that he injected too much or the drug was too strong. Anyway he survived, and he's going to be all right.

For a long moment I wondered if she had forgotten how to read. She stared at the words I had written for her, and yet her face hadn't changed. Finally, though, she looked up. 'There must be a mistake, Rose.' Her voice was flat. 'You know Max would never take drugs.' She tossed my words onto the kitchen table, abandoning them.

I picked up the paper and scribbled: *He was lucky. He was with friends. They took care of him, got him to hospital.* As I wrote it occurred to me that Max was fortunate with his friendships. This was the second time friends had saved him, looked after him better than he was willing to look after himself.

Suddenly my mother sat down, heavily on a kitchen chair, as if her legs had lost their brittle strength. I touched her arm.

'What else?' She said, her voice still flat. 'What else did they tell you? Write it down quickly.'

We need to go to the hospital. Bring him home.

She stood up and walked away from me.

Ten minutes later she was downstairs again, dressed and ready to go. She ignored the tea I had made for her. And stayed away from the fridge.

She was still sober as we travelled up to London. She had put a hat over the grey roots, and found a coat that didn't squeeze her like a bag lady. She wore good shoes, a good skirt and looked like anybody's mother.

But what would Max say when he woke and found her there, apparently twenty years older, not looking like *his* mother?

On the train she pretended to doze, but I could see her eyeballs twitching beneath the lids. I knew enough now to guess the way her arms would be itching and the morning hurting her. How long would she last? Hidden beneath her handbag, her hands were gripping each other tight. I wanted to take and hold them in my own, but I knew better than to try.

So I stared out of the window and tried to get used to it. The shock of it. We had never dreamt it was drugs that made Max disappear. I wondered if my mother hadn't been right after all. Maybe there had been a mistake. How *could* it be Max? Then I remembered another time, when the vodka had nearly killed him. No one had expected that either. No one had seen it coming. A Max none of us knew.

When the train stopped, my mother stood up like everybody else. She was steady as she walked briskly beside me along the London pavement, despite her heels, despite her added bulk. Now I could see how she had excelled all those years of my growing up, never giving herself away – at least not to me. A brisk walk and a set mouth, a face turned inwards. This was how it was done. Once by accident my hand brushed her hand and it was cool, just as I remembered.

Max was unconscious when we arrived, still hooked up to the machines in intensive care. Despite that, the nurse said he was safe, he simply hadn't woken up yet. So how did they know he was safe? Yet still they seemed to. No one on the ward appeared to be worried about him any more.

We stood on either side of his bed and stared into the face on the pillow. Max hadn't stopped eating in those days, was still healthy. He still looked like himself. The ward was hot, bringing a flush and a faint sheen of sweat to his cheeks. There was golden stubble on his chin, catching the light. He looked utterly relaxed, like someone lying down, enjoying a sun that shone exclusively for him.

They had told us he had stopped breathing twice, and yet here he was.

The Intensive Care nurse said, 'He really

should be awake by now. Everything's normal.'

She sounded impatient. I suppose she wanted the bed. There were other emergencies, other people, more worthy than Max, who hadn't taken their own poison, and brought this on themselves. Yet, when I looked at Max, this was how I wanted him to stay – asleep. This way he would be safe. The dials around the bed would continue to monitor him, the tubes to hold him down. While he slept, the sugar and salts would go on feeding into his veins, requiring no effort on his part, not even his consent. Keeping him alive.

But my mother wouldn't have it. She gripped his shoulder, and shook it. 'Max,' she said loudly. 'Wake up.'

Her voice startled me, sounding like it used to when we were young, unwilling to get up in the morning. A voice you couldn't ignore. 'Max,' she said again. 'It's time to wake up.' She shook him again, harder still.

Without thinking I touched his hand. A bird's touch, different from the shaking my mother was giving him.

But it was my touch that woke him. His eyes snapped open in a blaze of blue and looked at my mother. Already he was smiling, back to the Max we knew. Then his eyes slid past her, to me, and the smile turned into a grin.

'Hello Rosie.'

We walked alongside the bed as they wheeled him down to the recovery ward. He only needed to rest, the doctor said. A few days and he'd be right as rain – until he went back to the drugs. The doctor pulled a curtain around Max's bed, then took us to the nurses' room where he addressed most of his remarks to my mother. She was still making an excellent job of her front, fooling everyone around. Only the Intensive Care nurse had seemed momentarily interested in the slight tremor of her hands.

Nor was Max fooled. As we had followed the doctor, he'd caught my eye and winked towards my mother, making a small gesture with his hand, pretending to knock back a drink. He laughed at the shock in my face.

'Unfortunately your son is heroin-dependent,' the doctor was saying to my mother. 'The good news is that now is an excellent time for him to come off. Thanks to the last few days here, his system is clear. He could carry on being clear if he wanted to. The thing to remember is any addiction can be fought, with the right attitude.'

He raised his eyes at my mother, who nodded. Her hat was making her look impressively sage. The doctor looked at her and approved.

'A little help, a little backbone shown in

the right way, and you'll have your son back.'

He pulled open a drawer and took out a pile of leaflets. 'You might find these helpful. They'll give you the numbers for counselling and private detoxification centres, that sort of thing. I wouldn't wait for the NHS to find you a place. Sometimes it can be worth throwing money at a problem.'

My mother took the leaflets and folded them neatly in her bag. Beneath the hat, her face was smooth and set.

'By the way,' the doctor added. 'Who is Rosie? He kept mentioning a *Rosie*. Over and over again. Is she the girlfriend? If she is, it's probable she needs help too. In fact you can bank on it. Addicts tend to be co-dependent.'

I felt my mother stiffen. She found a point over his shoulder, and stared at it. Then indicated to me.

He looked at me, as if noticing me for the first time. 'Oh, it's your daughter, the one who can't...' He stopped himself saying any more. 'I see. Well ... good enough. Nothing to worry about so far as she's concerned. Got her mother looking after *her.*'

Isn't it funny? Everybody saw us that way. *My mother* looking after *me.* Even Mrs Platt thought the same. The doctor made his goodbyes and let us go back to the ward, to Max.

And Max was gone.

The bed in which they had wheeled him down was empty, as was the bag of clothes he had been given to carry on his chest. I saw my mother take one look and her lips part. And then it fled – all the front, the one she had been keeping up all day. She ran up the ward, screaming for the doctor, for Max, for anyone who would bring him back. She slipped onto her back in her good shoes, and screamed at the nurses who tried to help her up. She screamed at the security men when they came. Screamed at me in the cab.

She only stopped screaming when I stopped the cab, and helped her walk into a wine bar where I watched her take her first drink of the day. I didn't know what else to do. I was eighteen. I gave the bartender money so that in the corner my mother could drink herself into a better place. I had no idea how to stop her. Or even *why* I should stop her, blocking the one small route to happiness she possessed.

As she grew tired, I stroked her head, gently, so she barely noticed. Tried to let her know I was still there. That I wouldn't leave her.

A week later, I sent a telegram to my father. He phoned back immediately.

'Rose, little Rose. What are they putting

you through?'

Nothing. That's what I said. My father listened to my silence, then he said, 'Rose, I'm going to tell you this, even though he made me promise not to. I want you to know; Max is here, with me. He just turned up yesterday. "Taking time out", he says.'

I heard him and felt a stab of shock and hurt. Max had gone to my father, and run away from me.

'Now listen to me, Rosie. I know what you're thinking. But you'll be wrong. He's here for a reason. He can call it "time out", but I don't believe him. It's something else, and I don't know what it is. He's being incredibly charming. Charming the socks off everyone here. But they don't know him like I do. Rose...?' He paused as if I might still have answered him. 'Rosie, I'm going to keep him here as long as I can, but I don't think he's staying. He's got a – I can't put it into words – a *leaving* look to him.'

He sighed. 'I'll try and make him stay. I'll do my best for him, Rosie.'

He put the phone down. But a couple of days later he called again. Max had come, and now he was gone. He'd vanished in the night – together with the contents of my father's safe. My father said: 'I'm telling you this so you know he's all right in that department. He's got money. A lot of money. It will keep body and soul together.

He's not going to starve.'

But we both knew what the money would be used for. My father had mentioned keeping body and soul together. It seemed to me that Max was doing his best to prise them apart.

Chapter Seven

I read the leaflets the doctor gave to my mother.

They all said the same thing. A person would only overcome an addiction if they wanted to. Really wanted. I watched my mother drag herself around the house, and asked myself what it was she wanted.

Happiness, of course, if only for a little while. And forgetfulness. Yet most of the time the drink made her neither happy nor forgetful. In the mornings she was exhausted and angry. Her arms and legs ached and her skin crawled.

Surely she didn't want *this*. In the mornings addiction hurt her, every waking moment.

Come midday though, and things were different. By then she would have finished the first of the bottles from Mrs Platt's shop, and was safely on the way to where she wanted to be. She was like someone climbing into a car, getting ready for a journey to a short – a very short – stretch of happiness.

In the evening though, the journey seemed to be one only a worm would want to make, burrowing further and further into the earth, away from the light.

And it made you think. Is this what Max was after, too? Journey? Happiness? Forgetfulness? To get away from the light? Yet why would Max, beautiful Max, need any of that? More than anyone in the world, Max suited the light. He gleamed in the sun. Sometimes he looked as if he was made out of light itself.

I remembered the wink from his hospital bed. He hadn't seemed unhappy then. Just determined to get away. It was the journey he was after.

Some of the leaflets made it all so simple. They said addiction could be the result of genetic predisposition. They made it sound as if the world was full of people who were simply born to be addicted to something, doomed by a star-crossed pairing of their genes. I almost preferred to believe this. Star-crossed genes, wiping out entire fields of cause and effect.

The day of my birthday, and I ran downstairs to the letter box.

Silly, I know. It's what children do, desperate to see what the postman has brought them. I knew what I wanted to be there. And there was nothing. Not from Max. He was in a land where birthdays didn't exist. Or perhaps where every day was a birthday. He could make it that way – if my father's money was holding out.

Instead I opened a card with a lot more money inside and a printed greeting in Italian, along with my father's name. My mother appeared as I was slipping the card and money back into the envelope. She of course had been awake for hours. To my surprise, she took me by the hand and led me stiffly into the kitchen. Smiled at me almost shyly. She had laid out a breakfast – croissants, orange juice. Flowers on the table.

'Happy birthday, Rose.' She pushed a parcel into my hand with another quick, tight smile. I tried not to look startled. I hadn't even expected her to remember.

She watched me pull layers of paper out from under ribbon. Even now, my mother could still wrap presents like a professional. Finally, folded between wisps of tissue, I found my present – a bracelet. A thin chain of silver that reminded me of another chain, the bracelet I'd once had and lost, and never got back. But this one was different. It had charms hanging off it.

And I recognised it immediately. My mother had worn it when she was a girl, when charm bracelets were all the rage. She had kept it in the bottom of a drawer, and years and years ago we had found it, Max and I. All through my childhood I knew it was there, and coveted it. Now she had given it to me. I slipped it over my hand. Bicycles, cars, keys and boots, cats, pixies, bells and clocks hung suspended like tiny planets about my wrist, a solar system in miniature. And every one of them meant to bring me luck.

My mother said, 'I always knew you liked this. I'd find you poring over it when you were a little girl. It's not very fashionable, but then...' she gave a wry smile '...neither are you, Rose.'

She watched me a moment, and suddenly, as if the smile had somehow broken it, her face cracked. 'I'm so sorry, Rosie. About everything.' She began to cry, hiding her face in her hands.

I put my arms around her. For half a second she stiffened, her hands gripping the table as if to keep a purchase on herself. Then she gave way and leant into me. Her body shook against mine, and for the first time in years I was close enough to smell her, the scent of my mother, just as I remembered. Stronger now, and all bound up with other smells – alcohol and unwashed hair. But still she smelt of my mother, of long ago, and the very closeness of her threatened to overwhelm me.

I felt her stir, a signal for me to let go. She sat up straight. 'Well, we're a pair, aren't we,' she said. Somehow she'd managed to revert to her dry, morning voice. 'Whatever shall we do with ourselves?' She paused, then she whispered. 'Rosie, What am I going to do? I need a drink. All the time. Every minute of the day.'

There was a silence in our kitchen, broken only by the tinkle of the charms that were supposed to bring us luck.

I had thought there were no birthdays where Max was. But at midnight, the phone rang. Again there was silence. And this time I didn't tell myself it was a wrong number. I listened to the faint fizz of the line and tried to imagine where he was. Tried to imagine him standing next to me.

In silence I told him everything. How I wanted him to come home. How I needed help. Tears fell off my face, onto the receiver. I imagined them making soft pattering noises down the line. Max would know I was crying and I wanted him to know. I wanted him to look after me, us, even now, the way he was. I had just turned nineteen. I didn't think I could look after myself, let alone anyone else.

I held my breath. In the distance, I thought I heard something stir. The vibration of a word nearly spoken. I waited for

Max to speak to me, say something. Tell me he was coming home.

At the other end, the phone clicked and went dead.

Chapter Eight

Three days since Caroline died.

Three days, so you'd think they'd at least try to leave him in peace, down at The Centre. They need him of course, Max is needed everywhere. But look at him, the state of him. Max, beautiful Max, stoops as he walks, all the energy fled from him. He tries so hard to seem normal for my sake, but he can't hide it. Grief. Loss. Love.

And yet the telephone keeps ringing, and wearily he answers it. It's Ruth as usual, down at The Centre, not giving an inch. She's determined to bring him to her, determined to have him to herself. No sister to be in the way now. And best of all, no Caroline. This is what she has always wanted. I keep waiting for Max to make an excuse and stay at home, but he never does. Ruth calls, pretending it's urgent, and he goes.

This evening, though, when Max went out to The Centre, I switched on the TV. I needed to see what he is trying to keep from me.

And I timed it well. The first thing to appear on the screen was a photograph of Caroline. Max was there too. They'd been caught on their way into some kind of celebrity ball. Her arm is linked loosely through his, a careless joining of two bodies who don't need to cling. She is beautiful and so is he. They glow. They are utterly relaxed, eyes meeting the camera like an old friend. You can't imagine anything not turning out the way they wanted.

The picture vanishes and instead there's film of her front door in the aftermath, with hundreds of bouquets set against the railings. People must have watched her on television when she was alive and thought they knew her. Now she is dead and they think they are bereaved.

Outside the front door, surrounded by flowers, a policeman is talking to the camera, his lips moving not quite in sync with the words. I recognise him as one who has tried to talk to me, with Max always in the way. He is middle-aged, and wears a crumpled suit with what look like biscuit crumbs down the front. But his eyes are sharp, completely steady as they face the camera.

'Miss Caroline Marsh was a greatly admired woman who achieved much in a tragically short life. Whoever has done this has done the entire public an injury. But let

88

me make myself clear. This is one case in which we have a clear lead. Take my word for it, the person responsible will be found and brought to account.'

He seems to be looking straight at me, so that despite myself I blush. Kill once, kill twice. Forget once, forget twice.

But Max doesn't think that way. And so long as Max believes in me, then I can believe, and the blush dies away.

It's only the hole in my memory that draws me in, tries to pull me closer, threatens to make me fall.

Chapter Nine

The morning after my birthday I came downstairs, and my mother was clearing out the fridge.

'It needed defrosting,' she said. 'I'm throwing everything we don't want.' She kept her face hidden as she spoke, and tried to do the same with the shaking in her hands. She had removed all the wine bottles from the shelves.

After a moment I joined her in the task, extracting the hummus and the sausages that no one was going to eat. Threw them into the bin alongside the bottles.

By the afternoon the shaking in her hands had taken over her entire body. I wrapped blankets around her and put hot water bottles between her legs. Later, as she bent double on her bed dry retching into a bowl, I held her head the way she used to hold mine when I was very young, her hand cool on my forehead. Between fits of shivering and sweating, she lay back and closed her eyes, scarcely breathing, so there was no telling if she was asleep or unconscious. I stayed with her all night, afraid of what might happen if I closed my own eyes.

Just before dawn her mouth fell open and she began to snore and murmur into her pillow. My mother was asleep and dreaming, not by drifting into unconsciousness, but through sheer fatigue.

The next day was the same. A struggle with shaking and sickness and pain. Yet she didn't stop the fight, nor did she the next day or the day after. I began to think this was all there was to it, like having flu. It was as the doctor had said; you just had to have the right attitude, show a bit of backbone. The effort would make you ill, the way it was making her ill, but then you would recover. This was what I thought. I was nineteen. What did I know?

Three days after she asked me to buy cigarettes. Overnight, it seemed, my mother had become a smoker. She needed something to do with her hands. I cycled off on Max's old bike as the bells were ringing for the ten o'clock service in the village church, thinking I would be home in no time.

I was wrong. Mrs Platt's face beneath her Sunday hat loomed through the glass door of her shop, smirking as she tapped the *closed* sign. Sunday – of course. So I cycled to the pub, where years ago Max had nearly killed himself with the drink, and it was closed too. I went to the petrol station where my mother used to fill the car before she became unfit to drive, but the boy there only stared in amusement as I tried to make him understand what I had come in for. I didn't need a mirror to know what I looked like to him. A tow-haired girl who couldn't speak, miming the act of smoking a cigarette. Then pointing and pleading. A *mad* tow-haired girl who shouldn't be let out.

I had to cycle miles and miles, to the nearest supermarket where all I needed to do was stand in line at the tobacco counter and point. Only then could I turn for home – except that the bike had a puncture by now, and I didn't have anything to mend it with. Yet it all seemed worth it. My mother needed something that wasn't wine. Now bumping against the front wheel was a bag of lesser vice, cigarettes to keep her hands busy for a fortnight. I was triumphant.

It was almost dark when I got back.

October already and the evenings were starting earlier and colder. I wheeled the cycle up the drive, expecting her to have the house lights switched on. But she hadn't. The hall had a chilly, dark air that made me uneasy, already expecting the worst.

On the floor in the sitting room was my mother. She was slumped on her knees, her head buried in the sofa, an empty bottle of gin beside her. Never mind that it was Sunday, Mrs Platt must have arranged a special delivery for her best customer. I ran and touched her, terrified that she might not be breathing, but she was. Breathing and unconscious, in a place where nothing could reach her.

Then I saw the photographs. A box of them, emptied out and spread around her head on the sofa cushions. This is what she had been doing while I was out, passing the time until I came back – looking at photographs. Lots of them. Here were countless different versions of my face and Max's, staring out from squares of shiny paper. All those years of growing up and my father had never stopped taking photographs, part of the hope that we could still be normal. I picked one up at random – and there we are, Max and me. And it's just like in all the others; my eyes are guarded, thin face giving nothing away. It's my brother who is smiling, hard, as if to make up for me not smiling. Max is just smiling and smiling.

I concentrated on Max's smile – and allowed myself to look behind it. He can't have been more than ten in the picture, but here he was, the Max of all the days, our link with the past and with each other. I could see now how it had worked – Max and his smile, the engine of the family, keeping us going.

I found something else, half concealed in her hands. My mother had slid into unconsciousness like a woman who has died, clutching her last precious object. Not a photograph. Gently I prised her fingers apart and removed a piece of paper, its leaves folded like a church service. Which is exactly what it was. An order of service for the burial of a child. Benjamin Bryant.

Benjamin Bryant. I hadn't known his name, not until this moment. Somehow I hadn't even thought of him having one. A name and a date – two dates, those of his birth and his death.

And that was another thing: he was two months old. Somehow I never realised he had lived so long. Long enough to have burrowed deep into my mother's heart, and stayed there. The sheet showed the prayers they had chosen and the hymns they had sung. 'All things bright and beautiful', and 'Now the green blade riseth'. Hymns I had sung at school, and never realised what they meant.

Why? What had made her look at all this now? Why do this to herself? I turned the Order of Service over in my hands, and there was the date: 1st October.

Today's date.

I lifted my mother down onto the floor – she was too heavy for me to do anything else. I placed a cushion under her head and found a blanket. Passing the telephone I saw there was a message light on the answering machine. I played it and it was from my father, *'Pick up'*. His voice cracked, as if he or the tape was breaking. *'Darling, pick up.'* Whom was he addressing with that *darling?* Me or my mother?

My mother. I'm certain of it. He would have known what day it was.

Next day my mother replaced the bottles in the fridge, but I didn't replace the hummus and the sausages. I was adjusting. I was learning. There would be no Max to help me.

Chapter Ten

That's not to say we never saw him. Max had a way of putting us to the test. Or maybe it was himself he was testing. And for that he had to come home.

The first time was the night I had to have

my mother rushed into hospital. She had tried to give up the drink again. This attempt she had managed four days. Then she stopped – I don't know what tipped the balance. It was July this time of trying, a hot summer's day. She wasn't being sick any more but said the wasps were after her, buzzing around her head looking for a way into her mouth. They terrified her. I couldn't see any wasps, nor could I hear them.

All I know is, she stopped managing.

And this time she nearly killed herself. Her last words to me were to complain about the brand of gin Mrs Platt had sent her. Then, with what looked oddly like a wink in my direction, she slid into a coma. An ambulance took us both to hospital, and in the small hours they sent me home. Having re-balanced the electrolytes in her blood, washed out her stomach, and pulled the bars up high around her bed, they said she would sleep for a good while, and ordered me to get some sleep too because I would need it. In the morning they wanted me to be ready to take her home. Like every other hospital in the land they wanted the bed.

A taxi dropped me off at the end of our drive and, out of the dark, the house greeted me. Every light in every room seemed to be switched on. We had left in a rush, my mother strapped to a stretcher. But it had been daytime then, and the blue flashes of the ambulance hardly visible in the sunlight. Now it was three o'clock in the morning, and I walked towards my home knowing there shouldn't be a light switched on anywhere.

I let myself in and immediately I heard it – music playing in an upstairs room. Music from another age, not heard since I was a little girl. *The runaway train ran down the track...*

I followed the runaway train upstairs, to a door that no one had opened in months. Max's door. Now it was ajar, light and music pouring out of it. I hesitated, afraid, without knowing what I was afraid of. Then the runaway train blew loudly, and I pushed the door wide.

Max was lying on the bed, face down, one arm hanging off the side. Everything about him was motionless except for his hand, keeping the beat against the carpet. I was mesmerised by that hand and the movement it made against the floor. It was filthy and bruised, skin stretched over bone.

I was certain he had heard me, knew I was there. Yet he stayed as he was, his head buried in the pillow while his hand continued to beat time. It occurred to me he was taking his cue from the song, and he wouldn't move or turn until it had finished. And I was right. Only when the runaway train had blown for the last time, did he turn himself slowly on the bed.

'Hello Rosie.'

I looked at my brother and began to cry.

Beautiful Max. He had the fleshless pallor of a corpse, with a face sunk into shadows like where the dead people go. If he hadn't been moving, I would have taken him for dead himself. Only his hair was alive, brighter than it should have been, springing out of his skull as if feeding off his brain.

A filthy denim jacket hung off the end of the bed, leaving his arms bare. I tried not to stare at the veins standing proud of the skin below his elbows, blue ropes running down his wrists, knotted with scabs of blood.

Max bared his teeth in what was meant to be a smile. 'Hey, Rosie. I thought you'd be pleased to see me.'

I made myself sit on the bed beside him, touched his leg. I couldn't look at his face again, not straight away.

Mummy's in hospital. I wrote the information on a page from the notebook I carried and laid it on the bed beside us. He squinted at it sideways.

'What's wrong with her?' He didn't sound too worried. Probably he'd been in hospitals too many times to see the danger.

I stared at the floor. There was a smell in the room, heavy and sour. It was the stink of tobacco and body odour, and something worse – the taint of a bad chemistry escaping from his pores, of a metabolism poisoned. I

97

smell it on people all the time now, where I work at The Centre. I know it almost better than the scent of my own sweat. But I didn't recognise it then. I only knew it didn't smell of Max.

He said, 'She's still drinking then?'

I nodded. After a moment, I snatched up the paper again, and scribbled, fast as if I was angry. I *was* angry. *What's happened to you? Why are you doing this to yourself?*

He laughed out loud at that. It was as if I shown myself up as some kind of amateur, asking silly questions. All the same, he took the paper on which I'd written the question and smoothed it, put it carefully under his pillow. Only then did he answer me.

'Oh you know what they say about any-thing nice, Rosie. Once you start, you just can't stop. It's very ... *moreish.*' He spoke as if he was describing chocolate. This time when he began to laugh, I hit him, with my palm open, hard on the cheek. For a briefest of seconds, I felt the texture of his skin. It was clammy and loose, as if the moisture was oozing out of his body.

It stopped him laughing. His eyes grew wide for a moment, and I thought I saw a flash of life. Then they grew dull. Duller even than before.

'Oh God...' he whispered. '...you still don't know, do you, Rosie? You haven't even thought about it.' He spoke the words softly.

I stared at him in bewilderment. Thought about what? *What didn't I know?* I touched his leg again, gently this time. Immediately a spasm twisted his mouth as if he was in pain.

What didn't I know? I dug my hands into him, demanding that he tell me.

He looked at me, the dull sheen still there in his eyes – and tried looking away, avoiding me and the question. Yet somehow my eyes continued to hold his eyes, even while the rest of him squirmed; and kept holding him as his hands moved across his body, up and down his arms, as if somewhere among the scabs he would find a way to release himself.

What didn't I know?

'Rosie...' he whispered. 'If I tell you...' His hands moved faster, raking the skin on his arms. 'If I tell you, how could you ever...?' He stopped. His eyes searched mine, as if trying to know my thoughts even before I did. And still his hands moved, looking for escape.

I leaned over him and caught them in my own, laid them in my lap. Held them there.

What didn't I know?

The question hung between us. Yet he was going to answer me, I knew that. My eyes were forcing him, making it so he had to answer me. He was so close to telling me – then out of the dark the phone rang. Neither of us moved. A voice spoke into the answering machine in the sitting room, broadcasting its message through the house. A woman's voice, one of the nurses at the hospital.

'Miss Bryant. Just to let you know your mother has regained consciousness. She's nice and settled and you can come and collect her in the morning.' A click and then nothing.

I sighed with relief – and in my relief, let go of him.

And lost Max.

He relaxed against the bed and smiled at me, a lazy smile, almost smug. As if there never had been anything to worry about. Alcohol wouldn't kill her, his smile told me. It would take a proper drug to do that, take her to the place where people don't come back. The place where he was heading.

Suddenly I wanted to hit him again, harder this time. Something to make the sluggish blood flow, make him be Max again.

He saw it, the desire to strike and hurt. Without warning he darted forward and caught me first. And kissed me. A quick fierce kiss on the lips before he threw himself back against the bed. There, with his eyes closed tight, as if to shut me out he muttered: 'I love you Rosie. You know I love you, don't you?'

I sat, frozen by the kiss, the suddenness of it.

'Go to bed. I'll see you in the morning.'

And when I didn't move, he rolled over onto his front, pressed his head into the pillow, hand trailing on the floor the way he had been when I walked into the room. I watched him for a minute until I understood for certain that he wasn't going to speak to me again, not tonight.

In the bathroom I found a syringe and a length of rubber tube. They were laid out neatly on the ornamental wash stand that used to hold our toothbrushes, ready for him. But they were unused, as if he had changed his mind. The syringe still had its contents inside. I threw the syringe away into the bin beside the basin, and went to bed.

Then I got up again and wrote him a note which I put beside his head. A note to go with the one he had already slipped beneath his pillow. If he was aware of me, he showed no sign. The note read *Please stay*.

Later still, in the small hours I heard him again. Or rather it was music I heard – not the music of our childhood this time, but something different. It was synthesised, with a pulsing repeated rhythm, that rolled mechanically through the house, like the thump of a robotic heart. Roused from sleep I listened to it, disturbed at the same time as I was mesmerised. Mesmerised was the right word. As I lay, planning to climb out of bed, to find him, to talk to him again, the music worked like a drug and sent me back to sleep, rocked by that pulsing robot rhythm, dreaming of nothing.

In the morning he was gone, as I'd guessed he would be. So was the note. And so was the syringe from the bin. And so was all the money my father had sent me months ago for my birthday and which I had never spent. Only the smell he'd brought with him – so unlike Max's old smell – lingered. I opened the windows wide and let it all escape.

He came back a few times after that. Each time thinner, sicker, closer to the point he was always aiming for; namely the parting of the ways, the body from the soul. Each time he brought the music with him, and each time something else left with him – a piece of jewellery, an ornament, once even the television. Anything he could sell.

But he never came as close to telling me what it was I didn't know.

Nowadays, people always seem to think I've never been alone, never been without Max to protect me. Max himself is making the police think that way about me now, so they can't get near me, not without him being there. They think I'm helpless, scarcely able to lift my own head. Yet they're wrong, all of them. I've been alone before. Max made sure of that. I couldn't have been more alone.

Chapter Eleven

I told my mother that Max had come while she was away – and instantly regretted it. Her face, already puffy and bruised from a night pressed against the bars of the hospital bed, collapsed completely.

'And he didn't stay, Rose.' She wailed. 'Not even for a day?'

Then her face hardened. 'What did you say to him, Rose. You must have said something that made him go away. He wouldn't just have come and gone like that. *What did you say, Rose?*'

As if I could have said anything.

But it hardly lasted, the flash of anger. My mother was scarcely ever angry any more, not with anyone. Not even in the mornings and with me. She had discovered she could make the journey shorter, simply by drinking more and earlier. Mrs Platt must have been making a fortune out of her.

Neighbours came to the door, curious to catch sight of her. But more often they had to be content with me, the daughter who didn't speak. The child who had killed a child.

I suspect it might even have been me they

came to see. Everyone knows what a drunk looks like, but they could never be so sure about me, a girl who had taken to wearing her mother's clothes, thirty years out of date. Who didn't remember to brush her hair much. Who stared at them from the doorway of the house, blocking their view of the large decrepit woman they claimed they had come to see. Sometimes they caught a glimpse of her, moving slowly across the hall with her tea cup of clear liquid, drifting from kitchen to sitting room like some large animal in search of pastures new.

And you could see them looking at her and thinking: I was the one who had done this to her. I had driven her to this.

I binned the leaflets from the hospital with their talk of attitude and backbone. They couldn't tell me anything I didn't know. Last year Max and Caroline wrote a book which instantly became a best seller. *Racing Demons* he called it, which I suppose deals with the same thing. It's the story of what happened to him in his darkest days with the drugs and how he came through. He dedicated it to Caroline and me – both of us at the same time. He puts us side by side on the same page, calls us both his angels.

This book – I never read it. Somehow I could never bring myself to. I know what happened to my mother. I saw it every day, and at least I could help her, as best I could.

And now, years later, I see the same thing happening to other people down at The Centre. And I can do something for them, at least try to make things better.

But Max – I don't think I could bear to read about Max and what he went through when it's too late to help, when I wasn't there. Knowing he had faced it all by himself. Anyway, Caroline told me not to bother. She said he left out most of what's important. She helped write it so she would have known.

Some people might not have called it helping – what I did for my mother, every time she gave up giving up, the point when she was driven to ask:

'Rosie, there's something I've forgotten. A little drink and I'll remember. Help me Rosie.'

I would fetch the bottle for her, pour the first glass for her myself. Show her that I didn't, couldn't, blame her. I knew the reason for the drink, so who was I to judge? This was what I learnt from her, and it's knowledge I use every day down The Centre where every-one is abusing something. You don't judge the person, you just wonder about the reason. Because there is always a reason.

Chapter Twelve

Only once did I drink with my mother. It was the evening of my birthday, the second since Max had gone away. We were sitting by the window in the kitchen, the one that overlooks the fields. The late September sun was warm on her face. She hadn't remembered what day it was, but she was humming to herself and her eyes were happy.

Happy. On impulse I went into a cupboard and took down another glass, and reached for the bottle. My mother stopped humming and frowned.

'Rose...?' Not happy now. *'Rosie?'* Uncertain, she watched me.

The first sip took me back to when I was a little girl, to Mass when I used to freeze, remembering what the nuns had taught us. Terrified that the sweetness would turn to salt as wine turned to blood on my tongue. It took years and Sister Imelda's eagle eye before I learnt how to gulp and pass the cup along.

Today I drank the whole glass, in one swallow. My mother shuddered to herself, but when it was empty, she filled it for me again. She knew what I was looking for.

Sure enough, at the end of the third glass, I found it. I closed my eyes and felt the ground shift beneath me, and knew it had begun. I was moving; through space, through time, on a journey all of my own. When I opened my eyes again, I had arrived, and my mother was waiting, as if she been there all the time. Journey's end.

'Rose,' she said softly. 'Rosie.' I smiled at her and my mother's face was soft as her voice, soft like I remembered it in the Time Before. Behind her, on the kitchen mantelpiece, the clock ticked and showed the hour and minute of what could have been any day. Just for these moments time itself had turned and paused, snagged by a memory. Wasn't it like this we used to sit, all those years ago, she and I, accompanied by the tick of seconds? Believing this is how things would stay forever.

No baby then. Not yet. No Max either, for that matter. *So where had Max been?* In a blinding flash it struck me. Max would have been in his den. That's why I never could remember Max before the baby, before I became the child who killed a child. It had been like this all the time back then: my mother and me, together, just the two of us. No one else, not even Max. Just the way we were now.

Happy.

Happy.

Afterwards, my mother held my head for me as I was sick into a basin. The wine tasted of vinegar as it came back up and burned the back of my throat. In the morning I was another year older and everything was back to the way it was before. But I never forgot the sweetness of the journey.

I didn't drink again. I was afraid of the power of wine to turn back time. You have to be wary of the power and the draw of happiness, no matter how short.

Which all makes me think of the first time I laid eyes on Caroline in the flesh, and saw something, *someone,* more powerful even than wine.

She was drinking champagne, glass after glass, tossing it back as if it were nothing, as if it were water. A young woman who could turn wine into something *less* than water. A miracle in itself. I tried to catch Max's eye – I could always catch Max's eye, even in a room like this room today, packed with the press and the Great and the Good.

But this time I couldn't catch his eye. A radio journalist was talking to him, asking him about the role of The Centre in the treatment of addiction and Max was answering every question, making the journalist think he had his full attention. Only I knew that all the time he was watching Caroline, and the way she drank champagne as if it was water, as if it was nothing. Red lips on a glass, the slight swelling of a white throat. He could see the power in her, just as I could. It was the first time that he too had set eyes on her.

He wasn't watching me, not any more.

But that's all in the future, where confusion lies. I'm trying to concentrate on what I can remember, up to the point when the memories end.

Chapter Thirteen

My mother was in hospital again.

One day, she had begun to swell up. 'Like a Telly Tubby,' she said to me, in the middle of the afternoon. She observed her reflection in the glass, careless, as if it belonged to someone else. The whites of her eyes were an eggy yellow. In the evening it was difficult getting her up to bed. Even the stairs were too much for her by herself.

I should have called an ambulance then. I should have.

In the middle of the night, I heard a noise. My mother was sitting on the side of her bed, shaking and wild with panic. 'Rosie!' Relief flooded her face. She grabbed for my hand and her palm poured sweat into mine. 'Rosie, you can help me. I've forgotten something. What is it? Tell me what it is Rosie. Quickly, before it's too late.'

And when I didn't answer, she began to scream. Scream and scream like the day we lost Max at the hospital. Then suddenly she stopped screaming, and fell back on to the bed.

I had to leave her to run out into the road, wake up our next-door neighbours who were new to the village and couldn't understand at first, not even when I wrote the words down for them. But in the end they took my meaning and called the ambulance.

The paramedics were kind and let me hold her hand on the ride. They didn't try to move me aside as they worked on her – but then, there didn't seem much work they could do. Too weak to scream any more, she stared at me, her eyes eggy and pleading, begging the same question even now. *What had she forgotten?*

On the ward, however, the doctor wanted me out of the way. It was only because of the nurse I stayed as long as I did. She was Scottish and gentle, unlike the fat young doctor who tutted, wanting to know why I was still there.

'I think this lady is trying to say something to her daughter,' she told him. And it was true. My mother's lips were moving but no sound was being made. Down the bed, though, her hand found mine, and clutched it hard. The doctor made an impatient noise. 'I don't think this lady is in a state to say anything.'

At which moment my mother's eyes snapped open. Seeing them I caught my breath. Although swimming in yellow, the irises were blue and crystal clear with their small steady points of black – and looking straight at me. *And* they were laughing. My mother's eyes were laughing, *now?* And suddenly she could speak after all, with a voice that sounded young, like a voice from twenty years ago. A voice brimming with relief.

'You know what I've forgotten, Rosie? It's the baby! I've left that damned baby all by itself this last half hour. *That's* what I was trying to remember! Don't they always say – never leave a baby alone with young children, not even for a minute. I'd better go and pick him up, don't you think?'

On the bed, the grip of her hand on mine relaxed, became more like a caress. Her eyes smiled into mine. 'I never forgot about you, though, Rosie, not when you were tiny. I'd never have dared. Max was so jealous! I was half afraid he'd throttle you if I left you alone together! Rosie Posie!' The blue of her eyes intensified. Her smile grew wider and seemed fill the room. 'Rosie Posie, Lovely *lovely* baby that you were.'

She let go of my hand, yet the warmth of it seemed to stay, wrapped around my fingers like a glove.

The doctor glanced at his watch and using the bulk of his fat body pushed me out of the way.

An hour went by. The fat doctor strode down the corridor and beckoned me into the nurses' room. He was severe-looking as if about to administer a dressing down.

'Your mother has acute cirrhosis of the liver. If she drinks any more, *a single drop*, she is going to die. Do you understand what I'm saying, Rosie? She – you – both of you are going to have to change the way you deal with this. Do you understand what I'm saying. Change your attitude.'

I looked at him and almost laughed. It's not that I didn't believe the drink could kill her. It was his mention of *attitude*, as if it was some object you could lift off a shelf and exchange for the one you had. As if it was that easy.

Also I didn't like the way he called me *Rosie*, as if he knew me.

And so I answered him the only way I could, not having words. I shrugged.

It was the shrug that did it. He eyed me with distaste. 'Good grief, girl, I would have thought even you could take better care of her than that. What's the matter with you, letting her carry on like this? Can't you see you're killing her?'

Me, killing her? They made me reel, these last words. Made the whole world spin. And suddenly, I realised. He *did* know me. He was one of Max's old friends. One of the rank and spotty boys, all grown up and a doctor now. Roger Platt, that was his name. Mrs Platt's son, the one she was so proud of. And he'd recognised me, known who I was. I was the child who had killed a child.

Now he seemed to think I was killing my mother. Was sure of it. And all because of what he had heard when *he* was a child.

It's what everyone would think, even the gentle Scottish nurse, once they told her. This was how things were. It didn't matter what I did. Nothing mattered. Roger kept talking, but I had stopped listening to his words. I watched his lips move, telling me what the world believed.

There came the sound of heels along the corridor, the soft clip of the nurse in her hospital shoes. Without looking at me, she whispered something in his ear. He listened and then sighed, in what seemed to me to be impatience. But when he turned to me, he had another look in his eye. A look that said *I told you so.*

'Well it's all academic now. That was about your mother. She's beyond my help I'm afraid. She died five minutes ago. I'm sorry.'

Not sorry at all. It was all he could do to keep the contempt out of his face. He was so sure. So sure he knew me.

So sure that I had killed her.

It was then the world began to slide, slowly, beneath my feet. I closed my eyes, but a process had started, the beginning of things coming apart. In the dark I heard the sound of ropes snapping. I opened my eyes and this was worse. Everything around me was moving, rushing and rising like water broken from a dam, ready to take me with it. Straw caught in a flood.

I could see it coming, the drowning ahead. I flung out my hands, clawing for something to hold onto, to keep me from going under, and saw them fall like fists raining blows on the shoulders of the doctor whose lips stopped moving as he stepped sharply back. The sort of doctor who couldn't save a life if his own life depended on it.

So I began to sink under my own weight, beneath the world flashing past my eyes. I screamed for my mother, wanting her and knowing she couldn't come. For my father who couldn't have heard. And in one last gasp, I screamed for Max.

Who did come.

And that is the truth of it. Max came.

He was like an angel.

I saw him over the shoulder of the doctor, striding up the corridor towards me. The old Max, shining. Shining and softening the glare of the lights, stilling the movement of the world. Turning the air a liquid gold, like wine, like champagne. I saw him and refused to believe what I saw. Too much of a miracle.

He touched the doctor on the shoulder. 'Hey,' he said simply, and the doctor fell back, recognising him. Then Max stretched out his hand to me, and it was as if he was reaching across an abyss. 'Rosie, it's all right. I'm here. Everything's going to be all right.'

I stared at him, across the gulf between us, panting, still unable to believe. And with disbelief arrived the fear again, and I began to scream all over again. I screamed because I couldn't tell what was real or unreal, and carried on screaming until I felt a sharp pain in my arm, making me spin around. The fat doctor was pressed against my side, having arrived there by stealth. There was a look of triumph on his face. He slid the needle out of my arm, and I began to fall.

Chapter Fourteen

When I woke up, I was in bed. And Max was there, sitting in a beam of sunshine.

'Hey.' He said again. Just as he had when he appeared. He leaned forward to smile at me.

I tried to lift my head off the pillow to look

at him properly, see if he was real. But I couldn't move. He saw me struggle, and brushed my hair with his hand.

'Poor Rosie, old Roger went and knocked you right out. I suppose he thought he had to. He only wanted to keep you from hurting yourself.'

I tried to smile, but my lips were too dry. There was a terrible taste in my mouth. So terrible that when he stood up and put his face close to mine, I turned my own face away, afraid of tainting the air between us. Because I could smell him – Max – even over the antiseptic smell of the hospital. Max's own smell. Clean and fresh, and Max-like.

He was back. Returned from wherever he'd been. Yet how could he be? I looked – really looked – for the shadows in his face, and they were gone. Nothing left. He was Max. Beautiful Max. A tear rolled down my cheek, but I was so tired, so disbelieving, I couldn't even brush it away.

I didn't have to. Max reached and took away the tear, allowed it to stay, glistening on the end of his fingers where the sunshine caught it and made it gleam. He stared at it a moment, his whole body still, concentrated on that single drop. Then he looked at me.

'It's over, Rosie,' he said quietly. 'I'm back. I'm never going to leave you again. Never. You believe me?'

I shook my head. I believed in nothing.

Except perhaps the dryness and the taste in my mouth. Reading my mind, he reached across the bed and poured a glass of water, lifting my head so I could drink. Moistness trickled down my throat as if I was swallowing my own tears. He touched my hair again.

'Go to sleep now, Rosie. Properly sleep. I'll be here when you wake up.'

I frowned at him. There was something I had forgotten. I fought to remember what it was. '*Mummy...*' I mouthed the word.

'Sssh,' he said and held my hand more tightly than ever. 'She's safe.'

Safe? I fell back on my pillow. So I was wrong. It was only Roger, spiteful as his mother, telling me lies, teaching me a lesson.

Then I remembered that doctors aren't allowed to lie, not even Roger. A dream then, it could only have been a dream. My heart lifted and sang at this. Only a dream.

Except if that had been a dream, then so was Max.

I looked at Max again, and it was true, he *was* a dream. If I concentrated I could see right through to the other side of him. There were people walking behind him, and there was a door, a calendar on the wall. By squinting I could look right through him and see them all. Max was completely transparent. He smiled at me again, making me wonder if he even knew.

'She's safe,' he repeated the words to me.

'Go to sleep and I'll explain when you wake up. I'll be here waiting for you.'

I saw straight through him to the nurse coming behind him. The same gentle nurse as before, with a tablet to press upon my tongue. I closed my eyes knowing Max would be gone when I woke up.

But when I woke, Max was still there, still transparent, and I couldn't understand it.

The next day the doctors gathered at the end of my bed and discussed what they called 'issues' with Max. They talked about break-downs and psychotic tendencies and symp-toms, using words they chose with care, like grown ups forced to speak in front of child-ren. It was clear they were uncomfortable having the conversation here in front of me. I wondered why they didn't make things easier for themselves, and simply go somewhere else for their talk. Then something inside me told the answer. This was Max's doing, mak-ing sure I knew everything they said about me. Keeping me informed.

So Max made sure I was there when they told him I was fragile, hysterically aphasic to begin with and now deteriorated to a state hovering between over-stimulation and diminished affect. They said it had been too much for my mother to look after me. It would have been too much for anyone.

And now for sure I knew my mother was

alive, because then they started talking about long stay hospitals and drug treatments, places where she could recover. And afterwards the chance of a life in the community, perhaps in some kind of sheltered housing. I found myself smiling, imagining what my mother would have to say about that.

I struggled to sit up, pulling at the sheets to make them notice me. And notice me they did. They stopped talking, all of them to stare in my direction, as if embarrassed that I was there. Max peeled away to come and sit on the bed. He took my hand and smiled. He was thinking about what he was about to say, choosing his words. But he took too long because Roger spoke before him.

'See, Max? She can't even...'

I saw Max's shoulders tense but he didn't look behind him. Instead he continued to stare into my eyes, his eyes blue as my mother's were blue. Blue as the sky itself.

'Rosie...' For some reason the gentleness in his voice brought the tears back to my own eyes. He touched my hair and bent forward to whisper in my ear so only I could hear what he had to say next. Behind him the doctors watched to see what my reaction would be, waiting to see what would happen when I understood, when Max told me.

And now I did understand. My mother had died after all. This was what Max had meant about being safe. She was safe from anything else happening. Safe from the need to journey. Safe in the place she wanted to be all along. I opened my mouth, desperate to cry, to speak to Max and tell him I had looked after her, in every way I could. We had done our very best, the two of us, my mother and I. We had come this far.

Rosie Posie. In the end she had remembered what she had worked so hard to forget.

But the words wouldn't come and the doctors could only see me fumbling and floundering, hear the dry noises in my throat. The gentle nurse said, more sharply than I was used to: 'She's becoming agitated again.'

And I was, but not in the way they thought. Agitated because I couldn't speak, and Max couldn't know the truth, not unless I told him. Desperate, my hands left my bidding and flew away with a life of their own to tell their own story, but he caught them as he might have caught a pair of birds spinning in mid air. Held them gently in his own. One of the doctors nodded to the nurse, and she made a move towards me, a needle in her hand. They were going to prick me to sleep again.

But not this time. Max was there. He stopped her coming with a smile. Stopped them all.

'It's all right,' he said. His voice, aimed not at me but at them, calmed me. 'My sister doesn't need any of what you've just described. She only needs to be at home...'

One of the doctors broke in, 'Mr Bryant, I don't think you understand. A young woman in your sister's condition ... she couldn't, she *mustn't*, be left to herself. Home isn't where she needs to be at the moment.' He nodded and, as if it were a signal, all of them moved closer, including the nurse with the syringe.

Max shook his head at them, making me think of a lion, shaking his mane, defending his territory – or his family. 'You don't understand. You see, I'll be there. I'll look after her. It's the reason I've come back. I'm not leaving her.'

Again they stopped moving. They reminded me of a herd of herbivores, startled by the unexpected, easily halted. His old friend, plump Roger, said: 'Oh come off it Max, look what happened to your mother. It killed her, trying to cope with this sort of thing. Your sister needs proper medical intervention. If you think you can take something like this on by yourself, you're mad.'

Max sat back down on the bed and leaned in close to me so we faced them together. His hands still holding mine were warm, and seemed to vibrate as if a secret energy was stored up under the skin.

'But,' he said. 'I won't be by myself. Quite the opposite. I've got God to help me now.'

He smiled at them, relaxed and friendly. And that really unsettled them.

Chapter Fifteen

But it was true. Max had God.

Or was it that God had Max? I've never quite sorted it out, and whenever I've mentioned the dilemma to Max he's always laughed.

Anyway, they had each other, which is the best way I can understand it. They met in a dark alley three months before the day he came striding towards me in the hospital. He described it to me afterwards, when we were home, just the two of us. No doctors, no father, no mother. And a blank space of nearly two years between us.

We were in the garden, stretched out on mackintoshes laid out on the lawn. Early spring and the grass was wet, but we had come out anyway, because this was where the light was. We both craved the light now, sunshine on our heads. Inside, the house seemed dark. Too many shadows. Too dense a fog in my head.

And on the lawn, in the sunshine, Max tried to make me understand about meeting God.

'You read about it, Rosie – *Conversion*, seeing the Light, call it what you like. People talk about it, write about it, try to get across how it feels. But it's got to happen to you before you can understand. All I can say is it's like watching the whole fucking world being invented, all over again, right before your eyes. A great rolling act of recreation, and there you are, right in the middle of it. And then you realise it's a creation that's been going on all this time, and you're part of it, whether you want to be or not. Everything has a life of its own, and God is the life in everything. And suddenly you can see it.

'And the miracle is, it happens right at the moment you think there's nothing new under the sun, and everything is old, and finished. When you think there's nothing to stay alive for...'

Max stopped, picked a leaf out of my hair, examined it for a moment before laying it carefully on the ground. A small act reminding me of the note I wrote him long ago. A note which first he had mocked – but then stored under his pillow.

'I was down an alley. A dead end, of course. It's always a fucking dead end in conversion stories, did you know that? I was just about to shoot up. I'd got some cheap stuff off someone I didn't know and was hurting for it because I hadn't had the money, not straight away. In the end I got hold of it by ... well, it doesn't matter how I got hold of it.'

He paused, and the gleam in him faded for an instant. He was struggling with something I couldn't see – an image, a memory. Rushing his words, he said, 'Unless you want to know, Rosie. I can tell you how I got the money, if you want me to.'

I shook my head. But it ached so much I stopped and mouthed the word: *'No.'*

He looked pleased at that – not because I'd let him off an explanation, but because I had answered him. Most of the time I couldn't. My lips were too wooden to bend to the shapes of words, my head hurt all the time. Even the sunshine I craved made it throb.

At the same time, another kind of pain, more deep-seated and familiar, had disappeared. Vanished in the fog that filled my head. Sometimes I'd wonder where it had got to, that pain. It nagged me that it wasn't there. It confused me. No pain, not even when I thought about our mother, only a throbbing brought on by the sun.

And no pain now, even as Max began to tell me about the darkest moments of his life. About meeting God. To tell the truth it was all I could do to stay awake.

'I had the needle in my arm, Rosie, already jammed it in. It was sticking out of the vein like something in a cartoon. I just hadn't pressed the end in yet. Something in my head was telling me if I did, that would be it. The stuff was going to kill me. There was this junk going round, everyone knew about it. People were dying. And something ... don't ask me what ... something told me this was the same stuff. It had killed the other poor fuckers, and now it was going to kill me.

'And so I just sat there with this stick jammed into my arm, trying to make up my mind. Press the end. Or not. Suddenly, either way – it didn't seem important. I was sitting round the back of a three star restaurant. People inside were eating caviar while I was outside, perched on a bin bag with a bunch of brown rats for company. And a needle sticking out of my arm. And I just thought to myself *push* – what difference would it make?'

'*Max,*' I made the shape of his name sleepily through the fog. He shrugged.

'It's how it was, Rosie. That was the world then. Needles, rats and a fucking dead end.' He passed a hand over his eyes. Then took it away and looked at me. 'But then, that *same fucking world* changed. It just ... changed ... all around me. Same rats, same bin bags, same dead end, but suddenly I realised that wasn't all there was to it. There was somewhere else to go. I really did have a choice. Jam the needle in and end it, get rid of one more piece of rubbish in the world, *or* stay alive, stay in the world, the world that *he* was offering to me now.'

He frowned at me trying to gauge if I was

awake or not.

'God.' Max's voice was patient. 'He was the one offering. Because that's what happened, Rosie. He'd turned up in the alley. Like something that had stalked me, and cornered me. Probably been there all the time. Now he was waiting, like some great fucking dog staring at me. The hound of God,' Max gave a short laugh. 'That's it – the big Hound himself. All I had to do was make up my mind. Death or Life. Press the end of the needle or take it out. So I took it out, and suddenly the whole place – rats, bin bags, the dark itself – they all began to glow, all lit up, like every fucking molecule had a meaning, a message. All part of the plan, you see. And the best thing is, it didn't matter what I'd done. It's what I did next that counted.'

He paused, his eyes were serious, trying to make contact with my own, to make me come awake.

'Do you understand what I'm saying? It's what you do next. Can you see what that means, Rosie? How it lets you off? Takes the claws out of you? It's not about death or guilt. What you've done in the past. It's about life. What you do next.'

He stopped and frowned at the fog in my eyes. And sighed.

'You haven't got one fucking word of what I'm saying, have you?'

I stared at him, but there was nothing I

could say. The sun settled like weights on my eyelids, making the fog around him glow. I liked it like that – the diffused glow of Max. And I was so happy to hear his voice. I could have listened to him forever. But still my brother looked transparent and his words were like smoke. He could have talked about anything, and the effect would have been the same. I'd be listening in my sleep.

He sighed again and touched my eyes – my heavy, heavy eyes. 'Stop taking the pills, Rosie. Why don't you?'

I almost did smile at that. I couldn't not take the pills. We'd both heard what the doctors said. The pills were the only things that could keep me well, stop what happened in the hospital from happening again. And the doctors were right, they worked; they stopped the world snapping apart, and made every day the same. It was only my head that hurt.

Softly Max said, 'It's the fucking pills, Rosie. They're making it so you can't think. And the stupid thing is, you don't need them.'

And still I had no answer for him. My cheeks were numb. All I could do was smile. Max shook his head. 'Listen to me, Rosie. Trust me. You don't need them. Not these pills, not any pills. I'm here. For good. You don't need anything else.'

But I didn't believe him. He'd gone away

once, twice, how many times? What would stop him going away again? And that's what I told him, although not in words. Who needed words for a simple thing like this? All I had to do was look at him, and let my eyes say it all.

Max flinched, but he didn't look away. Instead he reached into the pocket of my trousers – my mother's old slacks – and found the bottle of pills. He took them out and gave them a little shake. I shook my head. And still he didn't look away. His eyes held me and held me until finally the shake of my head turned into a nod. He stood up and threw them over the hedge.

Next morning I woke to find that I didn't have a head, only a growth – huge and soft as a rotting pumpkin. So heavy I couldn't raise it off the pillow. And the fog was darker around me. Next day it was darker still, and so dense I was afraid it would fill my lungs and choke me. Then I began to understand; the fog was there for a reason – to hide things. Real things, monsters you could touch. They crouched in the dark, ready to pounce. They had taken my mother and now they had come for me. All they needed was for me to be alone, then they would take me.

But Max never let me be alone. He stayed in the room while I panted, trying to name the things that were there, hiding in the fog. Struggling and choking until at last I understood that I didn't have to say anything, not to Max. He knew about monsters. He had seen them for himself.

Then, one morning I woke to the sound of something popping inside my skull. I opened my eyes and the headache was gone, the fog was gone, and my tongue was wet and flexible as a small warm snake. Max was asleep in the chair beside my bed, but he leapt up, instantly awake, his hair ruffled and gleaming in the bright sunshine pouring through my window. He studied my eyes and smiled.

'Hello Rosie.'

He sat on the bed, and held my hand. Later I let him brush my hair and run a bath, find me clothes and shoes to go outside into the light. I could have done it all myself. The weights had gone from my lids. The sun warmed my head, but I didn't need it so much now. I had a kind of light of my own, inside me. A vibration under my skin, my own energy. I felt I might never need to sleep again. The energy stayed there, alive inside me for about a fortnight, then gradually dispersed, and I was back to being Rosie again – silent but lucid. Yet the memory of it remained, hummed and vibrated when he touched me, under the skin, like calling to like; and *that* never went away.

Max never spoke again about the God who trapped him in the alley. Not to me. I *heard* him – thousands of times, of course – telling other people, letting them know about the light and the difference in the world. But somehow he knew not to talk about God to me. So I never had to confess to him how, in some way, the idea of them both – Max and God together – made me blush. I've often wondered if it wasn't the fault of the pills, causing just the one picture to stay lodged in my mind: God as a dog, something not quite dignified, that slinks into alleys and waits. Not even grand like a lion, just a dog – long and low and louche.

And there was something else. If Max's God was real, how was I to know whether this same God wasn't going to take him away again, like some great animal straining and dragging at the end of its leash?

Max talks about God all the time these days. It's his job and his life. But he doesn't say anything about this. I'm the only one who knows that in Max's mind, God is a dog.

Unless, of course, he told Caroline. He talked about God all the time to her. And it never seemed to bother him that she never even tried to hide it – the look of amused disbelief that lit up her face. Indulging him as if he was telling her about a dream he'd had the night before. It was that very disbelief, mixed with amusement that made her so powerful. No one else looked at him like that, not by the time they met.

Did he tell her about the dog? It makes no difference. Caroline is gone and there's no one left to look at him with those eyes all lit up and disbelieving. Everyone is a believer now.

But I'm leaving out so much. This was all six, seven years ago. Max had only just come home and Caroline wasn't even on the scene yet. Not back then. She was just beginning to appear on the TV, doing little bits of this and that. Early days for her too. I don't suppose we even noticed her.

Chapter Sixteen

It's what you did next that counted. It was always what you did next. That's what Max had told me.

And what he did next was go in search of the God who had come in search of him. He enrolled at a college to study theology – an old place of stone and ivy which had turned out churchmen for centuries, all in the same mould. He didn't have to be told that he would stand out, throbbing and glowing, like the sorest of thumbs. Maybe that's what he wanted.

So what did they make of him, the other students – all those aspiring priests he had started to tell me about, and sturdy deaconesses? His hair was wilder than ever, there were holes in his jeans and his T-shirts came printed with messages that spoke like banners. *Sex. Love. Save the Earth.* At the same time the scars on his arms carried other messages for anyone who knew how to read them.

Max meanwhile was doing his own reading, feverishly yet systematically, like a man who had made a friend and was trying to track him down again through a forest of signs. I'd watch him at the picnic table he had turned into a desk – he avoided using our father's study. Books lay stacked in piles, reminding me of the fabric of his old dens. Sometimes they were piled so high I could only see the crown of his head gleaming over the top. He made copious notes as he went, every so often laughing to himself when he found what he was looking for.

One day I picked up one of his books and started to read. Max reached out and took it from me.

'*St Augustine and Predestination.*' He read the title aloud. 'Believe that and you'll lose the will to live. Not that you have a Will, according to Augustine. You only have a Will if you have Grace, and you only have Grace if God chooses to give it to you. And he might *not* choose to give it you, not the way Augustine sees things. There might not be room for a start. His Heaven is so terribly crowded you see, standing room only. Only so many people allowed in.'

He scratched his scalp through the mane of hair. Listened to my silence, before he spoke again.

'I know, hardly the embracing type is he, Augustine? And I haven't even mentioned his views on sex and original sin – or women. Half the time he's not even entirely sure women have a soul. Think you could follow the party line on that? I mean, does his Heaven sound like somewhere you'd want to go? And if you're a Muslim or a Jew or a Buddhist, forget it. You're carbon. Human toast. So how does that appeal?'

I shrugged. I'd never been sure I wanted to end up in a Heaven that included Sister Imelda anyway. He grinned at my silence.

'My feeling exactly. Kind of rules out being a priest, though – at least, not a Catholic flavoured one. Church wouldn't have it. No respect, you see, not even for the great Gus. They'd hold that against me.' He smiled ruefully into the sheaves of notes. There were arrows and underlinings, entire paragraphs copied out in full. And lots more writing, not copied from the pages of any book: Max's own words. Last time God had come after him. Now he was after God, chasing him down the centuries of other people's thoughts. Taking what he wanted and leaving

133

the rest.

'Anyway, it's a shame,' he said, putting pen to paper again. 'I'd been quite looking forward to heading up an army of altar boys, and changing the world. Putting the word around that there's more to God than sin and guilt and Hell. I'm going to have to find another way to talk to the fucking planet, Rosie.'

My brother spoke almost as if he was serious, as if he truly thought the Fucking Planet was waiting to hear what he had to say.

He made me go with him to the Theology Ball.

Even the idea of it had made him laugh for weeks in advance. *Ball*, he'd say. *Shall we go to the ball, Cinderella?*

But he was only pretending to joke. One night he tucked me into the front seat of the car, ready to drive through the May evening. I was all got up in one of my mother's old ball gowns which he had picked out for me, scratchy but splendid – a forty-year-old froth of coffee lace, stiff with starch.

'You look like Miss Haversham,' Max said, closing the car door for me. 'Or a mad film star. Not that you're mad, Rosie,' he added quickly, seeing my face change. It wasn't often that Max was clumsy. He poked me, quick to change the subject. 'Look at you,

you hussy. I can see right down your front. Watch out for the men, especially the ones planning for the priesthood. They'll think you're offering their last chance of a roll in the hay.'

He was right about the dress. The bodice was stiff and too big, barely making contact with my breasts. *He* on the other hand looked like a rock star out to pick up an award. Underneath the dinner jacket his legs were long and skinny in his oldest pair of jeans. In his lapel he had pinned a Celtic cross, a tiny crescent moon and a brooch in the shape of a scarab beetle. On our way out he passed the hall mirror without bothering to check what he looked like. Max never cared. But I knew: people would look at him and look again.

In the college cloakrooms, I stared at my own reflection, the way I never did at home. At home I was always half expecting others to be there, waiting to step out of the shadows and join me in the glass. And the thought made me stay away from mirrors.

Yet the dress suited me, suited the wiriness of my arms and the perilous arrangement of my hair. When I moved my head, pins tinkled into the wash hand basin like a fall of tiny icicles, leaving wisps to stick out like blades of straw around my face – and somehow that suited me too. I stole a glance at the others here; girls with neat bobs touching up their makeup, wearing long dresses without any distance between breast and bodice. Girls fresh and shiny, as if they had just been unwrapped from cellophane, and I knew I didn't look like any of them. The only person I half resembled in this building was ... Max.

At this my own eyes stared back at me. For the first time I saw they were Max's eyes except they were grey instead of blue, and filled with a satisfaction that seemed to have come from nowhere.

A plump girl in a red frock stepped out of a cubicle and filled the space next to me. She set about washing her hands, rubbing them with soap, so vigorously it made you wonder how dirty they could have been. Dried them methodically on a paper towel, every finger in turn till the nails shone – and looked at me.

'Oh I recognise you. You've come with Max, haven't you? Max Bryant. I saw you getting out of his car.'

She smiled as she spoke, determined to sound friendly. But the smile didn't quite make it to her eyes which were large and pale, and scanning my dress. Her hair was glossy and symmetrical, but beneath the fringe her features were unformed, the skin clean and scrubbed as her hands. A face you'd forget again and again.

And of course I couldn't answer. I made a

small sign with my hands, the one I use with strangers, flicking the air in front of my lips.

Her eyes grew wider than mine had been a moment ago. 'Oh I *see*. You must be the sister, the one who can't speak. Gosh, fancy Max bringing you to something grand like this. Honestly, poor thing! How on earth did he think you would manage?' She was looking at me in a different way now, like some creature she had found run over and dying by the side of the road.

As if dislodged by a vibration inside me, another hairpin tinkled into the sink distracting her.

'Oh dear, your poor hair,' she raised her voice, speaking slowly as if I was deaf as well as silent. 'I'm Ruth by the way. *Ruth,*' she repeated. 'Can you remember that?' Without waiting for a reply, she started pulling the rest of the pins out of my hair. 'Now don't you fret. I'll make it look nice for you. You know, *normal.*'

She reached into her purse and brought out a small metal comb, not made for unruly hair. The teeth dug into my scalp as she spoke.

'Has Max mentioned me ever? Silly me, you can't answer that, can you? Anyway, he must have said something. I have all my classes with him and I'm sure he does his best to sit beside me. Honestly, there's no getting away from him. He's quite clever, don't you think? But you know – odd. He will keep arguing with the lecturers. No respect, not even for Father Ignatius. I have to keep speaking up, try and say something jolly. You know, smooth the waters a bit. You can see Father Ignatius getting really angry, even if he tries to make out he enjoys having someone to argue with. *He* calls Max a pagan, and I'm pretty sure he doesn't mean it as a joke. Where did you get your dress by the way? It is awfully – *quaint.* Sort of old fashioned, like someone pulled it out of a drawer for you. Still, I don't suppose you even got to choose, not properly. I mean it *must* be difficult for you, buying things the normal way. You can't very well say "I'd like the lovely red dress off the top rack please". Don't you worry about it though – your dress I mean. It's not as if anyone here cares about fashion. At least the men don't – although I actually think they should. It would help them later, really it would. It's important for people in the Church to be – you know – *with it.* Show that Christians can be attractive as well as good. People mark you down as just a bunch of old fuddy-duddys otherwise. Although having said that, my friend – who isn't here yet – he has ever such a good eye. He's a doctor, so you can imagine he's pretty much seen every-thing – including people with no clothes at all! He's on call at the moment but he's going to do his best to turn up. But really, I almost don't mind if he doesn't. We're so close, all of us in the class, even Max. *Especially* Max. The thing is, people are so accepting, don't you find, especially in a place like this. Sometimes I think people don't understand *how* accepting and *how* close we've all become. You worry that others will end up feeling, you know, left out. People who aren't one of us. Boyfriends, sisters – that sort of thing.'

She stopped and drew breath.

'There,' she said putting the comb away. I stared into the mirror. She had pinned back my hair so tightly the scalp ached, leaving my face stretched and bony, almost skull-like, cheeks numbed from too much talk.

'Come on,' she said. She slipped her hand through my arm and led me out of the cloakroom to where Max was waiting. There was a crowd of people clustered around him, all of them with faces as round and unformed as hers. Students with sweet smiles and innocent eyes that later I would notice kept coming back to Max. Too innocent. I tried to imagine them as priests, knowing what to say at a funeral service for a drunk or a child. And I couldn't. Only Max carried his experience like a badge.

'Here she is,' said Ruth, triumphant as if she had snared a lost pet. 'I found her stranded, poor thing, all helpless and forlorn in the cloakroom. She needed help with her hair. It was falling all over the place.'

Max smiled at her. 'Thank you Ruth.' His voice was sincere, sounding as if he meant it, as if he approved of the changes she had made. Ruth blushed while something inside of me wilted. Then he leaned towards me, and briskly pulled long wisps of hair back out from under the pins digging into my skull, undoing all her work.

'That's better,' he said. 'Perfect. What do you think, John?'

He turned to a tall young man standing beside him, who I hadn't noticed before. He had the build of a rugby player and the shy face of a boy, and was wearing an ancient looking dinner jacket, shiny at the elbows but a perfect fit. Without knowing anything about him, I imagined it was passed down by his father along with his build – the solid set of his shoulders – not to mention the slow smile when Max addressed him now. A smile that extended to me.

It took him a long time to answer. 'M ... Miranda. Your sister looks like Miranda.' He blushed suddenly in my direction. 'S ... sorry. He did ask.'

'My God,' said Max in wonder. 'Miranda. I see what you mean.'

'Miranda?' Ruth's voice was sharp. 'Who's she. Anyone I know? Is she on the course?'

'From the T ... *Tempest*,' said John. 'After a

lifetime with only her father for company she comes to the feast of sailors at the end of the play and exclaims, "Oh brave new world that has such people in't." Overwhelmed because she's never seen people before.'

He turned to me. 'It's your eyes, if you don't mind me saying. They're so very b ... big. And the f ... frock. I do so like the frock. It's the sort a magus's daughter would have to wear.'

And now I was blushing, smiling back as he smiled at me. Despite the shyness, his smile was warm, a thousand miles from the acquisitive brightness of Ruth.

Who blinked, and said: 'What's a magus when he's at home?'

It was different when I met other people here.

'*So you're Rosie.*'

How many times did I hear those words that evening? If people didn't actually say it, they thought it; you could see the recognition in their eyes. Max and John had begun to talk earnestly about something, leaving Ruth to seize my arm and drag me around the room, making introductions to people I didn't know, but who seemed immediately to know me.

'*So you're Rosie.*'

And there it was again, always accompanied by a smile that reminded me of

141

Ruth's smile. Too bright, too knowing. I felt the colour take up residence in my cheeks. If I hadn't known better I'd have sworn it was common knowledge in this room: I was the child who had killed a child. Yet it couldn't be. Max wouldn't have told them, not about this.

And I was right. He hadn't. But someone else had. Half way through the evening, Ruth's friend, the doctor who was meant to be on call, turned up after all.

'Roger!' she squealed, darting a disappointed glance over at Max. But the squeal made sure that everyone turned, and there was Max's fat friend, the doctor from the hospital. Mrs Platt's son.

So now I could be certain. Everybody knew – even John. I was the child who had killed a child, and driven her mother to drink. That's what Roger would have told Ruth, and that's what she would have told everyone else before they had ever met me. Max's burden.

As if to drive it all home, Ruth left Roger's side and teetered over, caught my arm again. Her eyes were moist and shining, and a little golden crucifix bounced tipsily between her breasts. She put her mouth to my ear, her breath sweet from the chemicals in the cheap college wine.

'He's wonderful you know. Max, I mean. I don't know how he does it. This course, travelling, looking after *you*.' She hiccupped, and patted her chest. And giggled. 'It must be wonderful to have him for a brother – after – well, everything. You're lucky, lucky, *lucky.*'

Lucky. I stared at her in disbelief, and then turned away. But it didn't matter, because here was Max, coming to me just when I needed him, as if he could read my mind.

He dragged me on to the dance floor, and frowned into my eyes. 'What's the matter? Has someone upset you? Is it Ruth?'

I shook my head. Then nodded. His arms tightened on my shoulder. 'Fuck it. Forget them, Rosie. Forget them all. And try not to hold it against them. They're all babies, still learning. Except John. They don't know anything about anything.'

Fuck, forget, forgive. The language of Max.

And as the music sped up, he made me dance, in front of everybody, using his hands to curl my body around and around, until he had turned me into an eel twisting inside the starched walls of my dress. Men – Max's aspirant priests – were catching glimpses of my nipples, but that didn't worry me, any more than the pale eyes of Ruth. We danced, and as we danced, I had the sensation of everything falling away, as if we were leaving the floor and the people who were glued there; higher and higher, until finally we were dancing right above them all, two heads of gleaming unruly hair brushing the ceiling. A wonder to behold.

Looking down I caught a glimpse of Ruth's face, her mouth half open and envious. And others – an old man, smoking in the corner, who looked on impassively, and blew smoke rings that drifted slowly upwards as if to dance there with us. Father Ignatius, Max told me later.

The music stopped and we came back down, and Max bent me over in his arms, so I almost touched the floor. Strong arms, strong as walls – the only things between me and falling. I looked into his eyes, laughing at mine.

That night I realised that Ruth was right. I was lucky.

Lucky, lucky, lucky.

Chapter Seventeen

That's when I met them for the first time – Max's group. *The* Group – 'Swork. Short for God's Work.

Of course, they didn't call themselves that then. They were just his friends, John and Ruth and those others with their sweet un-formed features. Yet already he had added to their beliefs. First they had God. Now they had Max.

That's where it started, at college with Max talking. Because that is what he did – talk. In the intervals between tutorials; stretched out on the grass in the quad where they had their lectures; next to the coffee machine; lounging between the stacks in the library. He was Max and he was full of words and a gleaming secret energy that couldn't have stayed secret for long.

I heard him when they came to our house – Max talking about the God who had found him in the alleyway. God as Max saw him – with no time for guilt, breast beating or soul searching. No time for armies, or popes either. Max's God didn't bother with denominations or faiths. 'One ocean, many rivers' was his favourite saying. 'Why argue about water in the sea?' Max's God didn't mind where he found himself. And you could find him too. You only had to stop and look around you.

Or if that was too difficult, just listen to Max.

Max's God spanned time and beliefs, was both ancient and modern. He was under your skin and out there with the space men. A God who played in the sub atomic wonder world of superstrings and in the cosmic clouds of galaxies light years away. He was the stuff that everything was made of, the salt in the sea, the carbon in our cells, the bubbles in your cheap college wine.

In short He was everything you wanted Him to be. And Max's friends loved it, loved hearing Max talk. I don't suppose they had known anything like it.

And that's how 'Swork was born. You could see it happening that night even, another point hammered home, there, as they watched us dance. They knew that Max could talk, but they hadn't known he could perform miracles. That night they saw me change under his hands, become an eel beneath the skin, a different creature. Proof to them that everything could be recreated. Be new. Be different. Be like God.

Be like Max.

And they all fell. Little by little, their belief showed in their faces, in the hypnotised look they wore when he held forth. I watched them listening to him, and felt like reminding them to breathe. Or at least to close their mouths. After twenty years of sermons and creaking masses and sleepy services, I don't suppose they had ever come across this: charisma, the sheer animal draw of a man who seemed to have God in his fingers.

But that was just the students. The teachers were a different matter. People like Father Ignatius had seen it all. They listened to Max talk, observed the effect of his words. And in the end, they acted. They had been turning out churchmen for years, and here was Max determined to break the mould – what else could they do? A few months after the ball, Max made the journey home from the college for good.

I heard my mother's car in the drive and waited for his step in the hall. When it didn't come, I went outside and he was still sitting, his hands resting on the wheel, staring ahead of him. He looked as if he could be on the point of setting off again, a man caught between this place and another.

I opened the passenger door and slipped in beside him. Without looking at me, he said: 'I'm not going back. They won't let me. They've thrown me off the course, out of the college. No appeal. Nothing.'

There was wonder in his voice. And grief. His hands moved over the wheel unconsciously, trying out directions.

'They said I was abusing the institution, using it as a recruiting ground for my own beliefs. But Rosie...' He turned to me, and he was crying. 'I told them I didn't have any beliefs, not properly, not worth the name. Only ideas. That's what I was there to work out – beliefs. I *told* them that. But they said I was trying to start up some kind of a cult, all based around *me*. That's what they said. They sat there, and no one stood up for me. No one. Not even Father Ignatius.'

His voice throbbed with pain.

'I couldn't win. No one listened to me. I

told them all I wanted was to learn, for them teach me. I even said I would stop talking. I was ready to stop everything except thinking – I told them that. But they wouldn't believe me.'

Abruptly he opened the door, and got out of the car, leaving something in the seat behind him, a screwed up piece of paper. I picked it up. It was a note formally requesting the immediate return of all the books belonging to the college.

He had gone straight upstairs. Later I heard the sound of footsteps, moving across the ceiling and back again. It went on for hours. Max was pacing his room, rhythmically and pointlessly as a dog that has been caged. Then suddenly the pacing stopped, to replaced by music, the kind I had heard before. Music that pulsed and returned to itself in ever repeated rhythms. Hypnotic, mirroring the patterns that once were made by the drugs in his brain, making patterns in my own brain now. I heard this music and felt the shapes forming in my head, and suddenly I was afraid.

I ran upstairs and banged on the door, only to find it open. I stepped into the room, and music was there, like a wall. In the middle of it was Max, not pacing any more. He was sitting cross legged on the bed, his face calm, like a gleaming, breathing Buddha. He smiled.

He reached across and flicked a switch on his sound system, turning off the music. And the smile grew broader, more peaceful still.

I stared at him. He had changed again. The gleam was brighter than I ever remembered. I touched his hand and there it was, the shiver under the skin. Secret energy that hummed and vibrated against my skin. He nodded, knowing what I had felt. 'It's because of *Him*. He came back, Rosie. He – It – didn't abandon me. He was here. He made me see it doesn't matter. The college is just a figment of the past. It's what you do next that counts, what you make of the future.'

He took my hand. 'That's what He came to tell me. That good comes out of everything. You know, like mushrooms out of dung. Always something. What you can't change, welcome.'

And at that moment the phone rang downstairs. It was two o'clock in the morning. Max let go of my hand and rose to answer it, unfolding himself from the bed calmly as if he had been expecting it. His feet were bare, and made no sound as he crossed the floor. I stayed and stared at the heavy carpet beneath my own feet, laid when we were children to minimise the noise. For the first time I wondered how it had been possible for me to have heard him pace.

Max came back upstairs. He looked confused, and at the same time dazzled. 'That was John.' He waited to see if I remembered John, the sweetest faced of all his fellow students. Rugby John with the eyes of an altar boy. Who had smiled at me as if he meant it. 'He says everyone's there, at his flat. Somehow they just seemed to find their way, turning up in ones and twos right through the evening, until there was the entire class. They've just finished writing a letter to the college. And Rosie, do you know what they've done? They've dismissed themselves. All of them. We're all leaving. They're coming over in the morning. Then we're going to start again by ourselves. Do things our way.'

He stared at me, his eyes shining. And I remembered what he said about the army of altar boys, changing the world.

It made him famous – briefly – being dismissed and taking a whole class of twenty students with him.

The following week, the TV had news of it, a college with no one left to be taught. Now nobody knew where they were, not even their parents. A pretty female reporter with big hair and frantic clothes stood with her microphone in front of the old stone walls of the college and talked about the young man who had walked away with an entire year group, like the Pied Piper.

Halfway through her report, Father Ignatius walked by. Immediately she advanced towards him, microphone at the ready, triumphantly spotting her chance. And he ignored her. Walked straight past her as if she was no more than a small dog yapping in his path, leaving her looking clumsy and foolish, an amateur wrong footed in front of the camera. Now Caroline stood, blinking with the shock of it.

Max never saw it. I was sitting alone with only the TV for company. Everyone else – the 'vanished' year group – was upstairs with Max. They had spent all the days and nights having discussions, planning the future, how they were going to live. How they were going to worship. Even what they were going to call themselves. And since I had nothing to say, there was nothing they needed me for, not even to make the tea because there was Ruth, running back and forth, making herself useful, pretending she was indispensable. Laying down her role for the years to come.

When they were not talking they were playing music. Or rather Max was playing music, making them listen to those Trance tapes he had brought with him from the lost years, the music that until now he had played for himself and no one else.

Why was he doing this? Max's music – it must have been utterly strange to them.

Never the kind of people who went to clubs or raves, they wouldn't have heard anything like it. I watched them as they sat with their eyes, itchy from lack of sleep, now glued to the floor, trying to hide a bewilderment that bordered on distress. You could see them hating the sound of the synthesisers and the repetitive thump of the bass. To them, this must have seemed an appalling lapse of taste on Max's part. Something unexpected.

After the confusion came unease. They knew this was the music that was played at parties where, so far as they knew, drugs were the only things on people's minds; they had read about the children, brimful of ecstasy, who had danced themselves to death to sound of it. Music like in the fairy tales, where the devil had the best tunes. Now here was Max telling them that not only could *they* dance to it, they could pray to it as well. A new way to worship.

Only John looked thoughtful, listening hard, making up his mind.

Patiently Max tried to explain it to them, the power of music to create an altered state, a mind for prayer. Meekly they listened to the music again and waited patiently for their minds to be altered. Only to hate it even more.

And still Max persisted. Music was power, he told them, the reason Negro slaves were deprived of their drums and American

Indians forbidden to dance. Music could hypnotise and open up the mind, create roads to the invisible. Music made you strong. Music could pierce matter, carry you straight into the beating heart of God. You would dance as you prayed, take flight as your mind soared. Only connect. So yet again they listened, and kept on listening day after day, but still their arms and legs were heavy. No one soared. Only John showed any signs of understanding.

'Were there not other ways?' they asked at last, their faces numbed from thump of the rhythm. Other ways to pray and see what they were praying to?

Well, yes, Max admitted to them: they could view the miracle of unfolding creation through the lens of an electron microscope, or the eye of a radio telescope. God played in miniature and on a cosmic scale, His footprints were everywhere. Einstein knew that. But electron microscopes were locked away in laboratories, and astronomers guarded their observatories as closely as mediaeval priests deciding who was allowed a glimpse of the High Altar. That was the trouble.

No, music was the way. Anyone could hear music. Anyone could dance. And those who believed in God should want to dance. This was what Max had in mind. A new way of meeting God. Music and dance and prayer. Old meets new and touches the eternal.

This way people would find God.

And still they didn't understand, not at first. Ruth asked if Abba would do the trick.

Belatedly, someone remembered to ring his parents and tell them where he was. Hours later there was a bank of reporters, camped out on our lawn, although not Caroline this time. Perhaps she had blotted her copy book with that encounter with Father Ignatius.

Naturally Max was the one who spoke. Sauntering out of the house with his hands in his pockets, slouching and lean, the stubble gleaming gold on his chin. The people working the cameras did a double take when they caught sight of him. What had they been expecting? Some earnest Christian in a sweater. A plodding fanatic. Instead they had Max, in faded holy jeans and *fuck me* T-shirt. They asked him what he thought he was up to, and grinning, he replied:

'God's work,' The reporters wrote that down, then stared at him, suspecting irony, unwilling to believe he was being serious. But Max only grinned the harder, daring them to believe.

'God's Work,' he said again, cheerfully and blinked at the sky, pleased, as if he had just had an illumination of his own.

God's Work. 'Swork. Now the Group had a name.

Cameras snapped and flashed. Max ran

his fingers through his greasy gleaming hair and smiled sleepily as he talked about freedom and love and equality. Reporters frowned as they wrote, confused perhaps. No mention of Jesus so far, or sin or anything vaguely remembered from Sunday school. He told them about ecology and a cosmic pact to look after the planet, and some of them simply stopped writing. Then he talked about worship. He told them how 'Swork planned to use a two thousand-year-old liturgy, older even than the Roman, and set it to music – not organs and choirs but...

'Oh *now* I get it,' said someone. A last, lone camera flashed. 'You're talking happy-clappy. Guitars and all.' There was an audible sigh of relief amongst the crowd of reporters as they realised they had pinned him down. Max wasn't different after all. He was just another smiley face for Jesus. Only the sweater was missing.

There was a silence. Max smiled his slow smile. His skin seemed to ripple in the sunshine. I saw a woman journalist shiver, suddenly forgetting to put pen to paper. 'Fuck that,' he said carelessly. 'Fuck happy-clappy. I'm talking trance. Dance music. Heard of that, have you?'

And the journalist who was in his fifties, said nothing.

Max laughed out loud for what looked like sheer joy. He had the sun on his back and that secret energy running through his veins. 'Fuck it,' he said again happily. 'We're going to change the world.'

They looked at each other. Then suddenly they all had questions. The woman journalist called out, 'If you're doing God's work, what are your views on abortion?'

'The same as God's I hope,' Max replied promptly. 'Let every child be a wanted child. Only a woman can decide that.'

'War?'

'Dead against it unless it's in someone else's interests.'

'And sex?'

'Love it.' Was it an accident that his fingers brushed his groin briefly, careless as a boy in his sleep? The woman journalist's mouth fell open. 'And God does too. Every which way. Backwards, front-wards, inside out, upside down... If it works, do it. We're at it all the time.'

He was laughing at them, but the cameras set up a frenzy of flashing all over again. The journalists went away and wrote disapproving articles for their editors about a Christian who was pro-choice, anti-war and in favour of gay marriage. They asked how he could possibly call himself a man of God, then forgot all about him.

But the next day, other people appeared. They arrived in the night and now there they were, camped in our garden. And not just in ours. Mrs Platt looked out of her window to see a bender planted on her lawn. From inside came the moans of people (more than two?) leaving her no doubt what they were up to. She set her dog on them, then called the police who moved the occupants on to join the others camped outside our house. But she couldn't do anything about the strange smell of something sweet that remained hanging above the petunias. Not quite the scent of tobacco. Yet she could hardly complain; her shop had already sold out of cereal and snacks. French fancies were the first to go. In twenty four hours, thanks to these new arrivals, her profits, not to mention 'Swork, had doubled in size.

Max's invisible entourage, the one that had always followed him around – the life in our house – had become real and visible. And permanent. There were barely any shadows any more. There was no space for them. Ruth brought two hefty trunks from her family home and moved into my bedroom with me, filling it up with soft toys and mascots and posters of the Pope. At night she snored softly, and crooned Max's name.

I didn't mind, not to begin with. It was like being at school again, right down the snoring. At least there were no nuns, and Ruth didn't have the vicious strength of mind of a Sister Imelda. And anyway, Max made it clear that soon we would move somewhere else. We would have to. There were so many of us. An entire year group, plus the benders on the lawn.

But first they had to change. No one told them to, but change they did, all of them. First they grew their hair. Then they began to dress like him – like Max. Finally, and most startling of all, they began to talk like him, or tried to; experimenting with the *fuck*, and blushing. But they kept on trying, until they got it right and it became second nature and they all spoke like him, sweet-naturedly effing and blinding.

Max had done this. He got them breaking out of what had made them, smashing their own moulds. The result was a collection of new selves so unlike their old selves it was something close to a miracle.

Even then, they never quite lost their sweetness. John, still large, still clumsy, shaved his head and had holes in his jeans which I suspect he had drilled through himself. He was the first to see what Max was talking about, the first to understand; the first to lose himself when he listened to the music. Soon it was John mixing the tapes, improving on what was already there. He had been all set to follow his minister father into a country living, now here he was, creeping out of his former self with all the talents of an urban MC.

Yet he never lost the eyes of an altar boy,

and he still smiled at me as if he meant it. Out of all them, I liked him best.

Ruth, though – I was never going to be fond of her, even after the smug hair had disappeared and she'd taken to wearing ancient skirts and outdated frocks picked up from charity shops. There was something oddly familiar – and discomforting – about the Ruth who had begun to get dressed in the morning. I would watch her from my bed, pretending I was still asleep as she put on layer after layer. She reminded me of someone, although it took a while before I knew exactly who. Then one day I watched her, carefully pulling hanks of hair out from under clips and I knew.

Me.

Me – still wearing my mother's old clothes, still content to let the Past dress me; at the same time, knowing they suited me, these clothes from another age. Knowing that Max liked them – which was the reason Ruth wore them. But even with all the charity shops at her disposal, Ruth didn't look the part. She was plump not skinny. Her bones didn't jut out of her skin, and her eyes didn't set out to hide each and every thought that passed through her head. Ruth considered her own opinions entirely right and proper, didn't mind if her face gave every one of them away.

In fact, it was Ruth's face that let her

down, the reason she could never look like me. Ruth's face was still rounded, still scrubbed, and already betraying the first small traces of moustache along her upper lip which she dutifully anointed with peroxide. When she talked about Jesus, her features shone, like a naked bulb. And like a bulb, you could switch Ruth on or off, just by mentioning God. Or Max.

She kept a collection of pink nail brushes in the bathroom.

And now I did begin to mind having her around. I minded her voice when she talked to Max in her sleep, the way her eyes followed him when she was awake. I tried to feel sorry for her and all that scrubbed flesh and yet I couldn't. She had taken over my room, filled it with cuddly toys; she was there when I woke and when I went to sleep, and in all her waking hours, she never said one interesting thing. She brushed her hair a hundred times before she went to sleep, reduced the entire world around her to God and Max.

He must have been aware of her, but if she made him feel uncomfortable, he never let it show, not even when he turned to find her eyes resting on him, wide open and adoring. Sometimes I'd swear that Ruth forgot to blink. Only I knew how, deep down, she grated on him, like an old fashioned hair shirt, and still does all these years later.

160

Then again, you could say it was a kind of training for him, that sort of devotion, a taste of what was to come. Something to drive a normal person mad, but which he would have to learn to live with.

Caroline now, she was *so* much cleverer than Ruth; Caroline knew exactly how to look at Max. She'd catch his eye then look away, careless as if she had seen better, laughing at the idea that she could adore anything but herself. There was not a shred of devotion in Caroline. That's what he loved about her.

In time, I believe that will be what he misses most, Caroline's carelessness. Her determination to treat him the same as anyone. Except that it was a lie, that careful carelessness. Because Caroline loved him. Loved him so much she never could stop trying to understand him.

And now of course she never will.

Four days since she died and this morning the police came and took my finger-prints. Max wasn't here or he would have found a reason to stop them. As it was, I never even told him that they visited. He has enough on his mind. He cries in the night while I listen to him through the wall, wanting to go to him and knowing it isn't me he wants, not any more.

In the morning though, he pretends he slept the night through. I hear him telling people on the phone, utterly convincing, his voice strong. Max wants people to think he can bear anything, suffer anything. He wants *me* to think this.

Doesn't he know he cries in his sleep?

Last night, when I listened to him weep, I thought he sounded like a man who had never heard of God or heaven. Does it mean that Caroline, laughing and sceptical, has had the last word after all?

I wish she had never caught his eye. I wish she had stayed away from us, that she had died before we ever met her. I wish Max didn't have to cry.

I used to watch Ruth fall asleep, right in the middle of everything – late at night and all of them talking as usual about God and music and sound systems and lights. Then back to God again. It's funny, I read an article (written by Caroline) about how cults worked. It went on about how they brainwashed people by depriving them of sleep. And it made me laugh, because all I could think of was Ruth, dribbling slightly as she snored, only stirring when Max's voice pierced her dreams. I'd watch her and wonder what she was doing here, amongst them all. As if I didn't know the reason for that.

I'd listen, though. I listened hard, night after night, waiting for someone to say something that might change my mind, bring me on board, make me like them – a believer. Everyone else had changed, it was only me that stayed the same. Sometimes I would find John looking at me with his altar boy's eyes curious, wondering what I was thinking. More often it was Max, catching my eye and laughing. Max always knew what I was thinking. He knew I didn't believe.

He knew my faith was in him, only him. And he didn't mind. Like Ruth's good lord, he had promised always to be there.

Chapter Eighteen

When we moved from the village everyone came with us.

But where do thirty people go when they need somewhere to live? Max knew the answer. We took over a squat he remembered from his addict days. It was in north London, a former Mission building with planning permission denied. It was massive, big enough for us all. Only Ruth was less than delighted with the peeling walls and cold water baths. She took to finding more and more reasons to visit her parents or Roger, and each time I wondered hopefully if she would not be coming back.

The rest filled the spare rooms with their

sleeping bags and magazines, their bibles and their demo tapes, and set about painting everything white. Downstairs was an old meeting hall which Max and John decked with white sheets, stretched taut to fly like sails overhead. This is where they worked on the music and, just as importantly, the lights. Light was always going to be crucial to Max. Strobe lighting to begin with, oil on water – like boys trying to jazz up a school disco.

And really, school disco was the way to describe those first attempts to worship the way Max had in mind. The rest of 'Swork were doing their best, but still they hadn't caught on, not even now. Max and John played the music, but all they could do was shift self-consciously from foot to foot. Some of them had never danced before, not even at school discos.

Meanwhile John and Max kept on with the work, experimenting, refining, then unrefining to make everything raw again. Every week the music went on and every week the rest did their best to listen, waiting patiently for something mind altering to happen. A couple of them left, too mystified to stay and Max still hadn't found a way to explain.

Then finally it worked. The first Creation Mass was launched on Christmas Eve. It exploded at midnight, at the moment the year tipped over into Christmas Day itself. Which was the moment that, at long last, they understood what Max had been telling them.

He had got everyone to dress up – reluctantly – as if they were children in a nativity play. They stood around, assembled angels and shepherds looking sheepish, shivering in the draughts that stirred the paper decorations. Then John released the music, pulling a switch and stepping back as if he was letting something wild out of a box. Something dangerous. They gaped as a new sound, sinuous yet punctuated, closed around them. It coiled about their ears like smoke, or serpents: a John-created blend of modern trance and Byzantine chant, never heard before, not by anyone.

Gathering speed now. The girls in their frocks of angels began to be restless, tossing their hair like animals feeling electricity before a storm. Then they started to move, slowly at first, as though trying to resist. Then faster, and faster still, gradually losing the heaviness in their limbs until at last, weightless, their arms rose and became tangled in their wings. The boys watched them, and realised they wanted to do the same.

And that's what they did, all of them. They began to dance, exactly the way Max and I had danced that night at the ball, twisting and turning, free at last. Only Ruth was left behind, earthbound, glued to the floor, too busy wanting Max to know what she was missing.

In the midst of it, Max picked up a cup of wine and a loaf of bread and raised them above his head, his lips moving, talking to someone I couldn't see. He wore his usual jeans and T-shirt, yet he seemed trans-figured, separate from us. Tears ran down his cheeks. My brother was happy. Happy and distant from me.

Tears ran down my own cheeks, but for another reason. As with Ruth, the music hadn't touched me. When the music filled my ears, all I wanted was my mother who used to drink herself into the very place where they were now, which to my mind was no place. I crept back to my room, which was also Ruth's room, and covered my eyes to blot out the cuddly toys. For hours, as the music made the walls around me throb, I missed the shadows of our old house, the company of ghosts I had known. And mirrors where you were never alone.

Months passed. The holes in John's jeans had become real now. One day I looked at him and was shocked by how thin he had grown. He had spent a lot of time with the folk who had camped on our lawn before we moved, and picked up habits that didn't come from Max. The sweet dry scent that had drifted across Mrs Platt's garden crept out of his room now, and had taken away his stammer. You didn't find it anywhere else though. Max had no time for drugs, although he didn't exactly forbid them. He wouldn't have done that. But he made it clear he saw them as a distraction, an invitation to fail as he had once failed.

That first Creation Mass which exploded on Christmas Eve took place every week now. You could say that with us it was always Christmas. Music journalists started to turn up – the young, dour sort in leather jackets misted with dandruff. I led them through the Mission house and thought they would hate everything – the music, the boys and girls who made it, the people who danced to it. Yet they never did. They wrote about Max and John in their newspapers and magazines, and most of all on the Net. As a result people started coming who ten years ago would never have got to hear of us. They slipped through the doors at the beginning of every service, mostly young, tattooed and many of them pierced. People you never associated with prayer. At the end they stayed – ostensibly to help clear up, but really it was to speak to Max.

So many of them now, Max had to rent a bigger hall and ask for a collection at the door to pay for it, embarrassed because he knew it made them look like a proper church. But people didn't seem to mind.

They turned out their pockets as unquestioningly as they would to get into a night club, and suddenly there was money. Max called a vote on what to do with it.

Proper carpets and net curtains for the squat – that was Ruth's idea. She didn't like the neighbourhood looking in. She didn't even like the fact that we were becoming part of the neighbourhood. The rest voted with Max for a bigger sound system and better lights. John sat back and grinned broadly at the result, his eyes coming back as they so often did, to me.

More months went by. The numbers coming to the Mass rose then slowly settled. I thought this was the way things would go now, and wondered if this would be enough for Max. He seemed happy, as if just for now he could let things rest. Then I understood that this was exactly what he was doing – resting. Saving his energy for something else, something bigger.

Sometimes though, he needed all his energies for something more immediate. Increasingly, parents whose offspring were in 'Swork arrived at the door demanding that Max 'give them back their children'.

We should have expected it. Yet it always took Max by surprise. He met the mothers and fathers with puzzled courtesy, shocked that anyone should think he had stolen theirs or anybody's children. He spent hours with them, letting them know he agreed with them. He said families should stay together, and after a lot of soul searching, laid down the one and only rule of 'Swork. If you had parents who worried about you, go home to them. Show them you were still alive, still part of a family. Show them you cared.

All the more reason because that was the year our father died, out on his hillside with no family to be with him. Yet happy, by all accounts, right up to the moment that death had caught him by surprise. That's what the girl who called him *carissimo* told us and we had every reason to believe her.

Go home to your family, then – that was the rule, yet somehow the 'children' who left always came back. Sometimes within days. Often within hours.

''Swork's our family now. You, Max, everyone.'

One girl told me this after she had come back. Her eyes were shining with unshed tears and her hands were gripping mine. I tried not to pull away. She was one of the core group, one of the class who had dismissed itself for Max's sake, and I liked her – enough to wish she was the one sharing my room not Ruth; yet she didn't feel like a sister or related to me in any way. The fact is, she didn't feel like anything at all, just someone who was there because of Max.

She wasn't my family. My mother had

been my family. And my father. Now Max was *all* my family. No one else.

Then something happened that made us news again. Made us grow again. Something big. At least it seemed big to us.

The Church of England came to call.

The news spread through the Mission house, and people who had declared themselves free of all the trammels of the old institutions, who had walked away from the teachers, found they couldn't hide their excitement. The Bishop of the area had come to speak to Max. In person.

He was middle-aged and relaxed, elaborate in his appreciation of what Max was doing, and the way he was drawing in the youth. He told him the Church had been watching the activities of 'Swork – from a distance of course, but with enormous interest. His pleasant, unaccented voice sounded indulgent, as if Max and the others had been a bunch of puppies or small children gambolling at the feet of the grown ups.

But even Max couldn't have expected what happened next. The Bishop leant back in his seat, then dropped his bombshell. He said the Church wanted to take Max on, make him one of theirs. They wanted to appoint him curate, with his very own living. Of course, there would be an amount of training involved, but fast-tracked to minimise the time he spent away from his ministry. There was only one condition: he would have to leave where he was living with 'Swork members, although the Church itself would take out a lease on the Mission to allow the others to stay.

'I hope this doesn't make life difficult for you or them, Max. But you'll understand we can't have a minister of the Church living in what amounts to a commune. It would make it all look too much like a ... a ... *cult.*' He pronounced this last word fastidiously, as if it brought a nasty taste into his mouth.

I had forgotten how very cool Max could be when taken by surprise, the way his whole body would become still, like a lion watching the lie of the land change in front of him. Calmly, he told the Bishop he needed time to think. Even more calmly, he said he had never seen himself as anybody's leader. Or teacher. Or minister. If he had learnt anything it was from the people around him.

The Bishop smiled at this, and murmured that every servant of the church had to consider if he was worthy. Clarity of vision was perhaps a minister's greatest gift. His smile only faded a little when he caught sight of me, sitting in the corner of the room and realised I had been there all the time, and that somehow he had failed to register the fact.

When the Bishop was gone Max asked me

what I thought, and watched my face as I considered carrying on as we were now, a lifetime of sharing a bedroom with Ruth, with her cuddly toys and collection of nail brushes. And what I thought, showed.

So Max *(Max!)* became a curate in the Anglican Church. He will always swear there were good ecumenical reasons for it – for becoming a company man. But the truth is, he did it for me. He knew I wanted to be alone again, with him. I needed space for the shadows. For us.

And Max made sure it happened

And this was how 'Swork became headline news again.

'An experiment,' the Bishop described it to *The Times* when the press release came out. 'A radical test of ecumenism and practical theology in the city.'

'Sexy vicar employed to get them dancing in the aisles' is how the tabloids put it. Privately, I thought the tabloids had the edge.

Along with that press release, The Church sanctioned the first big photo shoot, the one that everyone uses, even now, four years on. There's Max in the foreground with his blue jeans and his sleepy smile, his hair glinting like a messy halo; and gathered behind him, lounging in black denims and black T-shirts – all the members of 'Swork. Piled up around them is the accumulated junk that goes into the making of a Creation Mass – speakers and turn tables, screens and columns of vinyl, lights and switches, a spaghetti of wires. Christianity was never as cool as this.

So there they all are, captured forever with their roll ups, and greasy hair. They look exactly like what they are – devout middle-class children gone off the rails. Except this was the paradox. They had gone to the good. They were on the side of the angels.

It changed everything, that photograph, and made Max famous in a new way. It even crept on to the front cover of *Rolling Stone*, together with an article that claimed to be watching the birth of a new religious move-ment, gleeful that rave music was set to give Christian fundamentalists a run for their money.

Yet the irony is, Max had done everything he could to have that photograph withheld. He didn't want anyone seeing it. The reason is me. *I'm* there, sitting on the floor, half hidden behind the legs, staring out of the picture. I look like a delinquent child who has crawled into the frame, and been trapped there. I wasn't meant to be any-where near, but the photographer had noticed me and waved me onto the set. Confused, I had done as I was told, and there I am, on my hands and knees, startled by the flash. Eyes caught naked and amazed, just this once giving everything away. Max says I look like someone's soul caught by the camera. *His* soul perhaps. I have his eyes.

Once you've noticed I'm there, you can't escape me.

And that's the trouble. It's the only picture of me that exists in the public sphere. Indelible, part of the legend of Max. I am the sister in the house, the one he famously refuses to talk about. Mad Mary Lamb to his Charles. Wherever people have heard of 'Swork, they have heard of me.

It's that picture the newspapers use over and over again. Every time a child kills another child. Every time they want to show the face of another child who has done just that.

And who let the cat out of the bag? Who told them about me? Ruth of course. Angry because she never made it into the frame, because no one remembered to wait for her. She'd been putting biscuits on plates in the kitchen, obsessed with finding cups with handles to give to the press. Saucers to go with the cups. So busy fussing they took the picture without her. She needed someone to suffer, so she picked on me.

Chapter Nineteen

Time is passing.

Coming closer to the present now, to the night that brought Caroline's beautiful sleek head in contact with those railings. Red against black. I remember now, those were the colours she liked to wear. They suited her.

You could see every memory from now on as a long slow march to that moment, her final moment. Makes you wish it could all slow down. That way Caroline stays alive, stays beautiful. Four years ago, she was just becoming famous in her own right, growing more and more visible, gathering audiences with that cool TV gaze. Her face was beginning to be everywhere – exactly the way it is now. Since she died, you see her more than ever. For Caroline it's almost business as usual.

She was famous before Max was. Four years ago most people had an inkling of her, whilst before the Bishop came to call, hardly anyone knew Max existed. They had forgotten about the Pied Piper and the vanished year group. Yet only last week a newspaper ran a poll to find the most recognised

Christian in Britain, and Max came third, ahead of the prime minister. Only the Pope and Cliff Richard got more recognition.

And it's not just in this country. Nowadays there are branches of 'Swork as far apart as Singapore and Israel, and every six months the numbers double, like some huge protean problem in mental arithmetic. Who would have thought there were so many people yearning? Sometimes I imagine them before Max came along, milling around in chaos, waiting for someone to open up the gates of heaven. Like the first day of a sale, or folk queuing up outside a club, desperate to get in. You'd have thought if they were so eager they would have found their own way in long ago, without Max. And yet they never did.

A month ago 'Swork's accountant wrote to Max suggesting it would make good financial sense if Max simply went out and bought his own plane. In fact he insisted. It would be cheaper, given the travelling he has to do. He said Max should see it as a kind of wedding present to Caroline and himself.

Max hated that. He showed me the letter with a pained look on his face. It's stuff like this that makes him embarrassed. It takes him back to the College and Father Ignatius who said that Max's God was all about himself. What would he say if he knew about the plane?

176

Father Ignatius was wrong then and he is wrong now. Max just wants to talk, to find a way to make the world a better place. An easier place when Max's God is in it, all-forgiving, all-embracing. Someone to fall back on. A God who is still busy, still creating, like a cook in a kitchen. What Max doesn't want is planes and ticker tape welcomes and little girls waiting at the airport with flowers, which is what happened last time he was in Taiwan, and which no doubt Father Ignatius knows all about.

All Max wants to do is talk. Is it his fault if people want to listen?

He has never even liked religion, not the organised sort. He says: 'look at the Spanish Inquisition.' Then he laughs and everyone else laughs too – and I'm the only person who seems to realise he's not joking.

Meanwhile the rest of the world has been waiting for something to happen, for the rot to set in. Something nasty. For four years newspaper editors have sat in their offices, praying for a story. Now with Caroline they've got one. What more could they ask? They have Max, a private plane, a world-wide following – and now a dead fiancée. It's almost as good as what they wanted in the first place. Namely, to see him fail, come tumbling down, exposed as being just like the rest of us – fallible.

Which only shows that they still haven't

got it. Max has never pretended to be any-thing but a failure. A walking, talking, em-bodiment of Fail. An addict addicted to the thing that nearly killed him. Failure is what it's all about, the reason he's here. Max's God absolutely adores failure, could eat it on toast. Failure is the only sure fingerpost to the future. It's what you do next that counts.

In the first days of 'Swork, when he talked about failure and where it took him, Max used to roll back his sleeves to show the scars running down his arms, like arrows pointing to where the future lies. Namely, in his own hands. In all our hands.

And later when Caroline came along, she was on a mission of her own, to expose him. She was quite open about it. Yet it turned out that she was a failure too. Because look what happened. She came, notebook in hand, to flay Max, to lay him open – and ended up planning to marry him.

Five days since they found her, bleeding outside her own front door. Poor Caroline. Poor Max.

And poor me. The police are surer than ever that I'm the one who killed her. That I'm the one they just missed with blood on my hands.

Part Two

Chapter Twenty

Five days since they found her. The newspapers are speculating about a vendetta
from her past, someone whose life she
uncovered and ruined. Maybe even a mafia
connection. But you only have to watch the
police to know what they think of that. Their
business is here, with us. More specifically
with me.

I lift the teapot and raise my eyebrows at
Detective Inspector Davies. He shakes his
head and stands up, brushes the crumbs off
the front of his polyester shirt. He's in his
fifties, overweight, asks for a lot of sugar in
his tea.

'Thanking you, but no. It was only a quick
word I wanted with the Reverend. See how
he was bearing up.'

He is a liar. He wanted a word with *me*.
Lots of words. Max he doesn't have much
time for. You can tell he doesn't like him,
despite what Max is going through. He
disapproves of him, being the sort who likes
his priests to go around in cardigans and
dog collars. Instead he has Max with his
jeans and *fuck me* T-shirts.

He'd have been so much happier if it had

been Max he had under suspicion. It would have given him a grim satisfaction to have him in his sights. But that can't happen because Max is accounted for. He was with Ruth when it happened, sorting out her problems. She was there, vouching for him from the beginning, a disappointment for the inspector with all his prejudices.

Oddly enough, he is nice to me, his main – his only – suspect. He smiles tenderly when I pass him the sugar for the endless cups of tea; talks to me gently as if I'm fifteen years younger than I am. He watches me, of course, because I'm the one with the past, the one that at some point he is going to pin down and skewer with her own evidence. The only person he knows who had a reason to want Caroline dead. But still he has to feel sorry for me, believing as he does that I'm 'Not Quite Right'.

Besides, he doesn't like Caroline, not one little bit. The more he talks to me, the clearer it becomes. He meets enough women like her in the course of his day. Women super-intendents promoted over his head, women politicians wanting to tell him how to do his job. Women like Caroline with ideas of their own. Noisy. Argumentative. Everything I'm not.

His apparent kindness cuts no ice with Max. The moment DI Davies says he's leaving, Max is there, ready to see him out. But although Max is standing by the door, DI Davies hasn't finished.

'Just one last thing, if you don't mind. Something I'm still not quite clear about. What were your plans, Rosie? For yourself I mean, after the wedding?'

DI Davies does this a lot – addresses me as if he expects me to answer. As if all it took was a moment while I gather my thoughts. And when he doesn't get a reply, he simply poses the question another way: 'Let's call them your domestic arrangements, I'm talking about your actual place of abode. Naturally you weren't reckoning to stay here, not once your brother had tied the knot.'

Max stirs, but DI Davies ignores him. He watches me, listens to the silence before he says, 'I mean, that wasn't going to happen, was it? The three of you ending up together. I can't see Miss Marsh agreeing to that, not from what I've heard.'

And there it is, unmistakable, the note of disapproval in his voice when he mentions Caroline.

This time, Max can't stop himself. 'What my sister would tell you – if only she could – was that we hadn't discussed it. There was no need. *This* is Rosie's home, with me. Where else should she live?'

DI Davies frowns, puts down his coat, feels for the notebook in his waistcoat pocket. 'Well let's see...' he flips through the notebook to find a page. 'I've talked to Miss Ruth Evans and she tells me Miss Marsh was all set to move Rosie into her own house. She was going to hand over the keys at the wedding reception. Another little ceremony to follow the first. Quite a gesture it was going to be, deeds signed and everything. Generous is hardly the word for it.' He looks directly at my brother. 'Ruth Evans says everyone knew about it – and what Miss Bryant thought about it.'

There is the shortest of pauses. Max says: 'Caroline *was* generous. Really generous. But...'

DI Davies waits. *'But?'*

'But as I said just now, this is Rosie's home, and ... and Caroline agreed with me. Rosie was going to stay here, with us. Caroline was looking forward to it. We all were. Everything was going to be fucking brilliant.'

And DI Davies visibly flinches. It's that use of *fucking*. Not what he expects to hear from a man of God, not even the unconventional kind. As for me, *I'm* startled. Max has always been a social chameleon. He knows what to do with words. Is this what grief has done to him, robbed him of what he knows to be appropriate? That *fucking* was out of place, sounding as if it came from a sixteen-year-old. In short, it was a distraction, leading DI Davies onto another train of thought... Leading him away from me. Immediately I

184

stop being startled. I know what Max is doing now, just like the old days. Taking the attention away from me. Building me a wall.

And it works – for now. I don't suppose that DI Davies goes to church – he prefers to keep his Sundays for DIY, or cooking his family a roast; he looks like that sort of man. But for the moment he is so flustered by Max's *fucking* that he lets the question drop.

The trouble with this though is, it doesn't help. Because if Max doesn't tell the inspector somebody else will. Ruth probably already has. Caroline made it crystal clear: she wasn't going to share Max with anyone. There never was going to be a place for me here, in the house that has been my home. Everybody knew that.

That's why she was giving me *her* house, so no one could say she was making me homeless. I would be the owner of a luxury house in Docklands with the benefit of shiny black railings and a home help. That was the plan. Then again, Caroline had plans for every-thing – whom she was going to marry, where she was going to live. Plans for career, honeymoon. Even plans for children.

And look where she ended up: dead on her own front doorstep, bleeding. All those plans leeching out to form a puddle on the floor beside her head.

Cruel to put it like that. But Caroline has ... Caroline *had* ...that effect; she made you

185

focus on the reality of things, whether you wanted to or not. Even when they're cruel.

At least I don't *look* cruel. DI Davies ignores Max and watches me, his eyes kindly. Is he this gentle with all his accused? To tell the truth, I am almost shocked by his kindness. What about Caroline? Where's his sympathy for her, the victim? Doesn't she deserve it?

And still he is not finished. 'Your brother has written a book, Miss Bryant. Isn't that right? Bit of a bestseller I understand.' He looks at his notebook. *'Racing Demons,* that's the name of it. Sorry to say, I haven't read it. I suppose I should get myself a copy.' He looks at Max as if half hoping that Max will offer him one and save him the money. But Max says nothing. He's just happy to show him to the door.

But at least Max is behaving like himself. I listen to him ushering the inspector onto the street, the pleasant tones of what Caroline once described as his 'posh hippie' voice. Laughing as she said it, and then turning to me, her eyes inquisitive.

And what did you sound like, Rosie? Posh like Max, all plummy and sweet like a little convent girl? I'd love to have heard your voice. Only Caroline could have asked the question.

But then my brother comes back into the kitchen, and already the Max that DI Davies knows has disappeared. Without realising it, his shoulders have drooped and there's a weight dragging on his feet. People don't see him like this. I don't see him like this. But sometimes, like now, in the wake of the questions, he can't help himself.

So he does the only thing he can do. Avoiding my eyes, he goes deep, deep into himself, where there's no following. Like the childhood days when he made those dens and climbed inside and there was no reaching him, not till he was ready to come out.

I don't have to ask what he's thinking about. Or whom. It's Caroline of course. Max was the one who found her. The one who called the police, the ambulance, everyone possible, and all of them too late to help. The only person left to call on after that would have to have been God, and I can't say He's been much in evidence.

But what's worse for him is that he had to find *me*, inside her house, only then waking up. And that's when they found *him*, in the bathroom with me, washing my hands. Both our hands wet in the sink. But too late, they saw it, the blood trickling down the drain. He told them it came from his hands, from having touched her, there beside the railings, touching and trying to call her back to life. But they didn't believe him then, and they don't believe him now.

I didn't know what was happening. I didn't even know there had been blood, not until I saw it in the basin. I didn't know anything except that, from the moment he found me, both his hands were wrapped around mine, determined to protect me, just like the first time.

Max protects me, and in return all I have to offer is silence. How can he stand it? Caroline was anything but silent. She was fuelled by opinions, bursting with questions. She always wanted to know more than anyone else in the room, the expert on everything. She wanted to be the expert on Max. And she would have succeeded. She had a thousand ways of getting what she wanted, and one sure way with Max. Sure as anything there would have been a day when she'd have turned and told me something about my brother that even I had never known.

All that noise, all that hot curiosity. All gone. Nothing left but me and silence.

No wonder he cries.

The phone goes, and as usual it's Ruth. And as usual there's a problem down at The 'Swork Centre. She has no pity, calling him at a time like this, but it doesn't stop her. She's been calling more than ever now that Caroline has died.

Max sighs as he puts down the phone. But at least he has come out of himself, out of that place where I can't reach him, and looks at me. And it never fails to amaze me.

His eyes are clear, suspecting me of nothing, blaming me for nothing. I saw the blood as it ran away from my hands, and yet his belief in my innocence is implicit. You can see it in his face. He doesn't hold me responsible for anything.

Why is he so sure of me? Why does he seem never even to consider that I might have killed her, the love of his life? Why does he still try to protect me?

What do I not remember?

The phone rings again. It will be Ruth checking, wanting to make sure he's on his way. If I had a voice I would grab the phone and scream at her to leave him in peace. Demand to know what makes her think she can call on him again and again and again.

Chapter Twenty-One

Caroline isn't the only person to make Max cry. He cried when John died. Everybody did.

But Max cried with a special grief because John had been his closest friend, the one who understood best what he was about. He was the one he depended on, the man who could carry every new idea into the real world. Max dreamt up the Creation Mass, but John made it happen. Max missed him for all these reasons, while I missed him for the slow smile, and the way he broke his own mould. And for the way he looked at me.

But most of all Max cried because he knew he was the reason for his death.

There weren't supposed to be drugs in 'Swork. The Church of England had taken over the lease of the Mission, making it officially no longer a squat. So that was one reason. But the real reason was Max. He didn't want drugs anywhere near us. He made it clear they were a cheat, a short cut that left out the main part of the journey. He said he wanted people to make up their own minds, but we all knew: Max hated drugs.

And John knew it too. Once, in our own house, I walked downstairs towards the room where he and Max had been working all night. Unusually Max had given in first, crawling exhaustedly up the stairs to his room while I was coming down, unable to sleep for the noise.

'Finished for tonight.' He smiled at me, tiredness creasing his eyes. 'Go and tell John to go home. The bastard won't listen to me.'

So, barefoot, I carried on downstairs and there was John, his body hooked over a small table with what looked like a straw in his hand. Hearing a sound, he looked up sharply and guiltily, the alarm on his face only slightly fading when he saw it was me, not Max.

He smiled his slow smile, but this time it didn't seem so real. And when he knew I'd seen it the smile disappeared, and he shrugged, half in apology and half in defiance. 'Got to stay awake somehow, Rosie. Too much to do. Too little time.'

Of course, I said nothing. I was observing the thin line of white powder traced along the table, thinking it looked almost benign compared to the needles and the tubes Max had needed. But John coloured and with an awkward sweep of his hand brushed the powder away, sending it flying off to join the rest of the dust in the room. He watched it scatter then said in a low voice: 'It's different for Max. Can you understand that, Rosie? He can do it. Stay up all night if he has to, talk to people, do whatever it takes to keep them glued to him. He doesn't stop. He has this ... this energy. Do you know what I'm talking about? This *fucking* energy he has?'

I nodded. Of course I knew. An energy that separated us from him, and would always make him different. John saw me nod and relaxed slightly. There was a hint of wonder as he spoke. 'And when you touch him, hand him a screwdriver or a disk, you can feel it, like there's electric running through him. Have you felt it?'

Again I nodded.

'It's that kind of energy I need, if I'm to be any good to him. And I haven't got it. I'm … I'm normal, Rosie. Ordinary. Sometimes I don't know if I even...' He broke off, then swallowed and forced the smile to come back to his face. 'You know what? I should have joined a fucking rock band. It would have been more restful. Just play the bloody music, and spend the money.'

I laughed at that. Because we both knew, John would never do that. There was nothing he would do that didn't include Max...

He reached out a hand to switch on the tape recorder on the table, still determined to work, but his arm fell flat under its own weight of fatigue. He stared down at himself in disgust, while the powder, his own expensive energy, continued to settle in all four corners of the room. He shook his head ruefully.

'Better go home, then, to bed.' He heaved himself up from his chair, his body heavy, acknowledging defeat.

The more so, because from upstairs in Max's room, we could hear the rhythmic thump of bass. Max was awake after all, buoyed up by that energy that no one else had. John shook his head again and shambled out into the night.

I didn't tell Max about the powder. I just

assumed he knew, like he knew most things. Sometimes I wondered if that was Ruth's proper role – a second eye to see and tell. Then I'd feel ashamed for thinking Max would do any such thing – use Ruth to watch people, even when it might be for their own good.

Anyway, he must have known about John. How else did he imagine he could keep up? And Max needed John to keep up. The Creation Mass had become so big, that with the Bishop's blessing we had moved it permanently out of the Mission House into a sports hall. After the encounter with John, I would watch my brother and wonder if perhaps *this* was where his energy came from, from the crowd of people moving around him, from the lights flashing and the drums beating. I'd watch him lift up his head and stretch out his hands, laughing, delighting in it all. Separate from us, part of something bigger.

Then I would turn to find John, who was always there, hidden in a booth. Crouched above a console of switches, frowning over the magic he was helping to create. The lights that made Max glow would have cast him into a shadow, made him look thinner, paler than I had ever seen him.

And tired. I'd see the weariness as it seeped out of him, and got lost among the dancers. We were always the only people not dancing, outsiders who should have been on the inside. Yet without him, none of this would be happening.

I watched him, and at once he was aware of it. His eyes found mine more often now, and held them longer. But in the end both our gazes would return to the same place, to Max.

The next time he stayed late, I came downstairs after hearing Max come up. This time John seemed to be waiting for me. There was no sign of anything on the table. He watched me settle on the floor. For a long moment we stared at each other.

Eventually he said, 'When you look at me, I think of Max. And when he looks at me, I think of you.'

It was a strange thing to say. John shrugged, acknowledging the fact.

'Other times, I look at you, and I forget that you don't talk. To me, it's as if you are talking all the time, but your voice is in my head where only I can hear. I tell myself I know what you're thinking, I pretend I know what it's like to be you, caught up in this. Part of the Max thing. And all the time, not believing a single word of it.'

I sat very still, saying nothing, denying nothing. At the same time shocked that he knew. I had thought that only Max knew that I wasn't one of them, that I didn't believe. Would never believe.

'You know, Rosie,' the words came out in a rush, 'I don't think Max knows you, not really. He thinks he does. But when he talks to you, it's as if you're fragile, ready to break in half. And I don't think you are. I think you're strong, like a ... a thin stream of light, concentrated. And you never waver. Never go out. Cover you up,' he put up his hands and cupped them upside down, 'and you disappear. But take away the shade,' he let his hands fall apart, 'and you're still there.'

I listened to him describe me, and didn't recognise myself. But I wanted him to keep talking, telling me about a girl who wasn't there, but wished she was.

'I watch you, Rosie, and I tell myself I know what you're thinking – that we're all mad or deceiving ourselves. And when *I* have doubts, I think of you, observing us – like you're seeing right through us. Your eyes are so clear...' He paused and suddenly his stammer came back. 'But I d-d ... don't want you not to look at me, Rosie. K-keep looking at me, let me keep telling myself I know what you're thinking.'

There was a movement upstairs, the sound of music. Max had started back to work again. I saw John wince, then something in him relaxed. He leaned back in his chair, and closed his eyes, deliberately not looking at me.

'Sometimes I imagine you're asking me

what I'm about, why I'm with Max. And I imagine I'm telling you, explaining myself, so it doesn't seem so mad. In my head I tell you how all I'm doing is trying to find out, poke at the fabric a bit, trying to see through the surface of things. You know my father is ordained? Everything I thought I knew came from him. But it's not enough. You have to look for yourself. That's what Max helps me do – to look at things, look through them. The trouble with looking, though, is you might actually see what's there – or not there. You might get right through the surface only to find there's nothing. Just hot air and wishful thinking. Nothing else.'

His voice was falling, words getting slower. 'I keep thinking how sad that would be, to search – and end up with nothing. But *then* I think how, even if that happened, you'd still be there, just the way you are, like that thin beam of light. And it doesn't seem so bad, after all. Because you're real. I could live with that, even if you were the only real thing in the world...'

He stopped. Without any warning he had fallen asleep, so abruptly it was obvious; he had taken something. Not the white powder, but something different that had loosed his tongue and now closed his eyes like a cosh coming down. Inside I felt a soft fall of disappointment. I had been listening so hard and all the time it had just been the drug that was talking. Probably in the morning he wouldn't even remember. Not a word.

I got up from the floor. He had started to snore in his chair, sounding uncannily like my mother when the drink would finally have finished her for the night. As I climbed the stairs, Max came out of his room. He smiled when he saw me, then the smile vanished, and he was alert.

'Something's wrong.'

I shook my head, but the light flickered in his eyes. 'John?'

I tried avoiding his eyes, something I never remembered doing before.

'He's taken something?'

I hesitated then nodded. Max's face, which had grown hard, softened. 'Oh shit, Rosie, what the fuck am I going to do with him?'

He stared at me, genuinely questioning. And I stared back, amazed that he didn't know the answer. They were in the middle of Max's biggest idea yet. A Mass that would take place, not just in a sports hall, but an entire stadium, the largest celebration they had ever had, and all happening in a week's time. This was the reason Max and John were working night and day. If Max wanted to do anything for John, all they had to do was stop. That was the answer.

And of course they wouldn't stop. The service was taking place on May Day – Beltane in the pagan calendar – and Max's idea was to make it a celebration for that as well, a mix of pagan and Christian. Thousands of people were going to be there, too many to leap through the flames of a fire, but Max had planned for lights and leaping of another kind. He needed music and images of a different magnitude.

And for that he needed John. Tired John. Who dosed himself with artificial energy, then spoke words that had nearly meant something. And ended in meaning precisely nothing.

I tried to stay away from John for the rest of the week. I didn't want someone watching me, thinking he could read my mind. But it was impossible; somehow he was always there. Or maybe it was me, putting myself where he was.

And I was wrong to think he wouldn't remember what he had said. I found his eyes on me constantly now, and they told me he hadn't forgotten. Meanwhile he'd discovered a new spurt of energy (no need to wonder how) and kept up with Max. They worked all the night through before May Day itself. No sleep for either of them, but by the evening they were ready.

Max had spent the morning arguing with

the Bishop. He wanted to call this service the Goddess Mass in deference to what he called the female aspect of God, and to women worldwide. The Bishop said no, and so Max had gone ahead and called it something even more pagan – the Beltane Mass. And that was the name that appeared on all the websites for the rest of the day. At seven in the evening the people began to congregate, filing through the barriers like a football crowd in fancy dress. By nine o'clock, the grass pitch of the stadium was covered.

Twenty thousand of them, maybe more, their feet muffled by grass and the emptiness of sky overhead. We watched them gather in disbelief. There were so many of them, more than we had ever seen. More than we could have expected. And virtually silent, that was the strange thing. These were Max's people, dreadlocked and pierced and tattooed, and all seeming to know that this was how Max wanted it to be; a Mass that started with silence. Darkness and silence, like the beginning of the world. All we could hear was the muffled tramp of feet and afterwards, the breathing of twenty thousand souls. A smell of patchouli and bruised grass rose into the night air.

In the players' tunnel, I waited with Max. He stood beside me, his own breathing light and fast. He was pale, not quite solid, trembling like someone caught in a stream of particles. It was if he was half empty, waiting to be filled.

People might have taken it for excitement, that sort of nervous emptiness. I knew it as fear. Max often dreamt the nights before the masses, and his most frequent dream was of failure. Of opening his mouth before a congregation waiting to hear him speak – and finding he could say ... nothing. A dream of being me.

Tonight, though, he was even paler than usual, haggard from days without sleep. He felt my eyes on his face and he smiled into the dark ahead of him. 'I'll be all right, Rosie. You know what it's like. Once we get going...'

So we stood and waited for John to pull the first switch. For the first chords and the first light. Max's cue. His release from the emptiness.

We waited and we waited – and nothing happened. Eventually Max craned around to find a clock in the tunnel, the last thing footballers might see before they faced a crowd. Already the minute hand had slid across the nine and beyond. Max shook his head. More minutes passed. Outside the crowd was beginning to stir. No one was heard to speak, yet the quality of the air had changed, become more charged, edging towards impatience.

Max took another look at the footballers clock, and muttered: 'What's he doing?' He meant John, of course. Nothing would start until John *made* it start.

I turned and headed for the box, John's booth where everything happened. Should have happened.

And inside John was asleep. I touched him and instantly he was awake, his hand reaching out as if to complete a movement that he had fallen asleep in the middle of. Outside the booth, the stadium exploded with light and sound, and twenty thousand people shook out their dreadlocks and began to move. It started with a slow solid stamp of their feet, like heavy birds looking for the rhythm of a wing beat that would lift them off the floor. I could feel the ground vibrating beneath me, pounding as if there was a secret life just below the surface.

Then that same life seemed to rise, through the pounding of their feet into their bodies. Arms, legs began to move – faster, and then faster still. Twenty thousand souls were moving together, never missing a beat, transformed into one great dancing creature, thinking like a single brain.

The stadium had come alive. John had done his thing – again.

He smiled at me, but his face was twisted by exhaustion, hands shaking as he moved them over his console of switches and dials.

I wanted to touch him again, but found I didn't dare. He was too powerful, too busy creating here, behind his screen. Instead I went in search of Max.

I thought it was too late to be close to him, right in the middle of everything; but I was forgetting how he could always find me, even in a crowd. I felt his eyes drawing me towards him through the dancing. I arrived at his side and his arm slipped around me.

'Is John all right?'

I nodded and Max squeezed my hand, then let it go. I knew what was coming next. It was close to the time when he would take his leave, peeling away from me and every person present, as if somehow we were part of his carapace, the thing that formed, then released him. The place where he belonged now was alone and free at the makeshift altar, waiting with its bread and its wine.

Afterwards people would talk, dazed, about this Beltane Mass, how something had happened, making it different from all the other Masses that had gone before. People talked of soaring and touching the sky, of flying. They talked about Max's words, yet no one seemed to remember exactly what he had said. They talked of images, but these, too, were muddled, created piecemeal out of a larger whole. They remembered and remembered, but patchily, frustrated by forgetfulness. But that was all right. Forgetfulness simply made them long for the next time, to be fully reminded. To do it all again.

Yet they remembered this – how Max had held the cup on high as people danced around him, and the light had concentrated, intensified in a way that seemed to emanate from, not onto, him. Several people fainted and had to be stretchered out, and afterwards described how it was the light that fazed them. Max's light.

Minutes, hours passed. The music changed, grew slower, quieter. It always happened at this point in any service, otherwise people would have danced themselves to exhaustion, into stupor. And as the dancing slowed something else happened that always happened. People began to turn to each other.

It was happening again now – the quiet winding down. Yet I always used to hate this part, the attraction flesh suddenly would have for flesh as faces softened and limbs relaxed. Most of all I hated the way Ruth would also begin to dance in a different way, abandoning the clumsy shuffle from foot to foot. Instead she would start to run her hands over her body, rolling her head from side to side, her eyes closed and dreaming.

I had always made a point of leaving at this stage. Never staying, never joining in. Hurrying to get away from Ruth, alone and touching herself; anxious to get away even from Max who stood at the altar presiding over everything, responsible for it all.

This time, though, I turned, and there was John. Watching me. I went to go past him, and he moved in front of me. I stepped another way and he did the same thing again, effortlessly. Then I knew whichever way I stepped, he would be there, reading my direction from my eyes. Blocking my path.

Reading my mind, just like he said he could.

Slowly John put out his hand. I hesitated then gave him my own hand, allowed him to draw me towards him, into his arms. But even here I was disappointed. I studied his eyes, and the dilation of his pupils gave him away, betraying the reason he was awake and able to stand up. He saw the disappointment in mine and smiled haggardly, recognising where he had gone wrong.

Yet all the same he kissed me, catching my mouth with his, catching me by surprise. There was the taste of water on his lips, cool and wet. He had been drinking from the bottle he had in his hand, and moisture drenched the kiss like an embrace in the rain. My first kiss. My only kiss. His arms tightened around me and I closed my eyes, pretending just for the moment that there was nothing wrong, that John's heart and head were clear, that he was his own man. That we were kissing in the rain.

Then I opened them again sensing some-one was watching. Sure enough, Ruth had stopped dancing and was staring at us, mouth open and gobby, like a cartoon character drawn to look surprised. Already she was tugging at the person standing beside her with his back to us.

Max, I had forgotten Max. Who turned when he felt Ruth's fingers pinching his arm. His eyes found mine instantly, as they always did, even in a crowd, and saw John's arms around me. I saw Max blink, his face expressionless, and suddenly I wanted to step out of John's embrace, to explain. Nothing would come of this.

But already Max had turned from me. I saw him bend towards Ruth and whisper in her ear. She listened then nodded, and with one more sly glance at us trudged away, vanishing into the crowd. Better without Ruth, though. Much better, because when Max looked at us again, the blank look had disappeared and he was smiling at us. The smile comforted me, made me calm again. But when I glanced at John I saw he hadn't even noticed – or cared. All he could see was me. He really did think the kiss had changed everything. That's what his eyes told me when he slid away back to his booth of lights and sound.

The crowds had nearly all left when the

police came, blocking the exits with their cars, the lights left flashing. They began hauling out the remnants of the crowd who were still leaving in order to search them. Meanwhile the officer in charge came and found Max who was standing helpless, white with anger, in the stadium changing rooms.

'This was a church service,' Max said at once. 'People came to worship, no other reason.' Despite the emotion, his voice was low and controlled.

'We had a tip off, Reverend,' the officer was saying. 'We were told someone was dealing in class A stuff. I'm sorry,' he sounded genuinely apologetic, 'we couldn't just let it go.'

Ruth interrupted. ''Swork has a no-drugs policy, officer. We make it perfectly clear at the door. Anyone found with illegal substances would be thrown out. We're not fuddy-duddies, but we are here to set an *example*.'

'Ruth,' said Max quietly. He wanted her to stop talking.

'Well it's true,' she said indignantly. 'You don't want these people to think you'd approve.' She turned to the policeman. 'Believe me, Max Bryant wants nothing to do with anyone who would bring drugs to our services. It would be a kind of pollution. A sin.'

The police officer was looking, almost embarrassed, at Max. 'Then this is going to

206

come as a bit of a blow, sir. The crowd is clean – those we searched. A bit of cannabis, but that's not what we came for. But it's your colleague – a Mr John Wreakin – who concerns us. We've just finished a quick trawl through his pockets, and frankly he's got the works on him, everything from ecstasy to tabs of acid. Can you tell us anything about that?'

Max exhaled quietly, then sat down slowly on one of the benches.

The police officer was still speaking. 'It means we're going to have to search all of you, the Group, and the people he knows well. You can see why we have to?' Again he sounded apologetic. Max inclined his head, avoiding my eye. 'Not my sister. Please. She's ... fragile. She...' The policeman shook his head. Max held up a hand, then let it fall, helpless. Softly, barely audible now, he said, 'Look, I'm begging you. Not her.'

The police man frowned. He knew the story of the sister in the house, everybody did. Finally he nodded, and turned to Ruth who stepped forward eagerly, thinking he was going to search her right then and there, only to be disappointed when he all seemed to want was her name. A police-woman would do the business with her.

Max glanced across at me, his face a blank. I knew why he had stopped anyone searching me. He was afraid that being with

207

John would have rubbed off on me. Afraid that somehow, they would have found something that put me in the same category as him. And when I glared at him, he had the grace to blush.

I never saw John after that.

Somehow Max persuaded the police to release him on bail. He went with him from the police station back to the mission and stayed with him there all night, leaving me alone and wondering. Just before dawn I heard Max's footsteps in the hall and came downstairs.

He saw me and his face, already drawn, became more haggard still. For a moment I could see him contemplating whether he could walk straight past, without talking to me. But he read the look in my eyes and led me into the sitting room, and took my hands in his.

'Rosie, John is gone. He's left the Group. He was all set to leave us, even before I talked to him. There was no alternative. He knows what we're trying to do, better than anyone. He knows we·have to prove to people – vulnerable people – there's no need for drugs, or alcohol, or any of that crap. We've got to get them to trust themselves. He knows we can't do any of that if *we're* using the very thing that's killing them. It would be lying to them. Hypocritical ... he couldn't stay ... he knew that.'

He watched me as he spoke. But I was thinking of the philosophy of Max. *Fuck, forget, forgive.* And he was doing none of that now. Max was being harder on John than anyone. Hard as he would be on himself. I tried to pull my hands out of his, but he gathered them to him, closer still.

'I know what you're thinking Rosie. You think I should have given him another chance. And maybe you're right. But John didn't see it like that. He knew I didn't have a choice. He knew before I even said anything. You've got to believe me. He'd made up his own mind.'

I shook my head at that, vigorously. Because he was talking about choice, trying to tell me there was no choice. And yet Max had made a choice. He could have argued with him, changed his mind. Made him see that there could still be a place for him. We could help him. That's what Max said we were here to do – help each other. It's not what you had done, but what you did next that was important. But Max had made a choice and he chosen not to say any of that. He had let John stay in the same mind – and now he was claiming he'd had no choice.

No forgetting. No forgiving.

All that morning I waited for the phone to ring, expected it to ring. John told me he could hear my voice speaking in his head. I thought he must have been deaf that day, because he never heard me and never called.

He didn't call because he was dead. I never heard the details, and I never asked. I know that after Max left him alone in the mission, he had begun to pack up his stuff – but he never finished filling his bag. He'd got distracted and stopped to do something else involving all the paraphernalia of tubes and needles. And what happened to Max happened to him, except that unlike Max, there were no friends to save him. Or family. No one went near him. And so he died, alone at the end of a needle.

Nonsense to call us *family*. All it showed was that 'Swork was nobody's family, especially not John's.

A few days later his *real* family – in the shape of his father – came up to London to speak to Max. He was a tall man with the build of a rugby player, clumsy and large, yet wearing a clerical collar with the ease of an old school tie. He had ruddy cheeks – even in grief – and shaggy, salt and pepper hair. Big hands that hung by his sides, determined not to form themselves into fists. He must have been seventy, yet he had the youthful eyes of an altar boy, and he looked just like John would have looked if only he had lived so long, if he had only stayed with his own, his real, family. Stayed away from us.

I don't know what he said to Max. I don't even know if he blamed him. I know that Max blamed himself. And I know that he cried after they found him, the way he is crying now for Caroline.

Did I cry?

What do you think? But I didn't blame Max. I blamed the choices he made – or didn't make. I didn't even let myself wonder why, out of all the people they could have chosen to search, the police picked on John. Never mind that. Max didn't kill John. Heroin killed John. Heroin was the enemy.

Six months later we finished turning the Mission into a refuge for addicts. A refuge from the enemy. We called it The 'Swork Centre, and anyone is welcome. It exists to try and make up for the loss of John and for the choices that were made.

And *I* run it. *I* make it work. I am not helpless or hopeless. That's a fiction Max is determined to make DI Davies believe. Determined I shouldn't be held responsible for anything.

Chapter Twenty-Two

Yet Max put Ruth in charge. Her name appears on all the literature, making out she's the one talk to.

And people believe it. They believe because she is the one who briefs the press, who turns up on the radio and on TV, whose photograph used to appear next to Max's in all the articles about him. It helps that she looks the part, her face as round as ever with its suspicion of a moustache. Those thrift shop clothes give her the air of a missionary, the sort of Christian DI Davies can approve of.

So that's Ruth's job, being the public face of the Centre, showing the world what we are for. Telling the world what we need. It's not as if I could do any better, even if I had a voice, because still no one would listen to me. I would always be the child who killed a child, and that's all anyone would be interested in.

Yet it grieves me that John's memory rests with her. She talks about him to the journalists, makes him sound like the lost sheep, the lost soul. Purse-lipped and frowning, she points to his name above the door, and turns his life into a cautionary tale. Makes him unreal, a sinner. It's only the music journalists, the ones who haunt the websites who properly remember him, see him for what he was. A creator who simply needed a way to stay awake.

But that's the beginning and end of Ruth's role: show. She's constitutionally unfit for anything else. When clients started turning up, drifting through the doors after we opened, she was horrified. Thin, ill people with dirty nails, children who looked ten years older than they were, old men with stained trousers – they all frightened her, convinced as she was someone was going to rob her for the sake of a fix or a drink. And when she finally got over being frightened of them, she was contemptuous. She didn't like the way they smelled – unwashed, bodies wrung out from trying to digest the chemicals in their cells. The truth is it still turns her stomach just to be in the same room as a client. It never seems to occur to her that Max would have looked and smelled the same if she had met him a few years ago.

So the real work has nothing to do with her. Down in the depths of The 'Swork Centre, in the canteen or the dispensary, people wouldn't even know her name. Yet that's where the real work takes place. That's where we make it up to John.

And here it's me who's in charge. You

don't need to talk in order to dole out soup and pen rotas of volunteers. You don't need a voice to do the rounds of picking up three-day-old bread from the supermarkets, to go searching for a pair of shoes for someone from the piles of donated clothes. You can exchange needles and bathe the sepsis in wounds without ever opening your mouth. The people who come to us are glad of it. They like silence. They prefer it that way.

The fact is, I've worked at the Centre from the day it opened, working in memory of John and other ghosts. That's my job. It's what I do. It's there I think of John and that one drenched kiss. My only kiss.

Max knows all this. Five days since Caroline died yet he lets DI Davies go on thinking I'm useless, fit for nothing. Too breakable for normal wear and tear, let alone for use in a soup kitchen. Ruth backs him up because it's what she wants to believe, and the result is, between the two of them, DI Davies must wonder how I can make it unaided from one room to the next.

Of course I know why. Max wants to make me seem as helpless as a person could possibly be. Helpless people don't prey on others. Helpless people don't bludgeon innocent people to death. Or if by some terrible chance such a thing does happen, it can't be seen as deliberate. Helpless people can't be held responsible, not for anything.

So this is the way Max makes me out to be: Helpless. So everyone has to treat me with kid gloves. Even DI Davies.

One thing is true: you *are* helpless if your memory lets you down. Helpless if you can't recall what you were doing the hour and minute a young woman was put to death. If you can't say a word to help yourself. I don't know what I was doing when Caroline died. All I do know is what everyone knows: I was with her the night it happened, and I don't remember anything about it. So you could say there is a sense in which Max is right after all, that I am helpless.

I tell myself that no one ever died of not being able to remember. But sometimes it feels as if it could happen. That I could die of helplessness.

When the Centre opened its doors for the first time, the press turned up and saw Ruth and Max together. They observed the way Ruth's body leaned towards his body, his smile and patience towards her, and they drew their own conclusions. It wouldn't have seemed odd; plenty of charismatic men have plain wives. Look at all those TV evangelists and politicians. It's almost the rule.

And poor hungry Ruth, she loved having them think that. Loved it so much she convinced herself it was true, if not immediately, then in the future. She had stopped

215

seeing Roger, probably without too much regret on his part. He married a nurse and invited Max and Ruth to the wedding as if they were a couple.

But of course, Max and Ruth never did become a couple. She waited and waited, until confusion set in, and after the confusion, depression. And finally anger.

Not with Max though. She couldn't be angry with Max. It was me she blamed, loudly, in front of anyone who would listen. But Max didn't know about it until one day he happened to read one of the endless series of interviews Ruth loved giving to the press. Here she explained sorrowfully why Max could never marry anyone, because there was always me, the sister in the house. Max's burden, standing between him and true love. The child who had killed a child.

And that was her mistake. Max went to speak to Ruth.

You can't help but wonder what must she have thought, opening the door to him in the middle of the night; the hopes that would have flown through her head. Only to find that he had come for a different reason altogether. Poor Ruth! What a let down it must have been. It's the closest I can get to feeling sorry for her.

After that, no one saw her for a fortnight. The 'Swork Centre carried on the work without her, in fact we hardly missed her.

Max took over the publicity for a while, and just for a change helped me pick up the bread, stir the soup (he added too much salt) and sort through the piles of second-hand clothes.

Then one day, Ruth appeared again, more intense, more nun-like than ever. She threw herself with a new fervour into the work she imagined she was there for, never seemed to stop working. That was two years ago and it's the same now. She never stops, never relaxes. Always finding something to do, without actually being much use to anyone. She's plumper than ever, yet I hardly ever see her eat.

Yet even then you could see she hadn't given up hope. At the Services she continued to dance with her eyes open and yearning, all that soft flesh quivering, never quite in sync with the music. Poor, plump, hungry Ruth. She really did manage to keep hoping and praying, right up to the day that Caroline arrived and everything changed. Right up to the day and after.

Caroline. I've only talked about her being dead, bleeding below her steps, her future leeching out of the wound in her head. Soon it will be time to talk about her alive.

In some ways it should be easy to talk about her. A story possible to tell because everyone already knows the end of it. And the fact is, there should have been no mystery about her, not ever. To look at Caroline, she was everything she allowed herself to seem: ambitious, greedy, beautiful, energetic, inquisitive. And cynical, very cynical. She was appalling in her honesty, never once pretended to be anything else.

No mystery there, at least not when she was alive. It's only now she's gone that she has become mysterious, full of secrets and enigmas. That's what happens when people die.

Caroline is dead. But now I'm going to think of her as alive.

Chapter Twenty-Three

The second I set eyes on her in the flesh I knew everything was going to change.

We had built an extension to The Centre, and had a big party when we re-opened the doors. This time it was more than just the press who turned up. Nowadays all sorts of people wanted to be associated with Max – politicians, the odd rock star, actors who wanted to be known for more than just playing parts.

The re-opening was Caroline's excuse to make her own appearance. I can't believe she was really interested in drug addicts –

unless they were famous of course. It was Max she was after. One of the newspapers had sent her, tempting her away from TV, thinking all they had to do was unleash Caroline for all kinds of vices to come tumbling into the open, an Eve with a notebook, just this once harnessed to the side of the angels.

So that was the first time I saw her. And I expect DI Davies would love to know what I thought of her, what thoughts sprang unbidden, etcetera. Motive, of course, is everything when trying to pin down a murderer. He'd have asked me all this anyway, but Max always gets in the way, stops me answering.

Yet I would tell him if I could.

I would tell him how I watched her that first time, hypnotised by the way she stood out, even in a crowd of people who were used to standing out. She was drinking the champagne we'd put on, expensive champagne provided by a French wine grower who had lost his daughter to heroin and admired Max, and now we were serving it to the Press. We had learnt it paid to treat them well. And here she was, the crown princess of them all, tossing the champagne back like it was nothing, like it was water.

So what would I say about her? Only this: I learnt everything that was important about Caroline that first night, in those very first few minutes, *just from watching her drink champagne*. Observing the way it had no effect on her, thus making her powerful, like no one else I had met.

And so beautiful. Caroline was blonde, as I am blonde and Max is blond. But not bony like me, with hair sticking out like straw. And not shaggy like Max. Caroline alive was smooth and sleek, and pale as snow. She shone, and I knew that Max, who also shone, would notice her. He couldn't help it.

And even before he set eyes on her, I knew this too: he would fall in love not knowing anything else about her – just from watching her drink champagne. All he needed to do was turn around and see her.

And it was at that very moment – as if I had been the one that willed it – Max turned. He looked once, then twice, then couldn't take his eyes off her. Over. Finished. For a wild second I thought of doing something to get his attention, falling into a faint or biting my glass, something to make the blood flow. But it was a moment of madness, thinking I could change anything. It passed. Instead I let myself become still, and watched my brother. A radio journalist was interviewing him, posing question after question. Yet Max never gave himself away. No one would have noticed how he was mesmerised by the tilt of a glass, the glitter of an eye. No one but me and another person. In the midst of her own conversation, the long, amused line of Caroline's mouth twitched, knowing it was being watched.

Absurdly, it seemed to me, she was occupied with Ruth. Ruth was doing the talking, waving her arms about, convinced that here was someone else interested in what she had to say. But she couldn't see what I was seeing. Caroline was *pretending* to concentrate on Ruth when all the time she was aware of Max, watching her, while Ruth gesticulated and smirked for nothing.

Yet Max didn't make a move towards her. Probably he was waiting for her come to him, the way people always seemed to come to him. It's what he had become used to, people gravitating towards him. And here was Caroline in turn, keeping her distance. So there you are – right from the start there was a battle of wills going on. Grist to their mill.

So he carried on, doing the rounds of the room, talking to the reporters and social workers and politicians. And only I could see how his eyes followed her, never really left her. I saw the flash of panic in his face when he saw her finally shake off Ruth and make a move towards the door, as if about to leave. The relief when he realised she was merely going in search of someone else.

Me.

He couldn't have expected that any more than I had expected it. But she came anyway. I watched her walk slowly over to me with that languid sway of a tall woman relaxed inside her body, her heels making her seem even taller than nature intended.

'Well, well. So *you're* Rosie.'

Her voice, not to mention her arrival beside me, came as a shock. Not because here was someone else who knew my history. Of course. Every person in the room knew. No, it was a shock because she spoke the words coolly, as if there was nothing to be excited about. As if there was no scandal in the world that could scandalise her, not even the scandal of a child who had a killed a child. I found myself staring at her, almost in awe, as if I was seeing her for the first time all over again. She was wearing wide black trousers and a black jacket with a mandarin collar. The only other colour was in the three tiny red buttons down her front and the line of red marking out her mouth. Yet she glowed in a way reminiscent of Max, with a brightness that came from the smooth fall of her hair and the paleness of her skin. And the smile directed at me was cool as iced water.

She said: 'Rosie by name, rosy by nature. Do you always go red when people talk to you?'

And it was true, I was blushing, for the

reason an animal would blush, fired up by the urge to fight or flee, not yet sure if it was recognising a friend or a foe. Ready to jump one way or the other. This was the effect Caroline had. She put you on your mettle.

Yet, as if on impulse she reached out and touched me; laid the back of her hand against my cheek. I shivered – then relaxed. The brief cool of her hand had taken the heat out of my skin and in that instant made me calm again. And curious, wondering what would happen next.

And what happened next was she took a step back, the better to examine me. Her eyes gleamed. 'Well I'm amazed.' Her voice was throaty, like a smoker's voice although she had never smoked. 'You're the little sister, the one we're not allowed to talk about. I thought you never went out, and he kept you under lock and key. For your own good of course.'

We stood a moment, both of us aware of Max in the distance, watching us. She said:

'I remember seeing an interview once on TV. Your brother walked out right in the middle of it. Someone had mentioned you, and started asking questions, and he just walked. He was completely wonderful. People don't normally throw away their microphones and stroll out of a TV studio like that, right in the middle of a broadcast. They think they need every moment of air time they can get. But not Max Bryant. That was impressive. It said a lot, I thought – about both of you.'

I hadn't seen that interview. Was glad I hadn't seen it.

She rested her glass against her lips, observed me over the top of it. 'You know, I've always thought you sounded rather romantic, the little sister he keeps from harm. It's like a fairy story, don't you agree? Who is it I'm thinking of – Hansel and Gretel? Or is it Sleeping Beauty? No, that's not right either. The Prince is supposed to wake the princess and take her back into the world, not keep her locked away. Rapunzel then. Is that who I mean, Rosie? Are you Rapunzel?'

I shook my head. I wanted to laugh, but still I was aware of Max. As if laughing would make me disloyal to him.

Caroline leaned towards me. 'So what are you, Rosie? The fairy in the house, too fragile to fly outside? I'm asking because I'd like to know, because I don't get it. Something happened – I don't know, how many years ago? – when you were just a baby yourself. And yet here it is still having its effect, keeping you behind doors, making your big brother march out of TV studios.'

She was smiling. And the way she smiled was as if it was nothing to have killed a child. As if she saw worse before breakfast every day of the week. *And now she was inviting me to see it the same way.* Caroline smiled and suddenly it was as if the wind had snatched my breath away. Made me gasp.

But what felt like exhilaration must have shown in my face as panic, because it reeled my brother in, finally breaking the resistance that had kept him from coming near her. Now he was here, right beside us. He thought I was in danger, that Caroline was dangerous. Which of course she was.

He put his arm around me and immediately Caroline stopped smiling. Her eyes became cool again. Financiers, captains of industry, her usual trawl of men had reeled under that look. But Max didn't. He stood firm, smiling a faint smile of his own. Yet I sensed the arm around my shoulder become tense. Caroline looked at him and something in my brother came alive, and would never lie down again.

For a moment no one spoke, yet already I had a sense of displacement, of having strayed into a story that was no longer my own. As they stared at each other, both determinedly in control, I made to slip away. Almost unconsciously, Max's arm tightened, then went slack, and I escaped. And once I had gone, he forgot about me, I know he did.

I went and found Ruth. She was standing by the canapés and never saw me arrive. She was staring across the room over at Caroline and Max. It was plain she had seen it too – the future about to change, and nothing she or I could do about it.

I touched her on the shoulder and she jumped.

'Oh, it's you.' She lurched towards me. She had been attacking the champagne this last quarter of an hour. It fizzed on her breath as her mouth came up against my ear, and fuelled the spite in her voice.

'She looks like a witch, don't you think? A horrid, horrid witch. There was me, thinking she was so nice, a minute ago. I was telling her all about Max and me, what we mean to each other. And she was nodding like she understood everything – how difficult it is for him. And me.'

Ruth was speaking without a hint of self-consciousness, too drunk to remember I was Max's sister, that I knew everything about her and Max. Now her voice grew vicious.

'But she's not nice at all. She's one of those awful witch women who just *suck* men in. Look at her, just sucking him in. She's like the Ice Queen. She'll eat him up.'

I glanced across the room, startled that we had both seen the same in Caroline. Ice. And snow. Yet Ruth was wrong at the same time she was right. Max was talking, while Caroline, although appearing vaguely to listen, wasn't even looking at him. Her eyes were trained on a point past his shoulder. She was anything but devouring. Only occasionally would she bring her eyes back to him, like someone who needed to be reminded who she was talking to.

As I watched, her eyes met mine and snapped into focus. She smiled at me. Properly smiled, so that deep in my head I thought I heard the sound of ice cracking, nothing but a thin surface crust after all, like frosting on a cake. The smile seemed to catch Max by surprise because I saw him stop talking, and simply stare. Ruth muttered beneath her breath and fell upon the canapés, cramming them into her mouth one after the other.

'She'll have him,' she said out loud suddenly, spraying me with pastry. 'She'll have him, and he'll be all hers. Then where will you be? She'll make sure he forgets all about you, just you watch. You'll be out on your ear, Rose. That woman won't have it any other way.'

Ruth's eyes glinted with transferred venom. If first impressions count for anything, DI Davies really should ask Ruth what she thought of Caroline. Ruth made up her mind that night and never changed it. She's glad she's dead.

But it means nothing. The night Caroline died, Max was with Ruth and Ruth was with him. I'm the only one unaccounted for, the one who was there. The one who can't remember.

DI Davies can't afford to waste time on Max or Ruth. The attention is all on me.

The day after they met, I sneaked a glance in Max's diary that he had left lying on the kitchen table. Sure enough, Caroline had got what she had come for. Marked down was a whole morning given over to an interview with her, here in our own house, where journalists had never been allowed.

And it was strange. Because I looked up from the page and gasped at the way the world had changed. All the walls around me seemed to have become wavy, on the edge of being transparent. Not quite solid. Just temporary structures built out of the moment, ready to be snatched away as time moved on. Already I was beginning to understand that Ruth was right. Soon there would be no place for me here.

Chapter Twenty-Four

A fortnight later, over at The 'Swork Centre, Ruth made a rare foray down to the soup kitchen to find me. She was trembling, literally vibrating beneath her long cardigan.

I had seen Ruth angry before, but not like this. Her face was flushed and beads of moisture stood out on her forehead in small translucent blisters.

'Look,' she spat. 'Look what that woman has written.'

She pushed the colour supplement of a Sunday newspaper at me, the pages damp, still hot from her hands. Slightly tacky to the touch.

'She can't get away with this,' Ruth said. 'Max could sue. He must sue.'

I glanced at the title – *Max Bryant: Shaman or Charlatan?* and handed it back to Ruth. I had already read it. Caroline Marsh had had a courier drop Max off a copy before it went to print – to warn him.

Ruth seethed. 'This is character assassination. Read it, Rose. Look what she's written. She's made him out to be a con man. She says he's using people, *abusing* them, building an entire empire made up of fools. Her words, not mine. She says he's not even a proper Christian, and he's just cherry-picking bits of the Bible to help himself, leaving out all the difficult stuff like guilt and sin. That's all she goes on about – guilt and sin, sin and guilt. The woman's a journalist – a *journalist!* What would she know about guilt? I bet she's never opened the Bible in her entire life.'

But it was Ruth who was wrong, and I

would have told her if I only could. Caroline knew quite a lot, as it turned out, about the Bible, about sin. If ever anyone was prepared for an interview, it would have been Caroline for this interview with Max. Because when it came to guilt – and the Bible – she knew exactly what she was writing about. More than Max probably. It was the first thing she told him, how much she did know. And Max had told me.

'She warned me, Rosie, told me before she even sat down. She gave me this short spiel about her own history. Her father is a minister in the Scottish Kirk, one of those splinter groups that branch off on their own because they're too extreme for the main stream. As a kid she never got to see television or even have a radio. Or books, apart from The fucking Bible. It was all she was allowed to read. And if she forgot any of it, he used to beat her – for her own good, he told her. And when finally she ran away, he gathered his congregation of tight-arsed souls together and told them she was dead to him. Made sure she heard about it. He told them she was *dead*, Rosie. Imagine. She tried to make it sound like nothing, but you can see the effect.'

He reflected a moment. 'Maybe it was a good effect. He killed his own child and set her free. She could make herself, all over again. Choose to be exactly who she wanted to be, an entire perfect exercise in free will. Do you reckon that could happen, Rosie? Or is it just cod psychology on my part?'

Max's eyes flickered. He was seeing her in his mind's eye so that I saw her too – a self-made woman, who probably had said none of this to him. But it wasn't cod psychologising. Already he recognised her, someone born out of her own dreams.

'She warned me her gut instinct was to loathe anyone who claims to have God on their side. She wanted me to know that. She said it would come out in her article and it didn't matter what I said because she would write it all through the prism of her own experience. She said I didn't have to speak to her, and she'd tell her editor she had changed her mind...'

She had said this to him, yet still Max had gone ahead. And she had written this piece and forwarded it to him, so he could see she had intended every word of her warning. And having read it, Max, who was used to criticism, and *thought* he was used to cynicism, was shaken. Yet the article hadn't gone to press by then. Caroline was still giving him the chance to do something about it. And what had he done? Precisely nothing.

Nothing. Because he was Max, a man who always tried to practise what he preached. And what he preached was that God would not be God if He gave a toss what people said about Him. God loved everybody – believers, non-believers, meat-eaters, vegetarians, arms dealers, even estate agents. And if God loved them, then Max loved them. And if God could allow anything to be said about Him, then so could he. He would take anything from anyone.

Even journalists.

Now, down amongst the soup pans Ruth wrung her hands. 'He's too trusting, Rosie. Look what she's got away with, the cynical heathen ... *bitch*. Excuse my language. Poor Max – he must be so *hurt*.'

But there was a hint of triumph as she spoke, a visible rising of the spirits. She marched over to the bins and tossed the magazine inside. 'Well, that's the last we'll see of her.' She pretended to wipe her hands, smiled fiercely at me. 'Thank goodness.'

Poor Ruth. She was showing her ignorance, betraying how little she really knew about Max. The night after the proof copy arrived, Caroline came around to the house. Her tall body was leaning against the side of the door when I answered the knock, and her head gleamed by the light of the street lamp. She smiled briefly at me before her eyes slid past me to Max, who just now had appeared in the hall.

There had been a silence, then he had stepped forward and drawn her into the house, leaving me to close the door behind her. They had slept together that night, as they had slept together every night since. They were together now, and there was nothing anyone could do about it.

And the strange thing was, both of them tried so hard not to be. Together, that is.

From the very start it was like watching a couple dance, with both partners trying to lead. Each one trying to govern the direction and the distance between them. Trying to make it seem as if it was no more important than a dance. Trying and failing. They belonged together, you could see it. It didn't matter if they stamped on each other's feet, if they hurt each other, they just danced faster, and closer.

I was alone in the kitchen that first morning after Caroline stayed over. She had stepped through the door and come to a halt, apparently startled; it was as if she had forgotten I might be there, forgotten everything but Max. For a moment we stared at each other, then she laughed, easy again.

'Hello Fairy. Don't look at me like that. There must have been others.'

I hesitated, then shrugged, raising my shoulders so it could have been a yes or a no. Yet immediately she knew it was a no, and she looked more startled still. It was the only time I saw her look remotely flustered. Suddenly she blushed a deep, rich red, the colour seeping all the way down her neck where it disappeared beneath the shirt she was wearing over bare legs, long and skinny as a girl's. Max's shirt.

But when a moment later Max appeared behind her, the blush vanished and she tossed her hair over her shoulder as if it were nothing that she was here, with him. Max glanced quickly at me and away again. Without a word spoken between us, it was over, the first shock; we both knew that things had changed forever. Now they were a given – Caroline and Max – even if they refused to see it for themselves.

Later, as she was leaving, neither of them mentioned seeing each other again. But in the night she was back.

Meanwhile in the weeks that followed, down at the 'Swork Centre, Ruth was screaming on a regular basis. Screaming at the volunteers, screaming at clients, screaming at everyone except Max. And everyone knew why.

She began appearing downstairs, in the dispensary and the soup kitchen where the real work was done, getting in the way. She hovered by my shoulder, her mouth pursed, as if she couldn't drag herself away. I had something she wanted, even if I couldn't work out what, exactly.

It couldn't have been Max. I didn't have

Max any more.

But gradually I saw what she was after. A reflection of herself, a fellow victim, as if we had both been hit by the same disaster. Two lives ravaged by the same force of nature. Namely Caroline.

'Of course it won't last,' she told me again and again, meaning that she was telling herself. She was devouring the biscuits intended for the clients. One after the other, whole boxes at a time, chasing crumbs when she had eaten them all. 'She's all wrong for him, and he just can't see it. Not yet. She thinks she's got him, but all he has to do is open up his eyes. Believe me, it will happen. Max is no fool. God won't let him be. God has work for him.'

Her own eyes glittered briefly. 'Let's hope it won't be too late for you, Rose, when he finally does realise. She's going to have you out of that house. I've said it before and I'll say it again. You'll be on your own. And whatever will you do then?'

She paused. Reflecting. Toxic. 'I suppose you'll end up back here, at the Centre. Don't know where exactly, though. There's not a room free that I can think of. Even John's old room is given over to stores now. Never mind, Max will have something done up for you. He'll find somewhere to put you. He'll have to.'

Ruth herself had two rooms at the top of

the building, with her own bathroom and kitchen. Two overheated rooms crammed with cuddly toys and frilly cushions and those old pictures of Pope John Paul when he was a young man on skis. Here she had lived all these years, waiting for Max, waiting not to be alone. I thought of those rooms and shuddered. And seeing me shudder, Ruth's eyes glittered even more.

'For goodness sake, there's no need to look so glum, Rosie. You won't be alone. This is 'Swork, remember. One big happy family. That's us.'

I turned away when she said that, defeated.

At first it was only the nights that Caroline came to the house.

They were still trying to pretend that it was simply physical between them, that neither had time or space for anything else. She made a point of arriving late, as if she had only made up her mind at the last minute. And Max made a point of seeming surprised to see her, as if Caroline had been the last thing on his mind. But I saw him watching the clock the first night she hadn't turned up as usual, forcing himself to smile and yawn at me as if bed and sleep was all he was hankering for. Then came the ring on the door and Max's exhaustion turned sweet with relief.

Gradually, though, Caroline filled space in other ways. She left notebooks and pens and tape recorders around the house, all of which began to pool in corners and turn up in drawers. Then clothes. Then make up. Then food, bits and pieces of things she liked to eat and insisted that we eat too. Expensive items that went off quickly, upsetting our tidy schedule of meals eaten only when we were hungry, and then only from tins of soup and packets of cheese. Sausages and hummus and oranges.

Caroline put paid to that. She loved food – good food – and feasted greedily on cream and smoked salmon and figs, filling herself to the point of bursting, knowing she would burn it all off the next day on some new project. She was working as hard as Max. In the evenings she arrived vibrating with energy, with all the chaos of a day lived in front of a camera, or running rings around editors. She would eat and talk and drink at the same time, throwing off her shoes. Then suddenly she'd flop, tired out, her entire body giving way to fatigue. It could happen anywhere – at the table, on the sofa.

Max would take her to bed then, leaving me to put off all the lights. There was never any point in staying up. They had disappeared together and all the life in our house had disappeared with them.

And finally, within weeks, as if it had only

been a question of time, Caroline moved in completely. Although she wouldn't own up to it, even then.

'It's only until we're finished,' she said. Words aimed not at me, but Max.

'Of course,' he agreed. 'Just till the book gets written.'

Now they were fooling themselves on a grand scale. Max was about to write an autobiography. Publishers had approached him, persuading him with an advance that would go straight into the coffers of the 'Swork Centre, where it was needed. But still it took Caroline to have the final say that swayed him, and then only by promising to help him write it. *Racing Demons*. She had already dreamt up the title, purloining the name without caring who else had used it first.

So this was their excuse: that she would be here, beside him to guide his hand and find the words for what he wanted to say. As if Max had ever needed someone to put words in his mouth.

But the book served another purpose for her. Caroline – who wanted to be an expert in everything – must have told herself this was how she would get to know him, better than anyone. The world expert in Max.

Yet even now, when they were together all day, every day, the dance continued. I watched them circle round and round each other, sizing up the faults in the other, the weaknesses. Pinpointing the places where they could never agree. Ruth could list them for me – and did, dwelling lovingly on each irreconcilable difference.

'The woman's a heathen for a start. An atheist. She doesn't believe in anything but number one, i.e. herself.'

Which was true. It must have been the first thing Caroline learnt, back when she was a little girl and her father had tried to beat God into her: namely to believe in nothing except herself. And Max, knowing that, respected her belief as he respected anyone's belief. In all the time they were together, I never once heard him try to convert her, or convince her of anything.

Ruth snarled, 'All she wants is to be famous. To be seen with famous people, and stand there, the centre of attention.'

And that was true as well. When people crowded around the two of them, when the cameras flashed and flared all around them, Caroline was utterly content. She breathed in attention as if it were oxygen itself. 'Max hates that kind of thing,' snapped Ruth, and with truth. 'Hates it. What's he doing with someone who just hoovers it all up, all that publicity, as if it's her right or something? *And* she's nosy,' she added darkly. 'She wants to know everything. Have you noticed that, the way she's always trying to winkle information out of you? She'd ask me all kinds of questions – *if she dared*. She's desperate to know about Max, and I mean *everything* about Max. And it's not just because of the book, although she says it is. I've said it once, and I'll say it again – she wants to suck him all up, make sure there's nothing left for anyone else.'

Ruth paused, panting. Breasts heaving. Smugly, she added: 'She'd get a thick ear if she ever tried pumping me for that kind of dirt. She's not getting anything out of me. What I know about Max will die with me.'

There was so much heat in her voice I glanced at her, wondering if, after all, there was something about Max she did know. But Ruth was all talk. She spoke the words, but they were, every one of them, empty. And when she spoke again, I knew I was right.

'It won't last,' she spat triumphantly. 'And I'll tell you why. Because she's everything he's not.'

And there it was – the very key to her ignorance. Because if Ruth had known Max, even slightly, she would know this was the secret of Caroline. Everything Caroline was, Max wasn't. That's why he loved her. I knew that.

Greedy, ambitious, self-seeking, cynical – these were words to paint Caroline. Yet hadn't Max once had a talent to be all those things himself? He could be all that now, if he chose to be. Yet he didn't. Instead, he had simply bundled up his vices, the very things that made him who he was, and handed them over to the great dog in the alley. And He, the Dog, the sin eater, had devoured them – Max's old self with all its faults.

Now here was Caroline shining with exactly the same faults. Human in every way, human the way he used to be. Gorgeous and sinful and vibrating with a life she had created all by herself, for herself. No wonder Max loved her.

Chapter Twenty-Five

Six days since she died. Poor Caroline, lying in a cold bed in a cold hospital mortuary, a true snow queen. Solid ice now.

Her father was on the television today. A camera crew filmed him in the small Scottish village where Caroline grew up. He was striding, straight-backed into his church, followed by members of his congregation, elderly men and women, all of them as grim faced as he was. In the background, mountains reared, their lines undulating against the sky. Granite peaks smoothed by time that seemed softer than he was. He ignored the lens trained on him, never altered his step, a wiry man, shorter than his daughter. And it would have made Caroline laugh – or cry. This was exactly the way Father Ignatius had walked past her all those years ago, making her look like a fool, live on air.

I wished Max had been there to see him, but of course he wasn't. Ruth had called yet again, first thing in the morning and like a lamb, Max had gone.

So I'm alone now, thinking about Caroline and her father, marvelling that another man of God had succeeded in winning her. And for the first time it occurs to me; maybe it was precisely for that reason that he did win her. Is *that* what she was drawn to in Max all the time? The God behind the man?

Then I remember the first time I saw Caroline at a Service. Watching her watch the dancers dance with a cynical eye, absentmindedly tapping her foot in time to the music. No altered state there. Her mouth twitched when her gaze came back to Ruth rolling her head in an ecstasy.

And most of all I remember how when Max held the chalice high, I suddenly saw him through her – through Caroline's – eyes. And he wasn't separate from everyone else at all. He wasn't even different. In Caroline's mind he was just a man with a talent to fool others and himself. And I saw then what I had always known – she didn't believe in

Max, not at all. Caroline had meant every scathing word of the article. She thought him a fool. A fool for God, a fool to believe he had something to say. A fool using his talent to fool himself and anyone else willing to believe in him.

And yet still she loved him, in the same way that he loved her, for all her faults. *Because* of her faults. She watched him now, thinking she was invisible and her eyes were soft. It was love I saw there. Real love, that made the music and lights and religious ecstasy seem like nothing, just an exercise in wishful thinking.

Caroline alive. You either loved her or hated her. Ruth hated her. Max loved her.

It's the same now, even when she's dead. Take DI Davies again. He's meant to be on her side, chasing the clues to her death, in search of some kind of justice for her. And yet he doesn't even like her. Otherwise he wouldn't talk about her with such a clear edge of dislike in his voice, keeping any kind of gentleness exclusively for me. She's the victim and I'm the suspect, yet I'm the one he seems to feel sorry for, the one he treats with kid gloves.

Maybe, at some level which he would never admit, even to himself, he thinks she got what she deserved. Punishment for being noisy and assertive and female. On the other hand, I must seem helpless and silent as the grave. I make him cups of tea, and sit with my hands folded in my lap. He doesn't enjoy the idea of what will happen to me if and when he turns out to be right. Max has done such a very good job, making him think I'm not responsible for anything, not even my own actions.

I'm guessing of course. Maybe he doesn't think anything like this. What I do know is that he has work to do. He keeps his questions simple, yet he keeps asking them all the same. All boiling down to variations of the same question.

'What were you doing, Rosie when she was killed? Try and remember, eh?'

Keep it up and keep it simple. That way he thinks sooner or later I'll tell him everything.

I used to leave Max and Caroline alone when they worked on the book. They never asked me to, but I went anyway. Yet even through the walls I would hear them, talking and laughing. Arguing. And often what they were doing didn't sound like work. Sometimes I would catch the sound of a key turning in the lock and I would know better than to disturb them.

Which was more than Ruth did. Once, when yet again I had failed to bring Max to the phone, I opened the front door to have her barge past me and make for the study where she guessed Max was holed up.

It was locked, yet somehow Ruth seemed not to register the fact.

'Max?' Her voice was imperious. 'What are you doing? I've been calling and calling you. Doesn't Rosie tell you anything?'

Behind the study door there was silence. Then smothered laughter. The sound of Caroline, only pretending to care who heard her. Ruth stared at the door and, too late, understood why it had refused to open. She stepped back as if she had been slapped.

'The bitch,' she whispered, and I was shocked to see how shocked she was. There was a rim of white around her lips where the blood stopped. 'The bitch,' she breathed again. 'What has she done to him?'

By the time Max came out of the room half a minute later Ruth was gone. Behind him I glimpsed a languorous hand reach for the pen and notepad that had fallen on the floor beside the sofa.

Who would have guessed the simple fact that they were having sex would shock Ruth so much? And yet it did, it shocked her to the core, when it shouldn't have shocked her at all. Hadn't she listened to a word he said?

Every day for weeks turning into months turning into years, in crowds large and small, Max had stood and talked about a

God who was at the heart of everything. A God who was in the molecules, in the DNA, in the squiggling, spiralling proteins and sugars in the cells. How can you demonise instincts that are bred in the bone? It was part of the message, the very thing Max was trying to make clear: flesh is God's creation, and with the flesh goes all the joys the flesh gives rise to. Part of being alive. Everything that is, tilted towards reaching its own potential, to give life to itself. *Evolutionary theology,* Max liked to call it. The very stuff of creation.

But it's just another word for sex. Anyone could have told Ruth that.

So most of the Group were having sex all the time. Lots of it. In all kinds of combinations. Most of them, that is, except for Ruth. And somehow she must have thought that Max wasn't either, even now with Caroline on the scene. Deep down Ruth still believed in the magic of celibacy. A pope on skis.

She was wrong, and discovering it pierced her side like a spear. She had left the house bent over double, clutching her stomach as though someone had taken a knife and sliced her.

As for Max and Caroline, they hardly noticed. They were too busy with the dance, still trying to pretend that nothing was serious.

Then the dancing stopped. Abruptly. Just like that.

No one saw it coming, not even Ruth who had seen all kinds of ends on the horizon. And when it came, it was a sign of how little each had really known about the other.

It had been a normal day. Normal for them. Max had flown back from America after a week addressing 'Swork groups as far apart as Seattle and Philadelphia. He had been photographed for *Vanity Fair* in New York, while at JFK he had been mobbed by a crowd of women whose T-shirts proclaimed them to be sex workers for Jesus.

And Caroline. She had just arrived back from Monaco, where she had been interviewing a minor European royal. She laughed as she described how halfway though the interview he had disappeared into his bedroom, to appear again wearing only a silk thong beneath a satin dressing gown. He had expected things to progress from there, the way they always progressed, because he was royalty. And of course they hadn't progressed, Caroline had carried on the interview without turning a hair, as if she hadn't even noticed the royal crest embroidered on the pouch, gradually shrinking. And she had come home, to Max.

Now she was here with him, relaxed on the worn-down sofa. Neither had slept the night before. Neither of them wanted to sleep now.

A normal day then – for these two, if no one else in the world. Caroline kicked off her shoes and pushed her head against the sofa, stretched out her long lean body. Max watched her, his eyes half closed, yet alert. Jet-lagged and happy to be here, with her. Waves of latent energy seemed to lap around them, ready to rest a while before they called on it again.

It made me tired, just looking at them. Something about them that made me weary, unable to stay in the same room. Max glanced up just as I was about to slip out of the door, and frowned. He didn't like it if I left the moment Caroline appeared. But for once I wasn't paying attention. Something that Caroline was doing had caught my eye, and now I couldn't look away.

She had sat up again, to reach for something in her shoulder bag – a tiny box. Now she was busy transferring delicate pinches of white onto the flat surface of the table in front of her. Max caught my gaze and turned, so now he had seen it too, the deft twirling of the twenty pound note, the fall of her hair as she bent forward.

'Caroline?' Max's voice was tentative, disbelieving.

She smiled behind her hair, too busy to look up. 'What?'

Max made a noise in his throat that could have been anything. She giggled softly, causing the fall of hair to swing. 'All right, but let me go first. The plane finished me. I'll fall over if I don't do something about it.'

'Caroline,' said Max. Suddenly his voice sounded thick. 'Don't.'

'Don't what?' She was still bent over, hadn't noticed the difference in him even now.

'Don't do that.' He drew a deep, shaky breath. 'Please, not that.'

Caroline sniffed hard, threw away the note and sat up. Her eyes were wet and laughing, like someone trying not to sneeze. 'What? What don't you want me to do?'

Then she saw the look on his face and stopped. Her own face changed. She glanced down at the table at the tiny grains she had missed. Looked at him again, and flushed.

'Are you serious? Is *this* what you're talking about?'

Max hesitated, then nodded.

Caroline's voice was mystified. 'But you must have known ... I mean this is just ... I don't know ... nothing.'

He shook his head.

Caroline stared at the table again. 'Max,' her voice was clearer now. Firmer. 'Max, this is me. This is what I do. Not often, not all the time. But every now and then. When

I feel like it.' Her voice became stronger still. 'Like when I've worked so damned hard the whole bloody world has started to spin and I decide I want to be more than just tired.'

'Then do without it.' Max's voice was thicker still. It was as if his tongue had grown too big for his mouth. 'Do anything but that.'

I watched Caroline. The sudden straightening of the mouth and shoulders.

'Why? Why should I?'

Max touched the table; his hands were shaking. And I knew he couldn't tell her why. He couldn't say it was wrong – a sin, a vice. Words he refused to recognise. All he could say finally was this: 'Because I'm asking you.'

He wasn't looking at her. And I thought he should look at her. Because the reality was there, in the straight, firm line of Caroline's mouth. Hardening. Suddenly I could see what he couldn't. This was Caroline, the same Caroline who could drink champagne as if it was nothing. As if it was water. Who would drink champagne because she could. The same Caroline who would take cocaine because she could. Because she chose to.

Not because she had to. Powerful, you see. More powerful than chemicals. The addiction lay in the choosing, in being powerful enough to choose, to create her own life. Now Max wanted to take away that power.

'And if I don't?' Her voice was low, but still firm. Much firmer than his.

He looked haggard. But he said nothing.

She stared at the table, at the shaking of his hands. Slowly, deliberately she brushed one of his hands with hers, and watched it quiver. Then her own hand moved quickly on and with the wetted pad of one slim finger she mopped up the last grains of white dust – and rubbed them into her gums.

Max looked away.

She stood up. For a moment she stayed, watching him while he kept on staring at the table, refusing to meet her gaze. Then she turned. I felt the heat in her as she passed me on her way out of the room, and I wondered how I could ever have thought she was cold.

Chapter Twenty-Six

Ruth's triumph was swift and fierce.

She grabbed me by the hand and dragged me into the pantry where we kept the dry goods.

'Why didn't you tell me?' she hissed. 'Is it true? *Have* they finished?'

Her face was inches from my own, her breath a mixture of chocolate and sugared tea. Her eyes were shining, hanging on what I would do next. All she needed was the last word of confirmation. The final nod from me.

And that's what I did. I nodded.

Ruth threw back her head with a strangled animal noise which somehow she converted into words. 'Thank God! Thank God for small mercies.' Except that it wasn't a small mercy, not to her. This was God in all his greatness, giving her what she wanted.

She lowered her head and bared her teeth at me. 'You must be over the moon, Rose, that's all I can say. You've got him back again. You're safe.' And with those words, she had reminded herself. Her eyes narrowed and became hard. With Caroline out of the way, I was the enemy. Again.

Briskly she said, 'I told you not to get into such a state about it. I told you. I know Max – better than anyone. It was never going to last. Anyone could have seen that. If ever two people were less meant to be together...' And she stepped past me, hugging herself.

At home Max was trying to be his normal self. In the evenings he wrote his web sermons and prepared his words for the next Creation Mass. He smiled at me and all the members of 'Swork, and he gave interviews. He travelled to Germany and then to France. He went to a reception in Downing Street. He met the Bishop twice to discuss plans for presenting a talk to the General Synod. He was as busy as always. It was only by chance, then, that he was at home a week after Caroline left, and switched on the television. And there, inevitably, was Caroline, presenting a fashion award. He watched her, his face flickering in the lights of the screen, taking in the eyes, the dress she was wearing, the way the camera seemed to caress all that lean golden flesh.

I touched his arm – and he flinched. I had never touched my brother and felt him shrink under my fingers, but he did now. My hand fell away.

Immediately he knew what he had done. 'Rosie,' he whispered. He caught my hand and held it against his cheek. We stayed like that for a long time.

A month went by. Caroline disappeared briefly from the screen. One day Ruth pushed a newspaper on to me, with a front page picture of a bikini-clad Caroline standing in the sea with a backdrop of Monaco behind her.

'Look who madam is with now,' spat Ruth. 'She'll be calling herself "Her Highness" next.' She pointed to the balding man with a paunch, standing with his arm draped over her bare shoulder. Yet when I looked at Caroline's face caught by the camera, he might as well not have been there. Despite the bikini and the sun blazing on the water, she had the chilly, snow-blind look of the ice queen that I remembered from the first time; before I ever knew that inside she was hot and greedy as a child. I hoped Ruth wouldn't show the picture to Max, but knew that she would, the very first chance she had.

Caroline. I remembered how her mouth had twitched as she watched Ruth dance and suddenly I missed her. *I miss her now.* There, I've said it. The woman everyone is so sure I killed. The woman I was supposed to hate.

I miss her.

And I don't know what I did to her.

Then one night, long after we had gone to bed, there was a knock at the front door.

We must have woken at the same moment because Max and I both came out onto the landing at the same time. We blinked at each other before Max glanced at the watch on his wrist. Three o'clock in the morning. And somehow we knew, both of us, who it would be.

I stayed at the top of the stairs as he went down to the door, listened to the low sound of voices from the hall. Eventually I looked over the banister and they were there, standing motionless in each others' arms, locked together, holding each other like lovers who had lost themselves. And found themselves.

I crept back to bed. In the morning it

would all be different again. The dance had stopped, and all the pretending. Now they were together, despite everything that should have kept them apart. And none of it surprised me. I had known it would happen like this, even when she left. Only a question of time.

This time I didn't feel sorry for Ruth. I didn't feel sorry for anyone, unless maybe it was for myself. No place for me any more, not now they had finally found each other.

That night – in the few short hours that remained of it, I dreamt of John, and the sheepish, resigned look that he wore when I caught him taking cocaine. Would he have seen it as unfair that he had lost his place at Max's side while Caroline was welcomed back? Things had been different for John. He had died because of the difference.

The sun was shining on my face as I woke up. In the room next to mine, Max would be waking up with the same sun on his face, to find Caroline in his arms again, closer than she had ever been. No pretending now. No dancing. Would he be thinking of John as he held her close and closer still?

This time Ruth kept her feelings to herself. Rolled the words up on her tongue and swallowed them, like poison that either killed you or else lent a kind of diseased tolerance to every kind of poison.

She knew now what I had always known: that Max and Caroline were together, were bound to be together. Like heaven and hell, or good and evil. I knew she had adapted the day I looked at her and realised that overnight she had stopped dressing like me. They were gone, the charity shop clothes, the oversized jumpers and out of date frocks. In their place a succession of smart suits and tailored trousers. She was even managing to be taller, thanks to the heels she had started to teeter around in.

Not quite there yet, though, wherever she was heading. For days she seemed to be caught between two states, the old and the new, as if in transition. Like a woman trying on someone else's clothes without any idea how to wear them.

Then one morning she appeared in the 'Swork Centre canteen with a bright golden fall of straightened blonde hair and a fitted black trouser suit whose bottom half clung to her behind and did nothing to hide its size. The transformation was complete, and she had arrived. Ruth had turned herself into a shorter, squatter version of Caroline, right down to the colour of her hair. People recognised the template and hid their smiles, nudged each other behind her back.

She hovered by Max's side and waited for him to notice, and of course he didn't. Max claimed never to notice what anyone was wearing, not even Caroline – apart from the times she wore nothing at all. It was the person he saw, not the clothes. At least that's what he said, forgetting the way his eyes would follow the swing of Caroline's skirt as she swept into a room, or the sway of her hips in skinny slacks.

But this was Ruth's signal to herself, the path she would follow, hoping this would take her where she wanted to be. Probably she didn't even know she was doing it, and had woken one morning with a burning desire for designer clothes and heels that tapped the floor impatiently as she paced between sofa and fridge. She must have wondered what it was all for, though, when Max gathered the core Group together one evening with champagne at the ready and told them the news.

He and Caroline were going to be married. I already knew. Max had told me when we were alone the night before. Clutching my hand and swearing that nothing would change. Knowing that everything would change

I looked around at the faces of the group, familiar after all these years – and yet almost unrecognisable as the people they had been before Max. So many years, you would have thought they would have known him better than this. Yet there was nothing in their faces except abject surprise. They had made the same mistake that Ruth had made. No one had taken Caroline seriously, believing she was too different, too much at odds with Max and his beliefs. Only John would have known Max well enough to see this coming.

Yet within seconds, the shock faded and the congratulations broke out. Everyone liked a party, another reason to dance. Only Ruth stood, the red buttons straining on her new black trouser suit, swallowing hard on one gulp of poison after another. Enough poison to fell an ox. Yet still she managed to keep standing, and smile. You had to admire her that evening, keeping it all inside.

Then her eyes swung across the room and found me, and just for a moment I saw them glint. Ruth was looking at me and taking comfort in the fact that here was someone worse off than herself. Someone who was losing everything.

In desperation I looked to Max. But he was standing with his arm wrapped around Caroline. He only had eyes for her. It's the way I will picture them forever now, like a snapshot frozen in a magazine. Two beautiful people with eyes only for each other. No room for anyone else. Caroline's face is glowing with the air of someone who has got what she wanted.

And now that she had him, she wasn't going to share him, not with anyone. It wouldn't even have occurred to her. Not malicious like Ruth, not spiteful like Ruth. Just careless and greedy. And powerful, careless with her power to hurt.

I left the room then, knowing that apart from Ruth no one would even notice I'd gone.

Seven days since she died.

Still only seven days and still Ruth phones all the time. It's getting worse, the calls more and more frequent. She phones in the middle of the night now, and he answers them. Does more than answer them. Invariably I will hear his tired step on the stairs as he tries to leave the house without me knowing, making his weary way back to the 'Swork Centre, to Ruth.

Maybe she thinks she is helping him. Keeping him busy, keeping him at her side. That would be the Christian view – that she calls on him for his sake and not hers. But I'm not a Christian and that's not what I believe.

Seven days since Caroline died. Last night we had our first Creation Mass since it happened. I knew it would be the test of Max, of whether his God can be found at a time like this. If Max could go through the ceremony, if he could stand alone in the space he makes for himself and yet not seem alone, I would think that he had come through. They would both have come through – Max and his God. Last night was the test of everything he believes.

And they failed. Max *and* his God. God. Last night the lights came on and the music played, John's legacy. Images moved in orbit above our heads, colours and faces and star systems. People danced and prayed and lost themselves, and Max stood in the middle of it all. Everything seemed the same.

Everything. I watched him as he lifted up the cup, and he looked the same. I listened as he spoke and he sounded the same. The crowd stood in silence as he told them about heaven and karma and souls that never die. Of love that lasts forever and never mind the world. People cried and held up candles, thinking he was speaking from the heart, believing his own words. But I watched and listened, and in the space he made for himself I could see that Max was alone. No God. Nothing.

Meanwhile on the dance floor, Ruth swayed and rolled her head of new blonde hair, and she was the one who shocked me. She danced as if she had found God all over again. Her hands moved over her body in a new way, as if she had only now begun to know herself. Her eyes closed as her lips spread wider and wider, until her entire face was a mask of pleasure, and I had to look away. Couldn't watch her any more.

And afterwards Max again wept in his room, trying and failing to stifle the sound so

I wouldn't hear. He wants to be strong, is so determined that I shouldn't see him weak. He refuses to cry in front of me. When I knocked on his door he went quiet, then called out that he had been asleep and dreaming, his voice normal. He is as talented as my mother through all the years of my childhood, talented at sounding normal. Even DI Davies is fooled, suspicious of a man who seems so cool in the face of bereavement.

But I know Max. My beautiful Max. I went back to bed, knowing that he would not take help from me. Half past midnight and the phone rang and of course, he answered it. Ruth again. Another so-called crisis, another reason to drag him to her side.

Why can't she leave him in peace? Why can't he ignore her?

And when Max weeps and will not let me see him weep, is he crying because he has lost Caroline, or God? Or both?

Chapter Twenty-Seven

The day after the wedding was announced, the Bishop came around to congratulate the couple. He smiled at Caroline, dazzled by her. No doubt he was telling himself this was what the new breed of churchman could expect in the World After Max; a bride who would be not just a pillar of the Women's Institute, but a wife who was beautiful and famous and ambitious, a true sign of the future. And, on balance, he approved.

Caroline caught my eye and smiled beneath her lashes so only I could see. She knew what he was thinking and it amused her beyond words. But her smile showed she was ready to be tolerant. Happiness was still there, written in the lines of her face. She had what she had never known she wanted. She had Max.

Only to discover that she wanted more.

Two weeks after the announcement of the wedding, the book was rushed into print. Max had given the go ahead, and forgotten to say a word to her.

Caroline was furious. They argued about it in front of me, forgetting I was there. They increasingly forgot. She didn't think it was ready, and Max couldn't see why not. He thought it was finished, and was impatient to move on, do something else. Caroline had been making him work, really work, and he was tired of it, tired of talking about himself. In recent weeks, there had been less laughter coming from behind the door, and more Caroline, her voice rising and falling in exasperation.

He had even complained about it in front of her, mildly, making a joke about the way she was forcing him to tell the story of his life, over and over again, greedy for every last detail.

'Just my luck to fall in with a hack. She's like a terrier, Rosie, trying to sniff out a story. She thinks she's got to know everything, right down to the colour of my underpants. Everything's important. Isn't that right, Caroline? Next thing you'll be wanting to know what age I came out of nappies.'

But instead of answering she had only looked at him, her eyes suddenly unreadable. I recognised that look and what it was intended to hide. I had caught sight of it in my own eyes over the years. Behind the cool blue stare, Caroline was hurt. Max had hurt her. He wasn't telling her everything. Not understanding that everything was important.

Yet he should have realised this was how she had made her name: finding out everything. Sniffing out the truth of a life, even if it turned out to be unsavoury. This was what she was so good at, discovering the secret. Gleeful as a child because she had so many truths – secrets about people we didn't know, and wouldn't want to know.

'How did you find that out?' Max would ask after she had let spill yet another detail about yet another celebrity, Something a newspaper would never print for fear of lawyers.

And she would just laugh, knowing she had a talent.

Yet now, what should have been a strength – that need to know – was slowly giving itself away as a weakness. It was the book that did it, the very book that was supposed to make her the world expert in the man she loved. Because Max wasn't going to tell her everything. Wouldn't, couldn't tell her. There was always going to be something he held back, because someone else was involved.

Me.

Me. He wouldn't talk about me, not to her, not to anyone. The wall he had built for me all those years was still there, and now it was becoming clear that not even Caroline could breach it. To write a book about Max, she needed to know what happens when a child kills a child and a family is ruined. Everything else pales into nothing. She would have told herself that this was at the core of Max, the thing that made him the way he was.

She needed to know. But he wasn't going to tell her, and she couldn't quite bring herself to believe it. Now they had finished the book and she had begun to realise that he never would.

That would have been the reason for the

sound of Caroline's voice from behind the door. Caroline's voice rising and still rising as she tried to prise the past out of Max. And his voice in return – never sharp, never cutting – telling her nothing she wanted to know.

The book came out.

The publishers sent a pile of copies to the house. They stood in boxes on the kitchen table. On the cover of them was Max, with that eternal look of a rock star, his hair tumbled around his face as if he had just rolled out of bed, cheekbones sharp, his eyes blue and sleepy. I imagined women picking up the book, meeting those eyes and shivering.

I picked one out for myself. All those months hearing them at work, I was curious to see what they had produced.

That was the moment Caroline stepped into the room. She was wearing Max's dressing gown and she had shadows under her eyes. There had been a publishers' party the night before and like Max she had slept late. She saw what I was holding and allowed her lip to curl.

'I wouldn't bother reading it, Fairy. That brother of yours hasn't told me a thing he wouldn't tell the mother of the bloody Bishop.' She walked over to the kettle and, did I imagine it, or was there a hint of defeat in the way she stretched out for a tea bag and a mug to put it in? Usually she would have ground herself coffee, steeped it with care. The tea bag betrayed a weariness I hadn't seen before.

For a moment she paused, her back to me. Then she turned. With one hand cradling her mug, the other she used in order to pull the hair away from her face, leaving it surprisingly bony and childish. School girlish and thunder-browed.

'I mean it, Rose. All that work, and he never told me one thing that was important. All that openness, all that so-called honesty of his. It's fake. And you know how I know? Because I meet fakes all the time. People who only tell you what they want you to hear. I'm sick of it. Sick of all that.'

And all I could do was stare.

Seeing me she stopped, and shook her head. A moment passed then she tossed out her hair and arched her back like a cat.

'Forget it. Forget what I said. I'm hungover and cranky. Too much to drink last night.'

I didn't believe her. She bent her head into her mug and ignored me after that. But I felt her eyes on me as I left the kitchen, asking herself what it was I knew about Max that she didn't.

So what could I have told her? Nothing. She wanted to know what happens when a child kills a child. And all I knew was the Max who had grown up with me, grown around me. His life twined about mine like ivy coiled around a branch. You couldn't base the truth of book on that. Could you? And why was it important anyway, what I knew or didn't know? It was all finished anyway. Life would start all over again now, and he wouldn't be there, not for me, not any more. Thanks to Caroline.

Soon I would be alone. Never the same again.

But I took her advice. I never read *Racing Demons*, even when half the country seemed to be engrossed in it. It was advertised in book shops, in magazines, along the sides of buses. For a while everywhere I looked, Max's face seemed to be looking back at me with that sleepy rock star stare. And still I never picked up another copy. Caroline had made it seem as if it could never be worth it.

Chapter Twenty-Eight

Eight days since she died, and something has happened. Unlooked for, unhoped for. Something that changes everything.

At least, DI Davies *says* it changes everything.

He phoned this morning, his voice sounding urgent. He said he needed to speak to us, both of us. He said he had information that threw the case into a new light. Ten minutes later he was knocking at the door. Such a short time it makes you wonder if he ever actually goes away, or is merely sitting there in the street all day, every day, in a car, watching.

'You might want to take a seat, both of you.'

So at his invitation, we sat down in our own kitchen and waited. Max's eyes were dulled with fatigue, although I don't suppose DI Davies would recognise it as such. He'd call that a look of sleepy insolence, and feel his hackles rise still further.

But Max *is* tired. The phone rang late again last night, with a call that caused him to leave the house, and only get back at dawn. No need to ask who it was at the other end.

DI Davies cleared his throat. 'The forensic chaps – pathologists and so forth – they've been re-running a few tests. At my request I might say. Angle of blow, alleged height of assailant, the kind of force required, that sort of thing. And the long and the short of it is, would you believe? They've changed their minds.'

Max looked up. 'Changed their minds?'

DI Davies hesitated then backtracked.

'Actually, no. Not exactly. But what they *are* prepared to say is they're not quite so certain about the *modus operandi* – the actual process of the killing. And having gone so far, they're prepared to entertain the thought that it might not be an open and shut case after all. For murder, I mean. They're willing to add the possibility of another situation. That is to say, an absence of *mens rea*, contributing to the way that Miss Marsh may – and I stress *may* – have died...'

'Inspector,' Max interrupted, 'I don't understand a word you're saying. And I don't suppose Rosie does either. What exactly are you trying to tell us?'

'What I'm *trying* to tell you, Reverend,' DI Davies's voice betrays his irritation at what he takes to be a command, 'is quite simple. It's possible – *possible* – that Miss Marsh met her end via an accident rather than the deliberate intent to murder. Before this, the pathologist bods were happy to swear blind she died as a result of a deliberate blow to the head. Now they're saying it's conceivable it was the result of a fall – I'm talking about the damage to her skull and facial injuries and so forth. They're saying it could all be made to fit with the shape of the steps and the railings...'

'So they're saying she fell?' Max said. 'And that's what killed her. Nothing unlawful.'

DI Davies shook his head. 'What they're saying is she might have been pushed. *Had* to have been pushed if they want to explain why she fell so hard, incurred the injuries she did. But there's a world of difference between hitting your head because someone has pushed you, and having your head caved in with a blunt instrument used for the purpose – if you follow me.' He paused. 'You *do* follow me, don't you Rosie. You understand what I'm saying?'

And the answer is that I do understand. He wants me to know there's a margin of doubt here, and that he's the one that's opened it. Scope to plead that nothing was intended beyond one short, sharp push in anger. But just in case I've missed it, DI Davies puts it into actual words.

'What I'm saying, Rosie, is that accidents happen. Courts know that. Judges know that. Damn it, even the police know it sometimes. That's what I want you to understand.' There's another pause. He watches me, wanting a reaction. But out of the corner of my eye, I'm watching Max, reading his face the way no one else could, not even Caroline. Yet Max's face shows nothing in the way of surprise. The only thing in Max's face is ... relief. And even this much he is not willing to show, but looks away from both of us, avoids my eye.

If the inspector expects either of us to

speak, he is disappointed. He waits a good half minute, but nothing happens. In the end he slaps his knees and stands up, looking exasperated, like someone who has had an act of charity thrown back in his face.

'Well there you are, that's what the forensics have to say. Maybe it's not sinking in. Let's say I leave it with you for now, give you time to think about it a bit. Eh, Rosie? Shall I do that?'

He never stops, never ceases to expect that one day I will answer him like everyone else, in spoken words.

But I do this much; I nod automatically, while I try to take it in. Not the news, but Max's reaction to it. Sheer relief, hidden from DI Davies but incapable of being hidden from me. So what does it say, a reaction like that? That he had his suspicions and kept them hidden from me all this time? A doubt, a fear that I did indeed take a blunt weapon and stave in the head of his beloved? And now it's possible that I didn't, and might only have pushed her, which makes me innocent after all. Half innocent. Whatever he thought before, it's there now – relief moving like something alive across his face. Max is relieved, and I should be happy. Instead all I feel is emptiness, a realisation of what he must have been hiding.

And anyway, what is there to feel relief about? Maybe it's not murder, as DI Davies says, not if you're willing to stretch a point. Just the unforeseen consequence of a push. But Max should ask DI Davies this: how much of a push would it take to thrust a tall, fit woman down a flight of steps so hard that her head hits the bottom with such a crushing blow it smashes her face and breaks her skull? Caroline was a woman who used to stand with her feet planted square, ready for anything. If I were DI Davies I'd have to answer that it would have taken force, hard and fast, to push her to her death. Do that kind of damage.

But Max doesn't ask any such question. The only thing on his mind is relief.

He doesn't see things the way I do, because after the first shock: nothing, not for me. It changes nothing. Caroline died. Someone caused her to die. The best they can say now is it might not have been deliberate.

Kill once, kill twice. Forget once, forget twice. What have I forgotten?

Thanks to Max and his impatience, then, the book came out. But Caroline – being Caroline – was bound to find a way of getting her own back, of redressing the balance. A punishment, in other words, for Max not letting her into the very centre of him, for keeping at bay all that curiosity. Something to show that he had not arrived at the centre of her either, not yet.

Max surely must have known it was coming – Caroline's revenge, a dish best not eaten too cold. Then again, maybe he didn't. Maybe he still didn't understand Caroline's need to know.

It happened at a service that had been months in the planning, a special mass to celebrate God as a woman. The Goddess Mass. This time Max had met no difficulty in persuading the Bishop. Nobody told him what was right or wrong now, any more than they could warn against a goddess's stock in trade.

Revenge.

He had persuaded over a hundred women to travel from peace camps across Europe and the US for this one night. Most had been dug in for twenty years in their different countries, sleeping out under different skies and rusting watch towers. But all had the same look to them, like mediaeval nuns, bringing with them the scents of another age. Woodsmoke and female sweat. A whiff of menstrual blood.

The hall was dimmed for their arrival. No lights or images – no music. The women walked in darkness, guided by a single candle. In silence they came to where Max waited by the cross. There they passed the candle into his hands and stood while he used it to light a larger candle of his own.

In the dark beside me, Caroline whispered in my ear, 'Trust Max to have a bigger one. Candle that is.' But I didn't pay any attention to her. I was fascinated by the women, by the otherness they seemed to represent. I was struck by the fact they were silent, like me.

But then, gathered around the altar, they broke their silence and began to sing – or rather to chant – their voices rising and falling in the surrounding blackness. Six, maybe seven hundred people, Max's congregation, listened in awe, ears more used to synthesizers than the strains of the human voice. As they chanted, some of the women used their breasts as drums, beating with their fists to create an eerie, muffled rhythm.

I wasn't used to it either, to the nun-like reediness of their voices, to people using their bodies as instruments, making sounds that never quite amounted to singing. I tried to make out the words, only to realise there were no words, just one long incantation. And the fact there were no words, that this was still a silence of sorts, was somehow pleasing. I knew I was falling under a kind of spell, quiet but compelling, a recognition of these women as nuns in actual fact. Devout as Sister Imelda and the rest, but wilder and witchier...

At which point came another sound, close beside me. Distracting and utterly familiar. It was Caroline, laughing, convulsed with merriment.

'Sorry,' she spoke through the side of her mouth. 'Can't help it. It always does this to me – lesbians when they will insist on singing. Why is it they always sound like they're blowing into teapots?'

Not witches or nuns, but teapots. Caroline laughed as if she genuinely couldn't help herself, and now it was happening to me, the desire to laugh with her. Suddenly the spell unravelled before it had ever taken hold, leaving me detached as Caroline was – an observer. Outside the web, outside the spell.

The Women had come to the end of their incantation, were standing with their heads bowed. There was a half a second of candled silence before the music exploded. Lights flashed down on seven hundred faces which in turn lit up, blinking and beatific. The crowd had liked the peace women, but this was what everyone had been waiting for. Girls and boys – Max's flock – rattled their piercings and began to dance as up on high the ceiling came alive with huge images of women rotating slowly like planets; kissing, working, giving birth.

On the ground, the Peace Women embraced each other, then began to move through the crowd, touching strangers to embrace them too. I watched as one of them made her way towards us. She was in her forties, slightly built, her long dark hair streaked with grey and with a face that was a perfect oval shimmering in the light of those giant, planetary women moving over head. She came and laid her cheek against mine and for an instant the cool touch reminded me of my mother. She smiled, and I smiled back, unable to help myself.

She moved on to Caroline and that's when I saw it, the wicked light in Caroline's eye. I would have cried out a warning, but how could I? No voice, no words. And anyway, it would have been too late. As the woman leaned towards Caroline, Caroline's own slim arms snaked out and twined themselves around her, drawing her in and close. The woman's eyes widened and then fluttered, surrendering to the kiss that Caroline was offering, deep and sensuous, full on the mouth. The woman drew away at last, her face soft, full of surprised love – only to crumble when she saw that Caroline was laughing, doubled up with amusement. The woman quivered with hurt, suddenly older, almost rickety, and moved quickly away.

'Caroline,' I mouthed her name in shock. But she didn't see me. She was staring over all the moving heads, past the women and the dancers, past Ruth standing motionless with her hands raised and her eyes closed, waiting in vain for someone to touch her. Staring past everything to Max.

He was standing by the altar, his eyes fixed in turn on Caroline. He had watched her kiss the other woman, she would have made sure of that. Caroline waved and he flinched.

Seeing this Caroline smiled, satisfied at last. I had to fight the urge to hit her – for Max's sake, and the woman's sake. She turned and caught the look in my eyes. She was so confident, so pleased with this small chastisement of my brother, even this look of mine made her laugh.

Now they were equal again, Max and Caroline.

Chapter Twenty-Nine

So that was that. Caroline laughed at everything. And most of all she laughed at Max.

But she didn't laugh at our house. She liked it, our tall, shabby terrace that came with the Living. It was full of holes, but also full of light, and she liked that too. She liked the windows without curtains, and the boards that creaked under your feet. She talked about living there, but she never talked about changing things. Except just the one thing.

Me.

Never mind the holes in the roof, this was where Caroline intended to live after they were married – by herself, with Max. So what was going to happen to me?

At first no one mentioned it. Max and Caroline steered clear of the subject. Or perhaps Caroline simply saw it as a foregone conclusion, nothing to argue about. She would move in and I would move out. Easy as that.

It was Ruth who brought it up, eager to stir, to make trouble. She had come around to the house with a pile of papers for Max. Caroline had let her in, followed her with the faint smile she reserved for Ruth as she marched into the kitchen where Max was drinking tea. Gulping would be more accurate. He had a plane to catch. Every-thing Max did had to be in a hurry these days. This was how he grew skinnier as the years went by, when other men start to fill out, waistlines expanding as life got more comfortable, less demanding.

'Oooh tea!' Ruth had squealed. She seized a cup, loaded it with three sugars and another one when she thought no one was looking and smiled at Caroline, bright with hatred.

'Only a few weeks now till the big day. You must be so excited. But you know, no one tells me anything. Where's Rosie going to be living after? Somewhere she won't find it *too* hard to manage, I hope. I mean, poor thing, it's going to come as a shock. All these years nestled under Max's wing like a little baby bird. How ever is she going to cope, I wonder?'

She made the question sound so innocent. Smiling at Caroline. Smiling and knowing perfectly well what she was doing.

There was a silence. Then Max said, his voice easy, 'Rosie will be living here.'

'Really?' Ruth let her eyes swivel round to meet his, big with surprise. 'Rosie's staying here, *after* you're married?'

Max nodded. Meanwhile Caroline was staring at him, her lips pressed close together. Ruth smirked. 'Well I must say I'm impressed at you, Caroline – having Max's family living under the same roof. Most people look forward to at least a couple of years before the in-laws take over.'

Caroline ignored her. She was still staring steadily at Max.

Ruth said sweetly. 'You're not saying a word, either of you. Gosh, I do hope I haven't...' Then she clapped her hands over her mouth, as if only now remembering exactly who was in the room. 'Oh ... I see, you can't, not very well ... not in front of...'

Max stirred. 'I'll think I'll come with you, Ruth, back to the Centre. If we go now I'll have time before the flight.' He spoke smoothly, as if nothing was wrong.

But we all knew. Ruth's smile said it all. Satisfied, she said, 'Not on my account, Max. Everything's under control – at least it is at my end. Let's just relax, enjoy our tea.' She turned her smile to me. 'While we're all still together.'

Max said, 'There's stuff *I* need to do. Shall we go?' He went to the door and held out his arm, offering it to her. Obediently Ruth set down her mug. Happy to have Max to herself. Happier still because she had started something that she'd thought had been taking too long to grow. But they were growing now – seeds of a dispute.

They left. Now there was silence in the aftermath. Caroline was frowning at Max's mug which he had left on the side. Then all of a sudden she lifted her head.

'You're a big girl, Fairy. You'll get by. You know that. You're strong. Strong as anything. Getting out of here will do you good.'

She spoke the words matter-of-factly, yet quietly as if not expecting me to believe a word she said.

There were sounds on the pavement outside, the excited clipping of Ruth's new stilettos. The slower, quieter tread of Max. Hearing it, Caroline's eyes flickered, spotting an opportunity and debating whether to take it. She decided to take it. Quickly she moved around the room, sat down at the table and beckoned for me to join her, watched me as I took a seat in front of her. For a moment there was silence in the kitchen. Caroline was searching for a way to speak, only to plump for the easiest, most simple way of all. Almost blurting out the words:

'Rosie, I'm just going to ask you, straight out. Why on earth does it go on? Why are you still *here?* I mean, look at yourself. You're living as if something terrible has happened, not years ago, but yesterday. And Max the same. Can't you see that it's strange? Wrong? Something happened that you can't even remember, that was never remotely your fault, and still the two of you live as nothing can move on. So Max treats you like you're a piece of ... of ... porcelain, as if you could break in half at any moment. And you let him! You live like this and you don't even seem to think about it.'

She listened to the silence between us.

'Rosie,' she said softly. 'You *could* move on. You're strong enough. Why is it only me that seems to see it? You could have a life of your own. You don't have to be the fairy in the house. You don't have to live in Max's shadow. Hasn't it ever occurred to you? You could have more, so much more than this.'

She paused. Tentatively, un-Caroline like, she reached across the table and touched my hand. Softer now, she said, 'Rose, think about your life. Think why it is you have to make yourself so small...'

I watched her lips.

'And silent.' A pause before she added, almost whispering, 'I know why you don't speak. Everybody knows. But it doesn't have to be like this. Children – little children – can't be guilty, they can't commit crimes, not unless you think we're all born guilty, just by being alive. And if you believe that, then you're believing a fantasy created by tired old men, centuries ago, wanting to pin the blame on someone other than God. They were wrong then and they're wrong now. Children can't be guilty. *You're* not guilty. Nothing matters the way you think it matters. Nothing.'

We stared at one another, feeling the words fall and settle around us.

'Think about it, Rosie. Everybody's dead. All the people you ever had to worry about. There's only you to think about now. And Max. Nothing else matters. Why is that neither of you can see it? Why can't *Max* see it?'

And that's when I turned away. Stopped listening right there and then. Because Caroline was right. Everyone *was* dead, everyone who could be hurt. And the reason they were

282

dead was because of me, killed by the damage done by a child to a child.

That's what Max understood. And that was why we lived as we did. No other way to live. I pulled my hand away, with a movement so fast that Caroline blinked. And though she tried, she couldn't hide the disappointment in her face.

I knew what she was after now.

Information. All she had wanted from me was information, something to take her right to the heart of Max. And after that she would have Max, all to herself.

She saw the look on my face and knew she had lost me, and she would have to find another way. Or simply stop trying.

Her answer was to keep trying.

So I had to be on my guard. What else could I be? On guard against Ruth, wanting to provoke. On guard against Caroline desperate to probe. And sometimes, on guard even against Max.

Like the day he said, 'Caroline wants to take you shopping. You know, just the two of you. Like if you were sisters.'

Sisters? Was this really Max talking? I stared at him in disbelief. He saw it and immediately had to hide his discomfort.

'You'll have fun. You can help with stuff. You know ... wedding stuff.' And then his face changed. 'Please, Rosie, go with her,' he said, and there was a note of pleading in his voice. 'She really wants you to. It would mean such a lot to me if you would only ... you know ... meet each other halfway.'

His eyes were desperate. Sometimes Max wasn't so different from other men after all, wanting life to be simple, the way God was simple, and love was meant to be simple. Trying to persuade himself that anything could happen between people, and anything could be made to work. Even Caroline's attempts to make me see the world the way she saw it. And believe what I see.

In the shops, sales staff recognised her as Caroline Marsh off the television, but it caused no flutter as they greeted her. The shops we were visiting were too expensive for that. Me they ignored. They assumed I was just some kind of assistant, maybe the girl who ironed her clothes.

In an exclusive lingerie shop whose very air was drenched with musk, she lingered and chose with care. Made sure I saw what she was doing. She picked up underwear so transparent I could see the glow of her nails beneath the fabric. Nightdresses and slips and camisoles. Clothes you might wear for a lover, but never in a house where there were other people to see, such as a sister, or an in-law.

She bought them all, not even glancing to

check if I was understanding the message behind the buying. Once she gave me a nightdress to hold, softer than skin and the colour of ivory. It shimmered and slid through my fingers, slippery as a mermaid's tail, with a fragrance all of its own.

And both of us knew what that said.

I was there too, in another shop, when she put on her wedding dress. She stepped out of the dressing room in a sheath of white satin that clung to the long lean lines of her body, limbs made for speed and strength.

'What do you think, Rosie?' She asked quietly. She was making me look at her with Max's eyes, seeing a shape that seemed carved out of marble. Hard and yet by some magic, supple. A pillar of strength, not a burden. Never a burden.

I knew exactly why she wanted me to look at her. Some things you can say better without words.

But there was something else she wanted to tell me. We had lunch in a small expensive restaurant where the people came and went, looking over their shoulders as they passed, recognising her. Normally, she relished the attention, but today she seemed oblivious to it.

'Eat up, Fairy.'

She was spooning up cream from the sides of her plate, slowly and greedily, like a magnificent cat with gleaming fur. Suddenly it occurred to me there was something different about her. Perhaps it was in the texture of her skin, no longer simply smooth. Now with a creaminess that made her need to eat cream. Between mouthfuls, she looked around her briefly, carelessly.

'Princess Di used to come here. All that crowd. They still do.'

I stared at my plate.

'The thing is, Rosie, so could we, any time we liked. We could shop and then we could have lunch in places just like this. We could eat nice food while I tell you the dirt on all the people feeding their faces and you sit with your eyes wide like they are now. Do you understand, Rosie? We could have *fun*, you and me. That's what it could be like.'

She listened to the silence between us. 'Oh look at you, pretending to be shocked at the very idea of having fun.'

And she was right. I was pretending. She nodded, put down her spoon.

'There you are,' she said triumphantly. 'I was right. You don't actually dislike me, do you? You think you should, you want to, even, but you can't. You and Max are more alike than you realise. What he likes, so do you.'

She paused, and met my eyes. They were cool and direct. Unsparing – a function of Caroline herself.

'I *want* you to like me, Rosie. I don't want

anything from you that isn't reasonable. Just a normal life in a normal house. Give me that and I can give you so much back, if you'll only take it. Everything you could be having now – and can't have, not when you're living with a brother who stands between you and the world like a great big dog. Stopping you from living. And don't try telling me working at the Centre is living. That's skivvying. Using up what little bit of a life you have. It's using *you*.'

She stopped, and gave a small bitter laugh.

'I said that to Max last night – that he was using you – and for one terrible moment I thought he was going to hit me, hurt me. It's the only time I have ever seen him angry like that. He simply won't believe you could be happy living any other way. And it wasn't just then he was angry. He's getting angrier all the time – with me. He wants me to change my mind about you. He wants me to say everything's all right and the three of us can go on living together. But I'm not going to, Rosie. I can't. You understand that, don't you? If you stay then everything stays the same – for you, for him. Everyone.'

Didn't she understand? That's all we wanted, Max and me. It was all I wanted. Instead, she sat back and looked at me hard.

'You need a life, Rose. Away from Max. And I'm saying you can have a life.'

Her eyes lit on mine, and there it was

again, the feeling I'd had on first meeting Caroline, of something catching my breath. A sense of what could be. Possibility. Of succumbing. For a moment I almost believed her. Almost...

And then she said:

'I'm pregnant, Rosie. I haven't told him yet. And I'm not going to tell him, not until after the wedding. By the time he knows, I want you to be used to the idea, and be happy for us. Max is going to be a father. There's going to be a child who will need him, and I need him to be happy about it. Not guilty or anxious about you. But that won't happen, not unless you set him free.'

She touched my hand. And there it was – the creaminess, even here, in the tips of her fingers. An opal glow that wasn't there before. Sometimes you see something before you even know what it is you see.

'Everyone needs to grow up, Rosie. And I think you have already – grown up. But Max doesn't know it yet. What's more, he needs to see it doesn't have to be a bad thing – growing up, growing away, making a life of your own. After all, look at me.'

By which she meant look what she had made of herself, by turning her back on her family. Having her family turn its back on her. A self-made woman, trying to make me believe I could be the same.

A baby, though. Something they had

made, and would continue to make for all the years to come. For the moment I was thankful that she didn't expect me to be happy – or be anything – not in those first seconds. She didn't even expect me to speak, not then. It meant I could turn my face away from the table, from Caroline, to look into the future, searching for the place that would be left there for me. But it was no good. There wasn't any place I could see. Little enough room before. No room at all after, now there was to be a baby. Another baby to change everything.

Except this baby – Caroline's baby – never did change anything. It never had the chance. Like Caroline it died, tucked away inside her, still a secret, a small shadow of itself.

Have the police told Max about the baby? They must have. He is the man she was going to marry, the father. But Max has never said a word to me. Keeps silent as if somehow this would have been the ultimate betrayal, the one thing he thanks his God he never had to tell me. One more reason to weep.

But I know. And now, remembering the baby, it comes to me in a rush, like cold earth falling around my ears. What if it's a case of kill once, kill twice? Kill three times? What if I did that?

Chapter Thirty

All those packages – Caroline's trousseau as she liked to call them, eyes and mouth ironic – she left in our house, on the landing where we had to walk around them. She didn't care if Max saw them, not even the ivory spill of silk escaping from the bag. The only thing she kept from him was the wedding dress. She hung that up in my room where he couldn't see it, surprisingly traditional suddenly. Even Caroline could be superstitious.

Maybe she needed to be. Because now the arguments had started, properly started. Furious rows waged in silence because I was there, and I wasn't meant to know. But everybody knew they were arguing about me, what would happen to me.

Ruth loved it. She had started it, and now she could taste the atmosphere that was filling the house as a result. She came around as often as she could to savour it. It meant she didn't have to give up hope, not even a month before the wedding. Not even a week before, telling herself it might not be happening after all.

'Why?'

Out of the near silence of the rows, this

was the one word that escaped. It leaked out of the walls and filtered through closed doors. It was the sound of Caroline forever wanting to know. The same question over and over. Why did he have to look after me so hard? Why did I have to stay with them? Why was he letting a sister come between them?

Why?

I listened for the answer, but I never heard it. Max could be as silent as the grave when he argued. Cool, but not cold. Never that. But he would make himself distant, shrinking deep inside himself, away from her. She had to watch him retreat from the arguments without a word spoken on his side, unreachable as when he used vanish inside his dens. Nothing for it but to huff and to puff...

And turn once more to me. But even this was becoming impossible. I was the reason for the distance, after all. Sometimes Caroline could barely bring herself to look at me. Yet other times I would find her watching me, speculating and angry as if trying to control the urge to shake the answer out of me.

Why?

But there were other times again when instead of being angry, her eyes begged me to speak up, to say what she had almost made me believe. She wanted me to make him believe it too: that there could be a life for me after Max, away from Max. And sometimes I really did believe it, enough to go in search of Max and tell him just that – I could live without him.

But then I would remember Ruth, who already lived without Max, alone in her two over-heated rooms with her bibles, her posters and her cuddly toys, counting out the days until everything changed.

That's where she had stayed all these years, always expecting things to be different, simply waiting for her life to begin. I thought of Ruth's life, and I thought about living like Ruth. A life without Max and no wall to keep the shadows away.

And it always stopped me, the thought of becoming like Ruth. I couldn't do it, I couldn't tell Max what Caroline wanted him to hear. It shamed me that I couldn't, and eventually shame threatened to make my wishes as simple and as brutal as Ruth's wishes. Wishing something would happen, something that would make Caroline go away, and leave us all in peace.

The closer the wedding came, the more I just wanted things to stay the same.

Nine days since she died.

Nine days. And Max still won't let me out of the house. He explains it all patiently, describing how there will be Press at both ends of the journey, waiting to pounce. He says it would be an ordeal just walking out of our front door. And I believe him, every word. You only have to look outside. The pavement is still being staked out by photographers. They haven't given up. They haven't even thinned out.

It means that Ruth is constantly being snapped as she comes and goes, and she loves it, of course. She walks smoothly through the mill, eyes cast down with a look of studied grief which only serves to emphasise her double chin. Shakes her head sadly when they call out to her. DI Davies progresses more grimly, cuts a swathe as he comes, ignoring the cameras and the questions as he would a cloud of mosquitoes.

But it means I am here, still housebound, the fairy in the house. That's how Caroline would put it, dryly. This morning I could have sworn I heard her laughing out loud. It must have been the sight of Ruth, lingering on the doorstep with a sigh, modestly turning to greet the cameras' flash.

But later when Ruth left – with Max of course – I was aware that something was different about the house, although for a long time I couldn't work out what. I had gone up and down the stairs ten times before I realised. For the past five weeks I had tripped over the pile of packages on the landing – Caroline's 'trousseau', with its fall of ivory silk, getting dusty on the carpet now. Somehow it had never occurred to Max or me to move it.

And it was gone. Nothing left except the suspicion of a scent, a trail of perfume already vanishing to nothing. And now I remembered. When earlier I had glanced out of the window, watching Max and Ruth departing through the banks of cameras, Ruth had been carrying a number of bags.

Ruth had taken them away. Carried away Caroline's things as if they belonged to her, along with so much else.

A fortnight before the wedding, things went quiet in the house. Not the quiet of the silent rows, but with a kind of exhausted hush. And still I didn't know what was going to happen, not to me or anyone. I thought about packing but didn't know where to start or *if* I should start.

One morning, Caroline came and found me at the 'Swork Centre. She made me come away from the canteen, telling me we were needed at her house – which was now going to be *my* house. We sat in silence as she drove me. I thought she would at least explain what we were needed for, but she said nothing. In these last couple of days she had given up pleading with me with her eyes. Now she had hardened, was merely determined to do things her way. Caroline had stopped trying.

Outside her house, with its steps and shiny black railings, a woman was waiting for us. She was middle-aged, neat, dark haired and olive skinned. Even from a distance she looked melancholy, solitary. Yet she smiled as we walked towards her, and there was a genuine warmth to her face. Close up she was younger than she looked.

Caroline said, 'This is Conchita. She's Mexican, but her English is well ... OK. Conchita looks after people. Isn't that right, Conchita? For years she looked after her younger brothers and sisters when their mother died, even though she was barely more than a child herself. You did a good job, didn't you Conchita? I know you did, because your youngest sister works for me. She says you were like a mother to her.'

The woman smiled anxiously. 'Maybe, please God. But now I...'

She stopped, too shy to go on. Instead she looked to Caroline, who said, 'But now they're all grown up. The youngest sister, the one who works for me, got married last week. So now Conchita needs someone else to look after. It's what she's good at, you see, Rosie, looking after people.'

Conchita's eyes smiled at me, already willing to give, to be kind. Her face was gentle and old fashioned, belonging to a woman who had spent so long looking after others, she couldn't imagine doing anything else. Without wanting to, I smiled back – and felt the helplessness take over. Caroline, catching the taint of submission in the air, allowed herself to relax.

We drove back to my house in silence. Except it wasn't going my house any more, not for much longer.

I went up into the attic and hauled down the old suitcases that had served our family all through the years. The last time I had seen them, it had been to come here, to this house, where Max made me believe I would always stay with him.

I packed, then sat in the hall, avoiding rooms that were no longer my rooms and waited for Max to come home. Caroline kept her distance, reluctant to come near, as if afraid I would change my mind. She would have preferred it if I had been gone before he arrived, settled in her house – now to be my house – with the black railings and Conchita to look over me. There would be no going back then.

But he would be home, any moment now. Tonight there was a Service, and no matter where he was – and today he had been in Amsterdam – he always came home.

Sure enough, the sound of a horn in the street indicated that he arrived. Max walked through the front door, bringing blasts of foreign places with him, wearing the same look that he always had when he came home. A face eager for the sight of Caroline, even now, in the middle of the rows. Lighting up as he laid eyes on her.

Then he saw the suitcases lined up behind the door, and his face changed.

'What...?'

Caroline tried to keep the triumph out of her voice – and succeeded only in sounding nervous. 'It's Rosie's choice, Max. She's met Conchita, the one I told you about, and everything was perfect, just like I said it would be. Rosie understands, really she does, Max. She knows it's better this way.'

She put a hand on his arm. But he snatched it away, as if she had been poison. She flinched, but said, 'It's what she wants, Max. Look, she's right here. Ask her yourself if you don't believe. Or *you* tell him, Rosie. Tell Max. Tell him it's what you want. Tell him you'll be all right.' And when I said nothing, her voice tightened, sounding angry now. 'Tell him Rosie, for God's sake. Don't just stand there. Speak to him.'

And Max and I could only stare at her. Because she had forgotten, completely forgotten: I couldn't speak. I couldn't tell Max anything. And then, too late, she did remember, and her mouth dropped open as a flush rose, setting fire to her face.

At which point Ruth stepped neatly into the hall from the outside. She took one look at the suitcases and me standing beside them and brightly she said, 'Oh well done, Caroline. You finally got your way. How on earth did you manage?'

Max swung round at this, and for the first and only time I saw him look at Ruth. Really look at Ruth, with a hatred so sudden and naked she could only blink. Yet when she opened her eyes, the look was gone, vanished so completely that to the end of her days she would believe she had imagined it. But I had seen it. And I hadn't imagined it.

But now Max had turned to me, 'Rosie,' he said. His voice was gentle. 'Is it true? Is this what you want – to leave?' And unspoken, the question: *to leave me?*

His eyes searched mine. I tried to meet them with an answer that would satisfy, but I couldn't help myself. I had no wall against Max. The truth was there in my face. Impossible to conceal.

I shook my head.

Without looking around he said, 'Ruth, do me a favour. Go upstairs with Rosie and help her unpack. Make sure everything goes back where it belongs.'

Ruth flushed with joy, unmistakable. She knew what this meant. With a toss of blonde hair, she picked up two of my bags. 'Come on, Rosie.' Her voice sang out. 'Jump to it. You're not expecting me to carry all this by myself, surely.'

But I didn't move. I was looking at Caroline. A frost had come over her. Eyes, lips, hands freezing. She was like a woman turning to ice, as all the warmth was sucked out of her. Max tried not to see, but the transformation was there, taking place in front of him.

Ruth saw it and she shuddered with delight. 'Come *on* Rosie.' She nudged me with my bags, pretending to hustle me up the stairs. But near the top she stopped and turned to look down at Max and Caroline, where the real interest lay. We both turned.

'Why?'

At the bottom of the stairs only Caroline's mouth moved. The word itself was soundless. Max stared at her. Suddenly, his hands shot out and caught her arm. He pulled her almost savagely after him, into a small room we scarcely used. She went where he led her, her body stiff.

And still we didn't move, Ruth or I. Then a minute later there came a noise from the room. Wordless, toneless. Sexless even. It could have come from either of them, and it could have meant anything, anything at all. But I knew exactly what it sounded like: the end of something. Ruth heard it and she knew it too, pressing her lips together hard to keep her own noise from escaping.

Upstairs, she took care to leave my bedroom door well ajar. Everything was quiet but she wanted to be sure. She didn't want to miss anything. Meanwhile she pulled open drawers and bundled the clothes from the suitcases into them, never bothering to ask where anything went. She had a smile on her face that was almost idiotic, trance-like. Finally, though, she opened the wardrobe and stood, stock still, gazing at what was there.

A short sharp breath escaped her, like air from the puckered mouth of a balloon. Slowly she reached out and took it down from its hanger – Caroline's wedding dress. She held it up against herself in front of the mirror, only to sigh with a kind of contentment as if the shape of the dress flattened against her was *her* shape. Long and lean, like something carved from marble.

Strange and horrific, the look of happiness on her face. As strange and horrific as a world in which any given dream of Ruth's became real. I ran to tear the dress away, but neatly she side-stepped me, her eyes still gazing at herself in the mirror.

And then it was too late. I should have shut the bedroom door when I had the chance. A footstep on the landing made me turn, made us both turn. Max stood in the door. He was looking at Ruth, her face a mask of idiot joy. His own face was unreadable. I thought he would say something, but he didn't. Instead he turned and moved away. He hadn't even glanced at me.

I snatched the dress from Ruth, and tossed it back into the wardrobe. She made an odd hissing sound which she tried to disguise as a laugh, but she didn't resist me. Then I went downstairs to find Caroline.

She was sitting on one of the boxes that contained the copies of *Racing Demons,* staring at her hands. When I came into the room, she raised her head. But her face was like a mirror image of Max's. Unreadable.

Without warning though, she moved. She stood up and took hold of my wrists and without a word drew me under the light. There, beneath the naked bulb she stared into my eyes, searching for something.

A moment passed, then a sigh passed through her body.

'It's true,' she whispered. 'Max told me and I didn't believe it. But it's true. You *don't* know, do you? You really don't.' There was wonder in her words.

Abruptly she let go of me. Straight away I missed the touch of her hands on mine. She put her fingers to her face and shook her head as if trying to clear it of everything, and most of all, of me. And left the room.

Outside it was still daylight, but soon it would be dark. Caroline stood in the open door. She was leaving. Her body was silhouetted against the evening sun as she looked past me, into the house. Max was standing on the stairs, watching us, his body tense.

And to Max, Caroline said, 'Tell her. Tell her what you told me.'

That was all. For a long moment she waited. And for a long moment he didn't say anything. And so she left our house and never came back.

I turned back inside, to Max. But Max looked away. 'I've got to get ready for the Service.' He looked at his watch, his face dull, then climbed heavily back up the stairs.

For a long time I stood staring at the place on the stairs where he had stood. *Tell her. Tell her what you told me.*

Tell me what? What had he told her?

Now I understood. Caroline had finally got what she was looking for. She had become the expert in Max, and she knew something that I had never known. Because he had told her. And now she wanted him to tell me. Needed him to tell me. She had waited those last seconds for him to tell me. But Max had stayed on the stairs, closed as a book and had told me nothing.

Tell me what?

Chapter Thirty-One

That Thursday night service was meant to be the last Max took as an unmarried man, which meant there was even more of a party mood than usual. Outside the sports hall, girls carried banners that they unfurled in the crowd. *We love you, Max* they read. *Don't forget us.*

Silly banners that would have made him laugh. But tonight he didn't even see them. Tonight Max truly was separate from all of us, like a man in a trance. Even Caroline would have seen the difference, found it impossible to mock. But she wasn't there. So she didn't see him stand, like a statue in the midst of the sound and vision, or watch him as he raised the cup up above his head with an air of a man offering not just the cup but his entire self.

Ruth saw it. Instead of dancing she stood and watched him, her face greedy, mesmerised by the look of him, the shape his body made against the lights. Once, one of her hands reached out, paw like, slyly, to touch him and I watched as a shiver ran down her body as if electricity had run from my brother into her. But again he hadn't noticed. She might as well not have been there. Despite the crowd, the people pressing close, he might as well have been alone.

Max was praying as I had never seen him pray. Pleading as he prayed, his lips moving. Praying, pleading. Eventually the congregation picked it up too, the difference in Max. And despite themselves, despite having arrived wilder than usual anticipating the party to come, they grew quieter. The dancing slowed until in the end, everyone stood, head bowed and a perfect stillness came over everything. But even then, in the silence he had made, Max was alone, different from all of them.

They trooped out at the end, sombre, a little confused. Something had happened and no one had explained what. They were happy though, as if confusion was to be expected, God-sent. As if they had forgotten how all this time Max had been trying to explain there was nothing confusing about God. God was easy. God was simple. Maybe they just had never understood.

I needed to be alone with him. Alone, I'd ask him the question: *Tell me what?* But as soon as the service was over he made it clear he didn't want to be alone with me. I heard him tell Ruth to come home with us, and the demand almost made her burst with joy.

Back at the house she made tea and fussed around, like in the old days when there had been no Caroline and she had been able to serve Max. She laid biscuits on a plate which no one would touch but herself, hummed as she made herself busy. And all the time, Max avoided my eyes.

Tell her, Caroline had said. But I looked at Max and knew. He wasn't going to tell me anything.

Later still, he announced he was going to bed. He smiled at us both, suddenly looking more normal than he had all day. I wasn't taken in. We were born of a woman who had a talent for seeming normal.

Ruth, though, gave him a sharp look. Followed by alarm. Maybe the wedding was going to take place after all. She followed him upstairs and without being asked, shut herself in the spare room. She had no intention of going home tonight.

Which left me, alone in the kitchen with the cups and the biscuits, and an absence of Caroline.

Tell her, she said.

She had planted the question in the earth and now it stood like a pillar in the middle of our lives, sending a shadow across the world. Only one thing I could do. I slipped out into the hall and picked up my coat, and let myself out of the front door.

I had to write down the address for the taxi driver.

'Sore throat, love?' He said sympathetically. 'Must be bad if you can't speak. There's lots going round. Try to keep your bugs to yourself, eh.'

He dropped me off outside the house with the black railings. Steps ran up from the pavement to a shiny red front door. Red and black – Caroline's colours. I knocked on the door. Already it was midnight, but I was sure she would be up still. So I didn't expect to have to wait as I did. A minute passed, two minutes. I rang the bell again, then stood back and waited some more.

And finally the door opened. Caroline stood in the doorway. Maybe I had woken her after all. The creaminess had vanished from her. Her hair was mussed and her face flushed. She had a glass of what I took to be water in her hand.

'Rosie.' Her voice was toneless, controlled. Yet full of hope. She scanned my face – and the hope died. 'He hasn't told you, then.' She went to shut the door. I put my hand in the way and stopped it from closing. Her blue eyes widened – then narrowed as she resigned herself. She stood aside wearily.

'All right, come in, Fairy.'

I followed the familiar sway of that long body into the house, the one that she was determined would be my house. Caroline's home was a collection of white rooms, as spare and elegant as she was. A beautiful house, and such a far cry from ours, draughty and cluttered. Yet our house was what she seemed to want. Maybe even still wanted. Now she sat down on a long low sofa and curled up her legs, looking up at me, waiting to see what I would do next. After a moment, I sat down beside her.

Awkwardly, though. It confused me, how shy I felt suddenly. I had been alone with Caroline more times than I could count – yet I was shy now. Maybe it was the sheer perfection of her house, with its planes and its curves of white objects. Its absence of shadows. Caroline's house, with all its order showed how much she had compromised to be with Max. How far she had come from herself. And I had never realised.

She saw me looking around, and gave a short laugh. 'It would have been all yours Fairy – if you'd wanted it. And if you hadn't liked it, you could have changed it. Done what ever you want. I never did. Someone came in and put it all together for me, some interior ... stupid ... designer. I can't remember if I chose one thing in this entire fucking room.' She glanced around her, careless. And then I saw I was wrong about what this house said about her – the order and the clean lines. They had nothing to do with her.

Max suited her. Max and all the chaos that came with him.

I looked at her. The flush was still there in her cheeks. Aware of the observation, she put up the back of her hand to her face and felt the heat. 'It's the vodka,' she said lightly. 'Evil stuff really. But it does what it says on the tin.'

Not water in the glass then. Instinctively I looked for the bottle and she laughed again.

'Stay there.'

She got to her feet, heading for the kitchen with its chill glow of chrome and slate. As she went she reeled a little – the first time I had ever seen Caroline unsteady. Then she reappeared, this time with two glasses, handed one of them to me.

A small glass with frost already forming around the side. I bent my head and inhaled a smell of oil and ice. 'In one, Fairy,' Caroline said, then threw back her head and swallowed what was in the glass. Emptying it.

'Should have brought the bottle through,' she said and got to her feet. When she was out of the room I drank what was in my glass. Cold rushed down my throat, to turn instantly to heat.

She filled our glasses and we emptied them again. Then we sat a while. A buzz started up in the back of my head.

'I know why you're here,' she said suddenly. Her voice had changed. Higher, younger. 'But it won't work, because I'm not going to tell you, Rosie. It's not for me to tell you. It's for Max.'

I looked away. *I* wanted to tell *her* about Max, about how he had prayed, pleaded. Whatever she wanted, he wanted too. But they couldn't have it, either of them. Not until I knew what Max refused to tell me. Maybe not even then. Maybe nothing could bring them together now.

And the reason was still me. Always me.

I watched her swallow another shot of vodka, closing her eyes and tossing it back. Face twisting as the alcohol seared her. This was a new Caroline, one I had never seen before, and not the Caroline who drank champagne. This Caroline was drinking as if every mouthful burned her, like a woman gagging on medicine, yet still greedy for the cure. Not thinking about the baby inside her either. Or maybe she *was* thinking. Maybe this was what she was doing, trying to douse the small flame of life inside. The part of what was Max and herself combined.

From the way I watched her swallow, I could see: Caroline was not powerful, not any more. Something she knew had taken the power away from her.

Tell her...

Again she caught me looking. And again she laughed. And each time she laughed, the sound of it grew more acrid, more harsh, as if together we were arriving at the bitter

309

dregs of something.

'So,' she said suddenly. 'What now, Fairy? Are you all going to go back to normal after me? Is Max going to carry on preaching the faith while you stay behind closed doors, creeping around like a little ... a silly little ... an ignorant little ... mouse.'

I shrugged. I wasn't contemplating life without Caroline, not yet. That was Ruth's mistake.

That shrug of mine, telling her nothing, seemed to irritate her. Goad her. She slammed down her drink. 'God help you, you sit there, taking it all in. Big eyes, watching everything. Judging everything – me, Ruth, everyone around you. Except Max, the one person, the *one* person, you should be judging. The one and only person you need to see clearly. And don't.'

She leaned forward. 'Why can't you understand, Rosie? *Max isn't on your side.*' She spoke the words, then saw the look on my face as they hit me. Immediately she drew back, laughing. No, not laughing. Crying. Or something. But not laughing.

'Fuck it,' she mumbled. *'Fuck* it. I can't talk to you. It's like trying to kill something with words. And I don't want to kill you, Rosie.'

She dived a hand into her pocket and took out a box, the same box of white powder as I had seen all those months ago. She turned away from me to lay a trail of dust on the table, with difficulty because now her hands had started to shake.

But I couldn't take it in, not her words or now her actions. *Not on my side.* What was that supposed to mean? What was she trying to say, drunk and desperate as she was, not powerful now, not with me? For a moment I thought I knew. She thought she had lost Max, because of me. So now she was letting the anger talk, telling me the things she knew would hurt.

Max, not on my side.

Of course I didn't believe her. Of course I didn't. Not for even for a moment.

Caroline sat back from the table, and laid her head against the back of the sofa. Her eyes were watering, a fine dust feathered her upper lip. She had jammed her eyes shut against the tears, and yet still the tears found their way out.

'Don't listen to me, Fairy,' she whispered. 'Don't listen to a word I say. I'm so fucked up. We're not even the same place, you and I. You're there, and I'm, well … here.'

I looked at the table. I saw now she had laid out two lines and there was another line left. I hesitated, then picked up the roll of paper she had thrown aside. She watched me from under her lashes.

'Oh Fairy,' she said wearily. 'What are you doing?'

And I didn't know. I couldn't have told her even if I had a voice, unless it was to say that I was trying to close the distance between us, to put myself where she was. But I'm not sure if even that was true. Maybe it was something else I was after – the making of a choice. Or journey. Maybe that was all. I put the roll to my nostril and breathed in the line of cold white dust. And waited.

And nothing happened. Unless you counted the buzzing in my skull which suddenly vanished, to be replaced by a high pure note, pitch perfect, resonating in my head. A clear cold sound that comes when a bell is struck or a tuning fork vibrates. I shook my head and the note ended.

I was still myself.

Caroline watched me, and whatever she saw caused her to nod. Quietly she said: 'He has to tell you, Fairy. He has to understand. Look at you. You're stronger than he is. I think you're stronger than all of us.' She stood up, still swaying, but calmer now. Looking down at me, she said, 'he *will* tell you. I'll make sure of that. He just needs to understand, how strong you are.'

She spoke with such conviction, so certain that she knew me – knew Max – that hearing her, I felt a surge of anger. Who was she to say she knew us, better than we knew ourselves? Who was she to turn our lives upside down, and make a praying, pleading creature of my brother? *Who was she?* Yet even as the anger spoke, another kind of wave hit me, cold and delicious and unexpected, like a surge of water thrown up by the sea. It took my breath way and made me come awake.

And yet. In the same instant that I came awake, I fell asleep, fast asleep, carried away on a dream of oceans.

When I opened my eyes it was all over. Everything. It was morning and there were noises everywhere – in and out of the house, and in my head. Lights were flashing and there were sirens and people. Lots of people. Two policemen in uniform were standing over me, both asking me questions, interrupting each other like badly rehearsed actors. Wanting to know my name, wanting to know what I was doing there.

Too many faces, too many questions. Then, in the middle of it all, striding towards me – Max. Fighting his way through moving bodies to be on my side, ready to keep them all at bay. My beautiful Max. My wall. My protector. And already carrying that dead weight of grief.

Max's hands reached out and wrapped themselves around mine. Just like the first time.

No time to think, though. Without a word, he had pulled me gently off the sofa, was hustling me to Caroline's granite-walled bathroom, pushing past the policemen who were too taken by surprise to stop him. The next I knew there was water gushing cold from the tap, so fast and furiously the drops flew up and wet my face, and the noise filled my ears in the same way as the hard bathroom light was filling my eyes. Max's hands were there under the water's rush, and without thinking I put mine in to join him. At once he started pushing the water over them – my hands – rinsing and washing and sluicing; and in the white gleaming bowl of the sink I saw it: the disappearing swirl of blood chasing down the drain.

And they saw it too, the two policemen who belatedly had followed us into the room, catching a last glimpse of pink before the water carried it away. Yet Max's face showed nothing but a desperate relief. He pulled my hands out of the sink as if to show them, so they could see. My hands were clean.

One of the policemen opened his mouth, but Max was ahead of him. 'It came off my hands,' he said quickly. 'You saw me. I was outside holding her – Caroline. Trying to ... trying to...'

But he couldn't finish what he had to say. Couldn't say another word.

And that was the first I knew: something had happened to Caroline. And already they thought I had done it.

And there was nothing I could say. No memory. No memory of what came after the falling asleep, dreaming of the sea. No memory of anything except of Caroline looking down at me. No memory of pushing, or striking. No memory of purpose or intention. None of that. Only that sudden flash of anger before the tide carried me away.

This is how you forget. This is how I forgot. Forget once, forget twice. Kill once, kill twice.

That's what the police tell themselves. And that's what Max keeps from himself, tries not to think about. This is how he is able to protect me.

Part Three

Chapter Thirty-Two

Ten days since she died.

'Oh,' says Ruth in her usual, more than bright voice. 'You're packing your suitcases, Rosie. Whatever for?' As if she didn't know.

I ignore her, fold another towel and place it in the bag. I have no idea of what I will need, what they will let me have. In films, on TV, when people go into the cells, they always seem to have their belongings taken from them. Maybe that doesn't happen in real life, and it's just for the sake of the drama, to show how far they've sunk.

Or maybe it is true. All true, and they will take everything away from me. Even my charm bracelet, still hanging around my wrist with all its tiny objects in constant orbit. Even that.

And there's nothing Max can do. This morning DI Davies came and spoke to us. He was very gentle, gentler than he's ever been. He told us they were getting a warrant from a judge that would allow me to be taken to the police station and questioned there. It's not an arrest, not exactly – he was insistent about that. And there will be people there to help me – a doctor, a solicitor, a family liaison officer. I can't remember even half of the people he mentioned. Lots of people, so I imagine a crowd of us, all packed into one small room.

And right there in the middle of them, me.

Max is somewhere, not in the house. He is talking to people, trying to pull strings, trying to make it all not happen. I can't see what use they'll be now, though, all those actors with a conscience, all those rock stars. It's going to happen. It was always going to happen.

Meanwhile, Ruth watches me pack, legs packed into tapered trousers neatly crossed, those stylish shoes already turning to the shape of boats on her feet. Her new, blonde head of hair is shining even brighter than usual, as if she has just had it dyed again. At the top of The 'Swork Centre, her two small rooms are full of mirrors, yet I don't suppose she has any idea what she looks like. Really looks like. I know who she *thinks* she looks like. And all the time she watches me pack.

'You know, Rosie, you mustn't fret.' Her voice is complacent. 'Nothing's going to happen to you. I've told Max tons of times. No one's going to make you *pay*. I mean it's not like America where they put children and idiots in the electric chair. You'll be fine.'

She follows me with her eyes. And

suddenly, is it my imagination or have they actually become misty? She has just watched me pick up the old teddy bear off the bed, and hold it close for a moment, remembering how I used to sleep with it at school. I've had it since I was a baby. It's the only thing I've kept from the old days, from the Time that came Before.

I have no intention of taking it anywhere with me now, and toss it aside. But too late, it seems to have touched something in Ruth. Probably it's herself she's imagining, saying goodbye to her banks of cuddly toys, not knowing when she will see them again. Whatever the reason, suddenly she blurts out, in a voice I can hardly recognise, it's so heartfelt.

'Oh Rosie, I mean it. Really you mustn't fret. Or feel guilty. Everyone knows you can't remember, not a scrap. Which is a good thing, don't you see? Better not to remember anything. That way, God gets his work done. *He's making sure you don't have to blame yourself.*'

I find myself stopping what I was doing, to stare at her. And she meets my stare, earnest, anxious that I understand.

'He needed her to die. It's obvious. He just needed someone to make it happen. God has to use people, He has to. People like you. He's all spirit, remember. He needs people to get what He wants, to be His hands and

His feet. His agents. And what God wants is Max. He certainly didn't want Caroline, stopping him, leading him astray. She was awful, Rosie! Terrible. And poor Max, he just couldn't see it. The woman was making him blind. If ever anyone was set on this earth to do the devil's work, it was her.

'So you've got to look at it this way. God used you as a tool. And then, most wonderful of all – He made sure you don't remember anything about it, so you don't have to worry. And that's how God gets to keep Max. Without you He would have lost him. *We* would have lost him. Do you understand what I'm saying.'

She smiles at the look on my face.

'Oh you should read the Bible more, Rosie! It's full of people like you. People who can't help themselves. Not once they've been chosen. But in the end they understand, they see what an honour it can be, to be chosen to do God's work.'

For a moment I stand in the aftermath of this. Frozen, never understanding until this moment how much Ruth had hated Caroline. Hated her so much she had convinced herself that God must have hated her too.

Suddenly I feel sick. I have to force my hands to begin to move again, carry on packing the bag with things I'm not sure I'll be allowed to keep. I close a drawer and move over to the wardrobe. At once Ruth becomes alert, watching me. And when I pull open the door, she's there, in front of me and only then do I remember what she is after.

The dress. Caroline's wedding dress.

Before I can stop her her hands have darted, greedy and deft, flicking the frock off its hanger. And it's there again, that appalling, idiotic mask of joy as she lifts the dress to her shoulders and looks at herself. And this time it is too much. I follow her and try to pull the frock away. But Ruth's fingers have clawed it fast and the more I pull, the faster the grip.

Then something tears and a panel of white comes away in my hands.

Ruth gasps in outrage. 'You stupid girl, you've ruined it.'

But I'm looking at the panel left behind, the underskirt that's been exposed. And typical of Caroline – underneath the virgin white, it is a deep, lustrous red. It starts me laughing, that red underskirt, as I recognise the humour behind it – Caroline's private joke on the world. It makes me laugh and miss her at the same time.

The way I am missing her more every day.

But Ruth comes and stands, thrusts her face where I can't avoid it. Eyes narrowed. 'You,' she spits. 'You're laughing because you think you've got him. Well, madam, you can think again. When they come to get you,

323

when they put you away, he'll be free. For the first time in his life.'

Her face pushes even closer into mine.

'And you know the first thing he's going to do? When he's free?' As she speaks she snatches the panel I've torn from the dress, gathers it in with the rest. 'He's going to marry me, Rosie. I'm going to be his wife. And I'm going to be right there by his side, looking after him, working with him. I'm going to be everything he deserves. He's going to be happy at last.'

Slowly I shake my head. Which only makes Ruth smile wider, clutch the dress tighter to her breasts. 'Oh you'd better believe it, Rosie. He's *promised*.'

She stares down at herself, at the folds of white gathered in her arms, and giggles. 'Hark at me, giving away secrets. And there I was, faithfully promising not to tell a soul.' The smile vanishes, like a snake diving down a hole, back into hiding. Suddenly she tosses the frock away from her, onto my bed where it lands with a soft whisper of silk. Turns her back on it.

'I don't need that. Somebody else's cast-off.'

With that, she stalks out of the room, getting more practised every day on those high heels, marches across the corridor to Max's door. There she waits to make sure I am watching and then, without knocking, she turns the handle and walks straight in.

I am left staring at a closed door. Ruth is mad of course. Wild imaginings finally having got the better of her. Only a mad woman would have spoken as she did. *'He's promised.'* As if that could be true. Max wouldn't, couldn't promise any such thing. Ruth is his hair shirt, the thorn in his side. The thing that tries him more than anything in this world. But more importantly, he loves Caroline, cries for her in his sleep. He couldn't turn from her like that.

Anyway, Max isn't in his room. He's out of the house, fighting to protect me, desperate to keep tomorrow from happening. In a moment Ruth will be out again, on the prowl, to find out where he is. Yet I watch the door and it stays closed. Then, from behind the door, I hear Max's voice, saying something I can't make out and a soft laugh peals out in reply. Max is home after all, and it sounds as if there is a young girl in there with him. Happy and young.

And I don't understand.

Later, much later, after I hear Ruth leave, I creep back to the door and knock.

There is a long silence, until finally Max opens it. He stands and forces himself to meet my eyes. And I am shocked by the sight of him, haggard and drawn as he is. This is what the last few days have done to

325

him – hours even, since he heard that I am going in to custody. Max has lost that secret energy, the vibration in his blood. But what shakes me, what makes me tremble is the effort that he makes to smile, just for me.

I am overwhelmed with love for him.

I hold out my arms and for a moment he hesitates, then steps into them, his head close to my shoulder, golden and gleaming. But even now he will not let himself bend. Within seconds Max begins to turn this embrace around, making it so I am standing in *his* arms. He is determined to be the one to offer comfort, to be strong. He will not take help, not from me.

And neither will he explain about Ruth. He can read the question in my eyes but wilfully he ignores it, pretends there's nothing to explain.

'Go to bed, Rosie,' he murmurs in my ear. 'Let's see if we can get a night's sleep. Better tomorrow, you'll see. Everything will be better.' He says this when we both know it's not true. Tomorrow I am going away and DI Davies is going finally to ask his questions.

Yet Max watches so hard to see the effect of his words that I make myself smile, just for him. And nod. Better tomorrow.

When I sleep, I dream of Caroline. Dream *with* Caroline. As if every night we have come together to watch the passing of these hours. Tonight we watch Max crying in *his* sleep and Caroline sighs, removes one of Ruth's false golden hairs from beside him on the pillow, a look of distaste on her face.

This is what I am dreaming when the telephone rings.

And sure enough, after a minute I hear Max's step on the stairs, carrying on down and out of the front door. His footfall is heavy on the pavement as he follows the summons. But no one else sees or hears him. Even the photographers have given up for the night.

Max.

For the first time in years, I attempt the impossible, try to call out his name, to make him stay. But my voice stays where it has always been, locked in my throat. The door slams, and I am alone.

And look, I thought I knew about absence, but it turns out I never did know after all. This is what I have discovered from the sound of a door closing, from Max leaving, telling me he is no longer there. Making me understand once and for all. Max is gone.

But he is not the only one to have left. I cast about in the darkness — and there is nothing. Even the shadows have become empty. They are *all* gone, all the people I sent there. The shadows in this room contain nothing. I am the only one here, in the dark.

If this is the dark, then I cannot bear it. I want to put on every light in the house, but now, in the absence of Max, in the absence of everyone, I find I cannot move.

So the darkness stays, nothing can chase it away. Outside my window, the street lights are no more than puddles compared to the ocean of black. Eleven days ago I fell asleep dreaming of oceans. Caroline died and what happened, I don't remember. Oceans cover everything, silence everything.

Max hopes that silence will be the saving of me. If I say nothing, admit to nothing, what can anyone – the police – know for sure? He thinks silence will be enough.

So here I am, alone, because Max is not with me to chase away the dark. And even if he were, he would be too tired. That light, that energy he carried around with him for so long has been eaten up, leaving everything so very dark, there almost seems to be an air of expectancy about it. As if in the dark something is there, after all, hiding, waiting.

With this, I feel my eyes starting in my head, as though there were shapes to be made out. Ears straining as if there are sounds to be heard. And yet there is nothing – until it occurs to me. Perhaps I am what is there. I am the Thing that waits in the dark. Born to be in the dark, to put others in the dark.

Oh I want Max.

Max would understand. This is where he was, all those years ago – in the dark, down in the alley. In the dark, just as I am now. The difference was he didn't care. He didn't care what was in the shadows, he didn't care what came next. So what *did* happen next, after he had given up caring? He said that was the moment everything changed, when the world turned and light came down all around him. Everything began to shine. *Every fucking molecule,* he said. And loping towards him, out of the shadows, long and low and louche – the Big Dog. The Big Hound.

And that was when Max discovered that he wasn't alone.

Makes me catch my breath, the idea of it. That I might not be alone, that we only have to be in the dark long enough, and the dark itself only has to be dark enough, and the future filled with precisely nothing. *If it happened for Max, might it not happen for me?*

Might it not happen? It happened for Max and the darkness vanished. *It doesn't matter what you've done; it's what you do next that counts.* With this one thought, I hold my breath and wait. And then, when I have to breathe, I breathe, waiting for the light to come, the way it did for Max.

And wait.

But nothing happens. What happened to

329

Max only happened to Max. In my darkness nothing changes. The people in the shadows stay where they are, and there's not so much as a scratching at the door. Wherever the Big Dog is – if it ever existed – it's not here, not in my dark.

But something else has happened.

I am here.

I am here. This is what I discover after giving myself up to the dark, breathing it in like a drowning girl submitting to the sea: I am still here. This is how John said it would be. Break through the surface of things, find there's nothing beneath – and *I* am still here. Cover me up with the dark – and see, I *am* still here. Look into the future, and it is filled with nothing – except for me, because I am there too.

John was right. Caroline was right. This is the truth, the thing that was hiding in the dark. And the secret of the dark is that I am strong. Stronger than Max knows. Stronger than Max himself.

And now that I know it, I can stand up, move through the dark like through water or air. Outside, inside, everywhere, it is still dark, but I am still here. And here in the house, in this room there is more than enough light to see.

Now I want Max to come home. I want him to see it too, how strong I am. Strong enough for both of us. Not the Rose he thinks I am, not the fairy in the house. Something we both should have understood. Years ago.

And here it comes again, that feeling of the wind in my face, snatching my breath away. Only Caroline could make this happen, coming at me now with such force I find myself glancing over my shoulder checking the dark that she's not here, making it happen. And of course she's not. Caroline is dead. This is me. All me. No Max, no Caroline. And no Big Dog.

This is how Max needs to see me. Strong. All the stronger for being alone. No need for him to carry me any more. No need to wear himself down.

And from downstairs, as if in answer to a prayer, comes the sound of the front door closing. Max is home. Tired Max who has never really known me. I can hear his footsteps on the stair. In a perfect, mended world I would be able to call his name, and he would hear it ring through the house. But that can't happen, so instead I run to the landing to be there to greet him as he reaches the top.

And Max is already there, shambling across the bare boards with his head sunk into his chest. So mired in fatigue that he hasn't even seen me. For the briefest of seconds, the wild feeling flickers and turns to rage against Ruth with her phone calls and her claws stuck fast into him and her talk of promises that no one would ever want to make her. But the anger disappears when I remember what I want Max to know about me, and thoughts of Ruth are sucked clean out of my head. I touch his arm as he passes.

Just that, a touch. But his entire body recoils as if I had touched him with a naked wire, and without a word he walks straight past me into his room, shuts the door. Leaves me to stand in shock, staring at the hand he shied away from. And from the other side of the door, there comes the sound of music.

It's the old song, the one we played when we were children. The one he played in his room the first time he came home with the all shadows clinging around him. *The runaway train runs down the track...*

I throw my body against the door, battering at the panels. But the doors in our draughty, shabby house are strong as oak and Max's door doesn't bend or give. All it allows is for the sound to make its way through the cracks, too loud, even from out here. Inside Max is lying in the middle of it, walling himself in with noise. I can batter and hammer on his door but my brother refuses to hear me.

After a while, I stand back. My knuckles are bleeding and the song is still playing. It seems that Max has it on a loop, unable to stand even a breath of silence.

And there is nothing else I can do. No other way to help him. I can't batter down his door, I can't make him hear me. All that's left is to find Ruth. I need to speak to Ruth.

I enter The 'Swork Centre by the back entrance. Out at the front of the building, in the welcome hall, in the kitchen and dispensary, people are milling around, working. Nights are our busiest time, when we are needed most. But here, where a back door gives onto the alley, no one comes and there is a staircase that runs straight the way to the top of the building and Ruth's two small rooms.

Normally the door is locked, but now, just before dawn, it is standing open. I have an image of Max leaving, striding away so fast he left the door swinging on its hinges. Max not caring what he did.

What happened to my brother to make him recoil from my touch? Only Ruth could know. Ruth will have to tell me. I am stepping over the threshold when the answer hits me, and I have to stop, doubled over as if somebody had punched me.

Ruth has convinced him. That's what has happened. She has done what no one else could do, not even DI Davies. She has convinced Max that I killed Caroline. Max never let himself believe it – until now. That is why he recoiled, so I can no longer touch him. I have lost him.

This is what she has done. This is Ruth's work.

For seconds I can't bring myself to move. I stay where I am, bent over, taking gulps of air. It's only gradually that it comes back, the knowledge that I am, after all, strong. But back it comes, until finally I am able to pull myself up straight, and where a minute before there had been horror, now there is rage. And strength.

A murderous strength.

So now I go quietly up the stairs. I am not giving her warning or time to prepare. Or time to gloat. Ruth is going to have to learn this truth as well: I am not the fairy in the house. I am strong. Stronger than she is.

But here, at the top of The Centre, is another door left open and a light left on. The entrance to Ruth's flat, usually closed and bolted against the people she is so loud about helping, is wide open so that anyone could walk in. Including me.

And so quietly, quietly, I tiptoe through the small hall with its religious pictures and its mirrors. Ahead of me is her bedroom, and yet again, the door is open. I can even make out the shape of one plump leg on the bed. Ruth is sleeping of course. Max has gone and now, idle, she will sleep for hours.

And the first thing she will do on waking is call him, as she has done every morning for eleven days. Not this morning, though. I will not allow her to wake him, not after this.

So I step into the room that has contained her all these years, her stuffy, frilly, over heated room filled with her over heated thoughts. And on the bed is the woman who has turned my brother's mind against me, the way Caroline never could. I take one look at her – only to turn away with nausea rising in my throat.

Ruth is lying with the sheets tumbled around her, her legs in disarray, a portrait of abandonment. She is wearing a nightdress, long and sinuous even on her, the colour of flesh itself; it's the same nightgown that Caroline picked out and gave me to hold, with its message written on silk, making sure I understood. This is what Ruth has pilfered for herself and is wearing now, thinking she could wrap her body in someone else's skin. Caroline's skin. And it's grotesque.

But this is not what makes me turn away, and makes my gorge rise. The plump abandoned body on the bed has no life in it. Ruth is dead. A single silky stocking is knotted around her neck, leaving her face to tell its story of this, the greatest shock of her life – namely the sheer unexpectedness of her death. Her eyes are wide and quizzical. There is not even pain there, just complete surprise.

And even as I turn away, I know. I could never have done this to anyone. Not even Ruth.

And for a moment, this is all I know. *I didn't do this.* I was somewhere else, awake, gauging the darkness around me, feeling myself adjust, like someone adapting to water. I was not here. But Max was. He was here.

And I know who did this.

My legs carry me to the door, and somehow to the stairs. And amazingly by the time I reach the quiet back alley, they are strong again. I am strong again. Caroline was right. John was right. Everything they said is true. I am strong, even enough for this.

At home, Max's bedroom door is open now. The song is nearly over, on its last loop. He is ready for me.

And for a minute I wait, watching him, dizzy with the feeling of life having spiralled around to meet itself, like the Big Dog chasing its tail. My brother is lying on the bed, face down with one arm trailing to the floor and the only thing that moves is the hand that is beating time to the music. The old song.

The runaway train runs down the track…

He knows I am here, but he is waiting for the record to end, as if taking strength from the music. But this time I will not wait. I walk over to the ancient record player, a relic from our childhood days and lift the needle, stopping the music.

Max doesn't look at me. The hand stops beating and falls flat against the floor. He lies, motionless, his head turned to the wall. And now I see what the beating hand had hidden from me – a small brown medicine bottle. Liquid morphine, the drug we keep under double lock in the dispensary. Not even I had access to it. Only Ruth had the key.

The bottle is empty. And now I know what else Max has done.

I reach for the phone beside the bed. At the Centre they know my silence. They will know it is me. Someone will help us. Help him. But the hand on the floor springs with a life of its own. It shoots out and grips my wrist, will not let me go.

My breath issues as a whisper and I sink on to the bed beside him.

And now, finally, Max turns. Effortlessly. His body hasn't begun to grow heavy from the drug. He is still strong. All the power in him is concentrated in that grip on my arm. This is where he will keep his strength until he falls asleep.

So this is what I will wait for. For Max to

sleep. Then I will phone for help. Then I will save him.

But Max knows. He looks at me and smiles, reading my mind, and the grip on my arm grows tighter still. 'Hello Rosie.' Then the smile fades. 'You've seen her?'

Pain flickers across his face. 'I'm sorry.'

There is a long pause in which nothing is said. Then, almost dreamily: 'That was me. I did that. All in a moment. I didn't even know I was going to do it.' The astonishment as he remembers what he has done flickers across his face, reflecting the same look I saw in Ruth's.

I nod, aware of my eyes trying to hide my own intent from him. He swallows. In a few minutes even this will become difficult. But before that he will be asleep, and then I will phone. Then I will save him. This is what I tell myself.

But in the meantime Max is wide awake, his words clear, although slow as if each one is being measured for its own truth, and its value to me.

'How can I explain, Rosie? She was wearing that ... thing. The nightdress, Caroline's. And stockings ... they were Caroline's too. She wanted me take them off her ... in a certain way. That's what she phoned me for, Rosie – to take off her stockings. So I went, and I took off her stockings – *in that certain way.*'

Even now, Max eyes can flicker with irony as he paints the picture of himself, removing a stocking. Then the irony disappears and in his eyes only a terrible blackness.

'But *then* she told me to tell her I loved her, to speak to her as if she was Caroline. Told me the words she wanted me to say. And I couldn't. Rosie, I couldn't. She told me what I had to say and that's when I...'

His face twists. For a moment his hand becomes loose around my wrist. I tell my hand to lie limp, to be deceptive. But this is Max, and he can read my mind. Even as the signal to be still runs down my arm, his hand reads it and the fingers lock around my wrist again. He is still so strong. But not for long. Like a man going under anaesthetic, soon he will be asleep. And then I will phone. Then I will save him.

And he knows it. His voice cracks. 'Please Rosie ... don't.'

For a long time, he doesn't talk. Such a long time I begin to think it is beginning to happen, the drug is closing him down; that in a minute he will be asleep, and the grip on my arm will fall away. And then I will phone.

But Max says:

'Ruth could make me do anything. It's because she was there when it happened. She saw Caroline die. That's when she knew she had won. All she had to do was tell you what she saw.'

For the first time inside his grip, my hand begins to tremble. He feels it shaking and for a moment the hand locked around my wrist softens, becomes a caress. This is Max, trying to soothe, to protect, even now. Then the hand locks hard again, as he continues with what he needs to tell me. Because Max *needs* to speak, this much I know. Words falling, one after the other, knowing he has only so much time.

'She came and followed me to Caroline's that night. I'd gone there to bring you home, make you safe. Make us whole again – the two of us, the way we used to be. But first I had to make sure Caroline didn't tell you, hadn't already told you.'

Once again my hand trembles under his. *Told me what?*

He blinks at me. And I can see it, the drug finally working its way to his brain. He is beginning to be tired now. He says:

'Caroline guessed, you see. Worked the truth out all by herself, that night. You had packed to leave, and I had to stop you, make *her* see I couldn't let you go, not when you needed to stay. You went upstairs with Ruth, and Caroline was alone with me. She couldn't understand. But then she looked at me, and before I said anything, I saw it begin to dawn, the reason why I couldn't abandon you. Ever.

'Caroline, she...' His tongue lingers on the name. He has to start again. 'For the first time, I understood how she used to discover the secrets of the people she wrote about. I watched her do it with me, looking at me that night. She was imagining the worst thing anyone could imagine, then testing it for truth. I watched her face as she imagined, her eyes when she understood that she was right. Terrible...'

He stops, has to force himself to speak now.

'And that's how she found out the truth about me. About *us*, Rosie.'

At the mention of my name, his hand loosens almost imperceptibly around mine, but the cloud that came over his eyes as he remembered Caroline, stays.

'And Caroline was going to tell you, I knew she was going to. That's why I went to the house – to stop her, and bring you home. She came to the door, but she wouldn't listen to me. She said that if I didn't tell you, she would. She tried to make me believe you were strong, strong enough for anything. I told her you weren't. No one could be strong enough, not for what she wanted you to know. I tried so hard to make her see. I begged her, and she wouldn't listen...

'Yet that's all I was trying to do – to make her understand. But already she was turning to go back inside to where you were. So I put my hand out to stop her, to pull her away from the door, keep her from coming to you. It's all I wanted to do. I never even thought of the strength I was using.

'I pulled her, and she fell. Not just an ordinary fall, but something hurtling and headlong, past me, right down the steps, all the way to the bottom. I tried to catch her, to hold her, but I couldn't. Five steps, and her head hit every one of them. It sounded like wood, Rosie, hitting stone. One step after the other. I can still hear it, the sound of wood.

'And at the bottom she stopped and lay there. She wasn't moving. And I realised I'd killed her. I'd killed Caroline. My beautiful...'

His fingers fall away from my wrist. There is nothing holding me now. But I don't move. We sit and look at our two hands lying side by side on the bed. Max's voice continues, but I don't know what makes him sound so dreamlike any more, so far away. Maybe the dream is all mine. And I am dreaming that I never killed Caroline. Dreaming that Max killed her.

'Ruth saw it all. She saw us in the doorway. She saw me pull Caroline, and she saw her fall. She knew it was my fault. Except she kept telling me it wasn't. She made me come home with her. She kept telling me it was an accident – but only at first. Afterwards, she started talking about there being no such thing as accidents, because everything is God's will. And for half the night I believed her. I wanted to believe her. It even seemed to make sense, because I hadn't meant to kill her. Not Caroline, not my Caroline.

'But then in the morning, I went back. I called the police. They found you, and decided you had done it. Meanwhile Ruth was telling everyone I had been with her, all night long. And I realised it was too late. I could never tell anyone now, because then you would have to know the very thing I killed to stop Caroline telling you. And if that happened, she would have died for nothing. I'd have killed her for nothing.'

His eyes begin to close. Slowly, thickly he says, 'So I washed our hands – yours and mine. And I told them the truth. I told them the blood had been on my hands, knowing they wouldn't believe me. They would think it was from your hands. They'd think you did it, and I was trying to protect you. Just like the first time...'

Max is falling away from me. The drug is taking hold, soon there will be no turning back. Now is the time to pick up the telephone, save him. Instead my hand stays next to his, not moving, while the words he has just spoken make a shape in my head.

Just like the first time.

343

Max has sensed that I am not moving. Not phoning. For a moment he seems to be smiling. But the movement of his mouth is too twisted, too sad for a smile.

'How did it all happen?' His voice is wondering. Dreamy. 'I wanted to *die* for you. Can you believe that? Instead I've ended up killing. I've killed people. Just so you'd never know.'

His eyes, heavy now, fall away from mine. Max cannot look at me.

'I told myself it would be all right, and nothing would happen to you. If you couldn't talk, if you couldn't remember, then how could they ever make you guilty? I thought so long as I was there, protecting you, letting you know I believed in you, it would be enough. You would be safe, and I would be strong. I thought...'

He stops. Swallows. And this time, I see it, what I've been waiting for – swallowing has become difficult. He hasn't long now. Max says:

'But then I killed again. I killed Ruth and now...' His eyes come back to mine and my brother stares in horror at who it is he sees mirrored in my eyes. Now he would turn away, stop what he has to say. But he can't, because still Max has not told me what Caroline knew. And he has to tell me.

Has to. The air is full of waiting, and suddenly I am aware they are back – all the people I thought were gone, shadows pressing closer, waiting for Max to speak, for Max to tell me. Ruth is here somewhere too, a weight of ether. And so is Caroline, although unlike Ruth, the air that contains her is humming, alive with her. And Max feels it. Suddenly his eyes are wide open again, swimming in blue. For a moment he stares right past me, as if into her – Caroline's – eyes, before he returns finally to me. This time his eyes are clear, almost peaceful. The horror is gone.

Now. Now he is going to tell me. Caroline has made sure of it.

Tell me what?

'Rosie,' he whispers. 'It was me. I killed the baby. Not you. It was crying and I was sick of it. You had a banana, so I took it and stuffed it in its mouth to stop the noise. And it worked. It was so simple, I couldn't believe how simple it was.'

I close my eyes. Seeing it. How simple it was. While Max says, his voice dreamy, as if describing a dream, 'Then I got scared because the baby wasn't moving, so I called for Mum, and she came. And I saw her face, and then I knew. So I pointed to you, I don't know why. I must have thought you would say something. Tell her what happened. And you didn't say anything, you just stood there, staring at her.'

And he's right. I stare at my mother,

345

knowing I've done something. But what? Max is pointing at me, so it must be something. Something I've done. This is what I do in these last few seconds before the world changes, splits into two. I stare and I say nothing, while Max points.

Max whispers again, 'You didn't say anything. That's why they believed me. You should have said something. You always used to – you used to have an answer for everything, don't you remember, Rosie?'

Remember? What is there to remember?

Max says, 'And suddenly it was too late to say anything. Even after the first minute it was too late. And anyway, I thought it would be all right. You were always in trouble, but then they'd always forgive you. You were the favourite, everybody knew it. I thought you always would be.

'So that's what happened. And there was no going back. We all just seemed to fall into our roles. And right away, in those very first seconds, I knew what my role was – to look after you, protect you, no matter what. Later, I told myself that one day, when you were strong enough, I would tell you the truth and what really happened. But you had to be strong, otherwise how could you bear it?

'And the strange thing was, you *were* strong at first, when you were little. But then I realised it was only because you didn't understand, not really. I saw how people treated you, the way it made you different. And then one holiday, you came home from school and you did understand. You had stopped talking and I knew why. I knew then you weren't strong after all, and never would be. Yet the truth is, I was relieved, because it meant I would never have to tell you. It only meant that I had to look after you. Never leave you. Never. That's what she couldn't understand. Caroline.'

At the mention of her name I move my hands away from his. Only a small movement, but the distance is there, widening. For minutes then, we sit in silence. A long silence. Outside the window, the dark is going, the world is waking up. I am waking up. It is as if I have been asleep for twenty five years. But Max is getting sleepier, his eyelids heavy as he watches the distance my hands have put between us.

I know without having to touch them that his fingers are cold, warning that the warm flow of his blood has begun to slow. Now, now is the time to phone The Centre, to use my silence as a scream. But I can't because my hands are heavy where they have fallen away from him; and I am staring at a past that seems to have rolled back like a carpet before me. I am looking at our lives and the things that changed us, and brought us here, to this room. And I can't move, so held am I by what I see.

Because I see them all – the baby, Caroline, Ruth. I see my mother turning away at the mention of my name; my father losing the woman that he married. I see Sister Imelda driving home her messages, robbing me of words. I see our family struggling not to fall apart, struggling to love what they have left. Loving and leaving and leaving and leaving.

And most of all I see Max, trying to keep us still woven together. At the same time, my wall, my protector. My beautiful Max. The reason for it all. The reason so many people are in the shadows.

And now he has told me, and I am waking up from that sleep. Yet somehow I don't feel the way I should. No sense of shock or dislodgement, but the reverse. What I feel all around me is the quiet movement of things falling into place. The end of a lifetime of confusion, the end of dreaming.

And suddenly I can move. I turn to Max, who has closed his eyes. Now, now is the time to phone. Save his life. And after I have saved him, I will be able to watch the world as it turns its face against him, the way it turned against me. Watch him trying to live in the aftermath, the way I lived in the aftermath. I can save his life just for this – a Hell of his own making.

I could do this to him. I could. I could set

the world on him. It's what will happen, whether I want it to or not.

My hand makes an unconscious movement towards the phone. With a final effort his eyes flicker and open, looking for me. Max is staring through a mist. His strength is gone, the words are gone, but he still manages to find my eyes – and hold them. And this is how he tells me that he knows all about the world, but he doesn't care. He never cared what the world thought of him. In that last flicker of my brother's eyes I finally know everything there is to know about Max. My Max. Staring at me with the eyes of a six-, nine-, sixteen-year-old. Max, the hair falling into his eyes. Max, always looking over his shoulder for me. Always there.

All he ever cared about was what *I* thought of him.

We were only children. They should have made us understand. They should have made themselves understand. We were not to blame, Max and I.

The phone stays where it is. Instead I take him in my arms and cradle his head which is golden and heavy against my breast. So heavy the weight of it makes me sigh. Except it's not a sigh, but a word.

'Max.'

The first word I have spoken aloud in nearly fifteen years, and the sound of it is as startling as a bell. My brother hears it and stirs – then lets out a long deep breath of his own. *Rosie*. My name on his lips, given back to me.

Max, my beautiful Max, is not dead. Not yet. But he is falling asleep forever now – a sleep of his choosing. And I am with him. As the sleep deepens, I feel that secret energy inside him beginning to stir again, ready to leave. It makes the air between us vibrate and hum, before it slides gently out of him. And into me.

Which means that Max is ready for his own leaving, ready to take all of the shadows with him like a troupe of actors leaving the stage.

And as they prepare to go, I imagine a scratching at the door, the sound of a Big Dog waiting patiently to come in. Meanwhile my brother sleeps in my arms, and I am full of secret energy. I am like that thin beam of light. Cover me up and I am still there. It's what you do next that counts.

I am still here. Max sleeps in my arms, my beautiful Max who tried to be good. And failed. But I am still here. Show me the world and I promise you, Max, I will shine.

This Large Print Book, for people
who cannot read normal print,
is published under the auspices of

THE ULVERSCROFT FOUNDATION

... we hope you have enjoyed this book.
Please think for a moment about those
who have worse eyesight than you ...
and are unable to even read or enjoy
Large Print without great difficulty.

You can help them by sending a
donation, large or small, to:

**The Ulverscroft Foundation,
1, The Green, Bradgate Road,
Anstey, Leicestershire, LE7 7FU,
England.**
or request a copy of our brochure for
more details.

The Foundation will use all donations
to assist those people who are visually
impaired and need special attention
with medical research, diagnosis
and treatment.

Thank you very much for your help.